To Richard a good friend and business aquantance

From his good friend
Pete Moella

HE DIED
A HERO?

HE DIED A HERO?

PETER MOELLER

Deeds Publishing | Atlanta, Georgia

Copyright © 2014 - Peter Moeller

ALL RIGHTS RESERVED - No part of this book may be reproduced in any form or by any electronic or mechanical means, including information storage and retrieval systems, without permission in writing from the authors, except by a reviewer who may quote brief passages in a review.

Published by Deeds Publishing
Marietta, GA
www.deedspublishing.com

Printed in The United States of America

Library of Congress Cataloging-in-Publications Data is available upon request.

ISBN 978-1-941165-18-8

Books are available in quantity for promotional or premium use. For information, write Deeds Publishing, PO Box 682212, Marietta, GA 30068 or info@deedspublishing.com.

First Edition, 2014

10 9 8 7 6 5 4 3 2 1

ACKNOWLEDGMENTS

I want to thank Dave Arterburn for the first reading of my novel—he gave me some good criticism. I don't like to impose on people but after his second reading he told me that he knew I was writing another book and asked if he could read that one when it was done. I especially want to thank Becky Beal for her help and encouragement during this ordeal. She did some editing, gave me advice, and saw it through to the finish. My granddaughter, Ashley Moeller, and Kevin Grogg helped me through the pitfalls of my computer. Also, thanks to the Atlanta Writers Club and the Southeastern Writers Association for all they taught me.

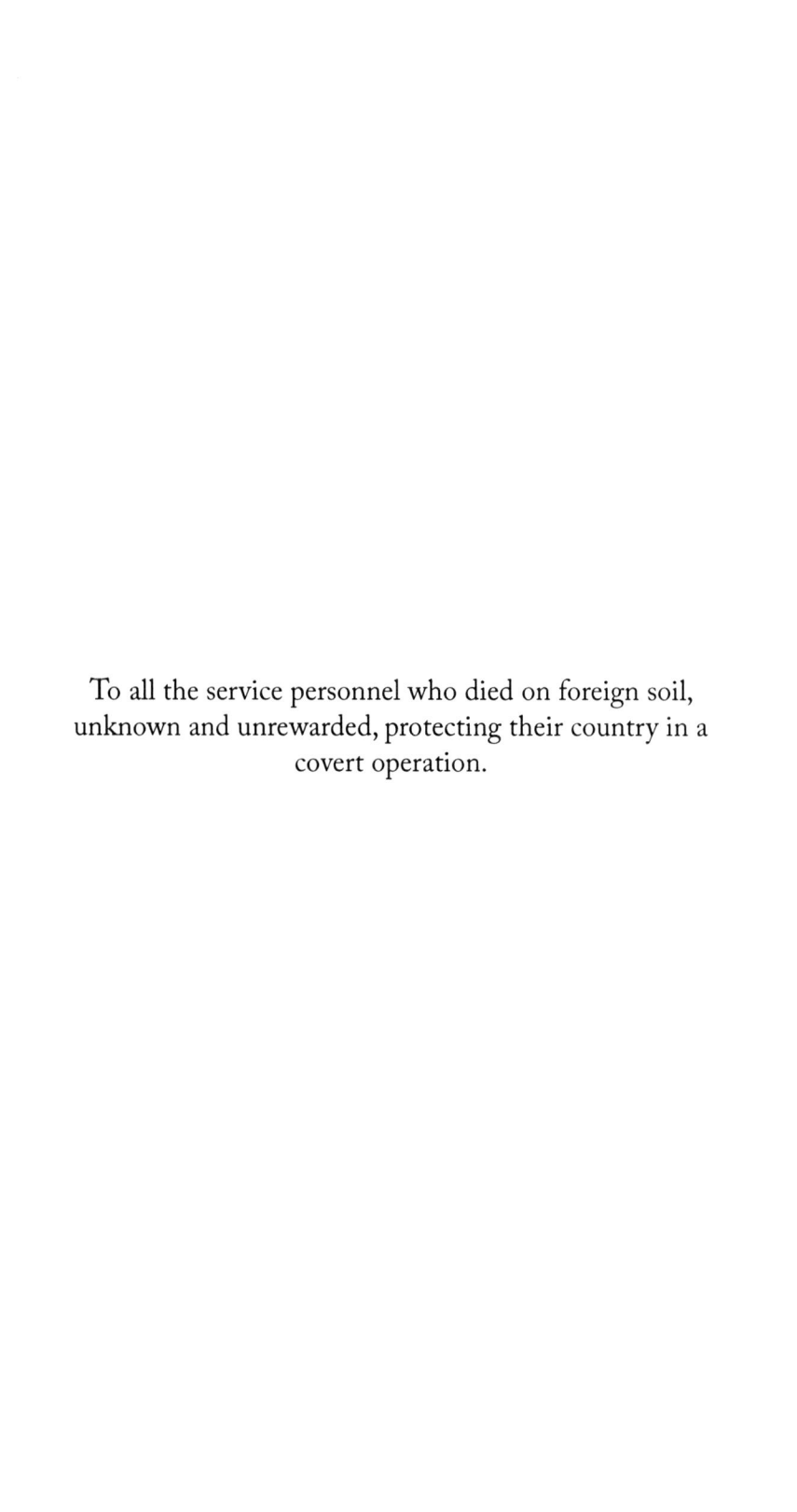

To all the service personnel who died on foreign soil, unknown and unrewarded, protecting their country in a covert operation.

Chapter 1

Atlanta, Georgia, February 4, 1994

Jack Nordone formed a hatred of war in his two tours in Vietnam. While others reveled in their kills, Jack never did. He thought the Viet Cong were poor bastards just like the Americans were, caught up in a war they didn't understand. This did not keep him from doing his duty and doing it well, as the fist full of decorations, including a Purple Heart with cluster that he earned, attested to. When he returned from the war he vowed never to kill another human being; it was a vow he couldn't keep.

Now a family man and attorney, Jack slammed the kitchen door shut against the cold February wind and threw his briefcase across the room. It just missed the chair. Hell, he thought, I can't do anything right today. He was not a happy person. Driving in Atlanta's five o'clock traffic could do that to you and screwing up in court today didn't help.

He headed straight for the den and wet bar, lit the gas logs and poured himself a Jack Daniels Black Label over ice, with a splash of soda. As he finished it, his wife came into the room, making things a little brighter. He held up the bottle, asking if she wanted one.

She shook her head. "Bad day?"

"Worse," Jack answered, and watching her walk into the room he knew hers wasn't much better. There wasn't much that could bring her down so he knew she had talked to their son. "Did Tim call?"

Nancy nodded with a sigh.

"Did he tell you anything new?"

"No, and I finally came right out and asked him."

"And?" Jack prompted.

"And it took that son of yours about five minutes stumbling around, trying to tell me that everything was good. I hate to say it but I don't think he is telling us the truth. Something happened there which he can't, or won't talk about, so I decided to go to Ocotal and see for myself."

Jack looked at her in surprise. "You know we can't do that; I'm right in the middle of this trial."

"I know we can't, but I can. I booked a Delta flight to Miami and a TACA flight to Managua."

Jack flopped down on his favorite, overstuffed chair and took a long swallow of his drink. "I can't believe I'm hearing this."

"Believe it," Nancy said. "Maybe if you weren't so pig-headed about his going to Ocotal, he would be able tell us what's wrong."

"Pig-headed," Jack repeated, "I'm not pig-headed. I know he is a great teacher, I just don't see why he had to go all the way to Nicaragua to do it."

Nancy sat down in Jack's lap and put her arms around him. "I'm just worried and didn't mean to guilt trip you, except, maybe, for the pig-headed part." She gave Jack a big kiss, and then took his head in both her hands. "At least you don't look too much like a pig," and they both laughed. She sure knew how to ruin a bad mood.

"I also did some checking," Nancy said, "and found that the USA Conference of Churches started a sister-city program with Nicaragua, and Hartford became a sister city with Ocotal. They have a full-time staff member there and I talked with a woman who had been down there. She said it was a nice quiet place, friendly and safe. They have been sending people down there since 1985. She was impressed when she found out that I had a son teaching there."

"Oh, so now he is your son." Jack protested, trying to hide his smile. He still wasn't sold on the idea, her going down there alone, but the information was reassuring and he knew she had made up her mind. He would be fighting a losing battle so he decided to give her a hug instead of an argument. "By the way where's Ralph? I miss his welcoming drool."

Nancy smiled. "I really don't know. I always let him out, he does his stuff and comes right back. Lately he hasn't been doing that. He's been gone longer and longer, even in this weather. The other day he came in and, I swear, he had a smile on his face. I think he found a girlfriend."

Jack shook his head, "Well, you had better start putting him on the chain. I don't have time for a paternity suit."

Chapter 2
Atlanta, Georgia, February 8

The gym was stifling. It was cold in Atlanta, even for February, and the maintenance people made up for it by turning up the heat. Jack wiped the sweat from his eyes and tried to dry his hands on his damp shorts.

He moved past half court and glanced up at the clock. They were in their second overtime and the score was still tied with just enough time for one more shot. As the ball was brought across court, Jack saw that his favorite spot was open. He feinted to his left, and then moved quickly to his right, signaling for the ball. Walt Kutch made the pass. Jack caught it and went up for the shot, all in one movement, and the ball just cleared the outstretched hands of the defender and fell through the hoop, touching nothing but net.

Walt raised his fist in victory and gave Jack a pat on the back. "Not bad for an old man."

Jack returned the pat, "Not a bad pass for a banker."

It had been a long game and most of the players had to leave after their shower, but Jack had agreed to meet Walt in the club's bar.

The old man part still rankled, taking a little off the flush of victory but Jack smiled. Mid-40s was not old by any standard. After Jack showered, he called his answering service and then joined Walt in the sports-club bar. An ice cold Rolling Rock was waiting for him and he took a long swallow. Man that tasted good.

"I'm sure glad you made that last shot," Walt said, "I almost didn't pass it to you. I could tell that your brain wasn't with us today. It looked like you were doing some serious thinking. Tell Uncle Walt what's happening."

Jack turned his beer bottle around a couple of times and took another swallow. "It's a little convoluted," he said.

"Well, I'm not exactly chopped liver. I'm the executive vice president of a very large bank and deal with the world monetary system on a daily basis, so tell me." Walt smiled and looked at his watch." I've got the time, and maybe I can help."

Jack took another drink and sat back in his chair. "You know that after Tim graduated he went to Ocotal to teach in a Catholic school."

"I do know he went there and always wondered why. Where is Ocotal, anyway?"

"It's in the northern mountain region of Nicaragua, near the Honduran border, about 140 miles north of Managua. Tim met some kids from Connecticut when he was at the University and they sold him on the place. Apparently Hartford had become a sister city with Ocotal in the mid-80s, around the time Ollie North was furnishing weapons to the Contras in Nicaragua. I guess the Hartford people were trying to show the Nicaraguans that not all Americans want them dead. Most of those kids had been to Ocotal."

"Anyway, he had taken a couple years of Spanish in high school and off he went. His first year was really great; he loved it. He called once a week giving us all the news, running up some great telephone bills. Then, a few weeks ago, things changed. His calls were different, kind of erratic, short and stilted. We both felt something was wrong, but Tim wouldn't talk about it. Nancy got worried and her motherly instincts kicked in. I was in the middle of this trial and couldn't get away so she flew there herself. Funny, I was getting used to worrying about Tim and now I have to worry about both of them."

"I don't blame you. It's kind of a mess down there and their politics suck. I think the Cubans and Russians are running Nicaragua right now."

Walt emptied his beer and looked at his friend. "Now that you have another case in the win column, are you going to Nicaragua?"

Jack smiled for the first time. "No, I intended to, but I checked my answering service after I showered and Nancy left a message that she and Tim are on their way home. They took a TACA flight from Managua to Miami this morning and will take a Delta flight to Atlanta. The only thing bothering me now is Tim coming home. It's not like him to leave in the middle of the semester. I think his problem could be more serious than I figured."

Walt signaled for another beer and Jack agreed to have one more.

"And when I finish it I'm going down to Hartsfield, hug and kiss them both, and get reacquainted with my son."

They were talking about friends and business when Walt, who had a good view of the television set over the bar, saw that Channel Two had interrupted their programing. Something was said that grabbed his attention. He pulled Jack to his feet and steered him toward the bar. They couldn't hear every word because the television was muted, but they could tell the newscaster was excited and he had mentioned Miami. Walt took a stronger grip on Jack, steadying him, as they both listened in mounting anguish and horror.

"TACA flight from Managua, Nicaragua to Miami, down in the Gulf…"

"No warning or radio contact…"

"No known survivors, five passengers from Georgia…"

"Names withheld until notification…"

Jack made a noise like a wounded animal and collapsed in the nearest chair.

Chapter 3

Miami, Florida, Tuesday, February 8

THE SKY WAS DARK AND overcast, much like the atmosphere in the room where the five richly dressed men were gathered, trying to show how calm they were. The room, a library of sorts, was on the first floor of the rambling two-story villa on the shore of the Atlantic Ocean, south of Miami. It was a man's room, with oak floors partially covered by thick rope rugs and heavy, leather furniture. Three of the walls were constructed of floor to ceiling bookcases crammed with an ill assortment of unread books. The fourth, facing the sea, was of solid glass. It offered a magnificent view of green, well-manicured lawns that sloped downward to an Olympic-sized swimming pool and continued to the ocean. The property was protected on the other three sides by large walls topped with razor-sharp wire, and if you looked closely, you could see the guards move through the thick foliage.

The men were powerful businessmen and landowners from El Salvador who fled their country in 1980 to avoid the civil war. They planned to return, and now that the fighting was over and the peace accord signed, it was time. The first free election was to be held on the first Tuesday in March, but Nelson Martinez wouldn't let that happen.

"I still think there is a better way," Miguel Casstillo, the oldest man in the room muttered.

"If you have a better plan, let's hear it," Nelson Martinez, their host, snapped.

Miguel shrugged. "Why not let the election take its course?"

"You saw what happened in Nicaragua when the people decided," Jose Blanco intervened. "They voted the leftists in and we can't let that happen in El Salvador."

"But ARENA is the favorite to win," Miguel persisted, "and we are still members."

"The Republican Alliance is not the same party we left and any control or power we had is gone. No, this is too important to let the people decide; we will do what we must."

"I worry that the Americans might intervene."

"The new President is not a Ronald Regan," Martinez answered, losing patience. "He is weaker, more indecisive and will not attack us. Besides, many people that are in high places in their government approve of us. They know we will stop the Soviet movement in Central America from moving north."

Nelson Martinez was a dark-skinned man with a full head of graying hair and a distinctive, hawk like nose. He wore his age well, was impeccably dressed in a black silk suit, gray long-sleeved shirt, and black alligator loafers. He sat behind a highly polished, cherry-wood desk, absently drumming his fingers on the surface. The noise, the only sound in the room, was irritating, adding to the anxiety of the other four men, but not one of them dared voice a complaint.

After all these years, Martinez thought, it was finally coming together. He had been away too long and it was right that he return as the head of his country. It is his legacy and if he is forced to destroy the country, so be it. He will rebuild it, brick by brick, rebuilding it his way.

A soft buzz emanated from the telephone and drew five pairs of eyes, interrupting their various thoughts. Martinez knew who it was and knew that now they were committed. He let it ring once more before picking it up.

"Your order has been filled," the caller said, and without waiting for an acknowledgment, Martinez heard the click of disconnection. Still he held the telephone to his ear and then with an audible sigh, replaced it in its cradle. The eyes of the other four men were riveted to his and he nodded. That solitary movement released the tension and a babble of voices.

"Madre de Dios," Miguel Casstillo exclaimed as he crossed himself, "all those innocent people."

Jorge Lupe, a heavy set, moon-faced man, the youngest one in the room, started to retort, but was silenced by a look from the man at the desk. Martinez needed these people; they were his pawns. What he didn't need was to listen to the fools. That teacher had to be eliminated after he had taken possession of the statue and had to disappear without raising suspicion. Security at Managua's airport was non-existent; the bomb was an easy solution. It was too bad about the other people on the TACA flight, but collateral damage was a part of every war. Now, no one could stop him. Captain Loring had assured him the mercenaries would be ready when needed.

San Salvador, El Salvador

Colonel Rafael Gomez replaced the telephone and fell back on the too soft bed with a sigh of satisfaction and a sense of accomplishment. He ran a well-manicured hand through his dark curly hair, and down his slightly pox-marked face that some women found fascinating.

It had been easier to plant the bomb on the TACA flight than he thought. Even the bribes were less than anticipated, so he would make a nice commission.

Still, he had wanted to take out the teacher while he was still in Nicaragua, but Martinez wouldn't hear of it. He didn't want any undue attention paid to the American. He was tired of taking orders from those greedy, senile old men. The good news was that it wouldn't be for long. They had the money, but he had the power, and power would win.

Less than four weeks now and he would be what: king, tyrant, or maybe even beloved president. He smiled, felt himself harden as the excitement began to build, and reached over and pulled the lovely dark haired woman on top of him, feeling her lush breasts against his bare chest. He kissed and caressed her, murmuring words of endearment as he pushed her head down his chest.

"Hurry, my darling," he whispered hoarsely, "I must meet your husband at the Ministry in less than an hour." He knew Martinez was anticipating the surprise he had planned for the people of El Salvador—what Martinez didn't know was that the biggest surprise would be on him.

Chapter 4

CIA HQ, Langley, Virginia,

Thursday, February 10

Cathy Stanfil's office was on the third floor of the six-story office tower, which was added to the original CIA building in 1991.

Joe Ellison, the CIA station chief in El Salvador, sat on an uncomfortable chair, too small for his large posterior, and watched Cathy with a sense of pride and admiration. She bent over her keyboard, frowning in concentration, alternately punching keys and making notes on a long yellow pad.

Cathy Stanfil, in her late twenties, was a graduate of Boston College, majoring in political science, and spoke three languages. Joe had met her at the Georgetown University library where she was doing her graduate work. It was not by accident. A friendly professor had passed along a paper Cathy had written regarding the political situations in Central America; Joe was impressed. After heated debates, many discussions and a lot of patience, Joe had recruited her to the CIA. Surprisingly, both of them were glad that he did. After her training period and the usual time at the farm, Cathy was assigned to the office of Asian Pacific and Latin American analysis where she had made her mark.

"I never could get the hang of those things," Joe said, breaking the silence and indicating her computer.

"You never really tried," Cathy said without looking up.

Joe smiled; the lady really had a way with words.

"Ha!" Cathy exclaimed as she turned away from her computer and Joe caught a glimpse of long pretty legs. Joe was old enough to be her father, but he could still appreciate a great pair of legs. That had been her only drawback as Joe saw it—she was just too good-looking. She was tall, with light brown curly hair and a figure that other women would die for. She had delicate features and green eyes that sparkled when she laughed or smiled, which was often. She also had a quick focused mind and a good sense of humor.

"Ha, what?" Joe asked.

Cathy looked up from her notes, dropped her pencil and folded her hands in her lap. "Remember when we were at lunch yesterday and you told me about those people in Guatemala?"

"You mean those guys playing soldier in that camp at Puerto de Jose?"

"Yes," Cathy answered, "and that started me thinking. You know how much traffic I have to go through every day?"

Joe nodded.

"Well that scenario sounded familiar so I went over some of the info I should have thrown away but didn't, and bingo, I found not one, but two similar situations."

Joe shook his head, "What situations are you talking about?"

"Just listen," Cathy said impatiently. "About two weeks ago I received some information from the DEA, relating to a drug lord in Honduras. Apparently the DEA and the Hondurans have been keeping an eye on this scumbag for some time and lately they observed a big increase in activity around his place. The guy owns a few thousand acres, most of it jungle, near the town of San Marcos. Anyway, they decided to take a closer look and found that he set up some kind of training camp. They figure the camp will hold two to three hundred people. The Hondurans are getting a little nervous, wondering why the guy wants his own private army."

Cathy paused for a breath. "More recently, I came across another scenario, source FBI, and much closer to home.

Someone set up a training camp in South Georgia near the town of Folkston, abutting the Okefenokee Swamp. They don't appear to be breaking any laws so the FBI is just watching, trying to get a closer look and see what they are up to."

Joe rubbed his jaw thoughtfully. "You think there's a connection?"

Cathy shrugged, "boys being boys, I can understand playing soldier, but three camps starting up at about the same time?" She let the question hang. "Then I started thinking about the locations, another coincidence?"

Joe pushed himself up with some effort and ambled over to the map of Central America taped to the wall of Cathy's office. Joe didn't look much like a CIA agent. He was about 60 pounds overweight, had brown thinning hair and wore suits that looked like rejects from the Salvation Army. Cathy knew the rumples and broad chubby face hid a sharp, intelligent, well-disciplined mind.

Cathy joined him at the map. "If the people in Guatemala had a mind to, they could cross into El Salvador here," and she pointed, "near Santa Anna, or if they wanted, go by boat and land in any number of places, possibly here at La Libertad. From there they could move to San Salvador, taking control of the airport on the way. The people in Honduras could cross over in a number of places, like Metapan, an important communications center, or here in the South, near San Francisco, or both of the above."

Joe continued to study the map and mused. "So you think I'm going to have trouble in my back yard?"

Cathy nodded.

"You're thinking the election?"

Cathy nodded again, and then shrugged. "Hey, it's just a guess, but I'm sure something is brewing down there."

"O.K., and knowing you, young lady, you've made that conjecture on more information than you're giving me, but what in hell do the people in Georgia have to do with this?"

Cathy walked back to her desk, picked up a folder and told Joe to sit. "For some time now we have been interested in a company called the El Sal Corporation, ring a bell?"

Joe shook his head.

"It's owned by five well-heeled business owners from El Salvador who came to Miami in the early eighties to escape the civil war."

"The company's organization has more twists and turns than a maze and we suspect they are into illegal arms, money laundering, drugs, and God knows what else. So far, we haven't come up with any proof. Then I got lucky, with hard work and persistence, of course." She looked up, smiled and then turned serious. "I found that one of the subsidiaries of the El Sal Corporation leased three Hercules C-130's, from International Transportation, for the fifth of March, just three days before the March eighth election in El Salvador."

Joe frowned and sat up straighter as he took the folder from Cathy and studied it.

"And did I mention," Cathy asked smugly, "that our Honduran drug lord, Carlos Camejo, has an airstrip on those two thousand acres of his, which is capable of handling a C-130?"

"Let's see," Joe said scratching behind his left ear, "if I remember correctly, a C-130 can carry about…."

"Eighty-five men with full equipment," Cathy interrupted.

"So you think the Georgia boys will join the bunch in Honduras?"

"I have that suspicion and it's getting stronger."

"You know," Joe said slowly, "something happened in San Salvador recently that puzzled me, but if your projections are right, then it would make sense. I was attending a big-wig army reception, fulfilling one of my many duties as our cultural attaché."

"Boy," Cathy laughed, "someone in State sure has a sense of humor."

Joe gave her his most offended look and continued without comment. "There were a bunch of military types in attendance and the booze was flowing. I was talking to this Gomez character, Rafael Gomez, a real piece of work. He's a Colonel in the PNC, the new National Civil Police and would cut up his grandmother for a buck and sell tickets on the side. While we were talking, something happened that set off the old alarm bells. I couldn't figure it. We were talking about the election and this Captain Navero walks up and says, 'what election,' and laughs. The Captain was pretty drunk and I wouldn't have thought about it twice if I hadn't seen Gomez's face. He was livid and he hustled Navero out of there in one hell of a hurry. The good Captain never returned."

Cathy sat at her desk, making notes on her yellow pad, and chewing on the end of her pencil. "That would make sense if my scenario is right. These Miami people would need a military connection in El Salvador and who better than a Colonel in the Police Force. Most of the PNC members are from the old death squads and the Colonel probably knows where all the bodies are hidden. They could coerce a few reluctant people into seeing things their way."

Joe nodded. "Sounds right to me, and who are these Miami people you keep talking about?"

Cathy rifled through the file again and pulled out a sheet of paper. "Nelson Martinez," she read, "is the head honcho, a large property and coffee plantation owner; Jose Blanco, coffee and sugar; Pablo Matus, banking; Miguel Casstillo, manufacturing and transportation, the oldest member; and Jorge Lupe, who replaced his recently deceased father. We know that these people are the El Sal Corporation, and they want to return to El Salvador, but under their terms."

"Wait a minute," Joe said as he waved a hand, "I'm sure the Miami people you mentioned are all members of ARENA, the National Alliance party, and ARENA is favored to win the election, so why do they need all the fire power?"

"I think they lived the good life too long. They have been here over ten years and lost control of the party. No matter who wins, they will be out in the cold. Like most situations today, it's not about country; it's about power. They want control and won't trust an election, especially after Nicaragua's election went to the Communists."

"Even if you're right," Joe protested, "our esteemed President promised a free election down there and he meant it. I think he would use the Marines if he had to."

Cathy continued to chew on her pencil, "What if…" she speculated, "something catastrophic happened? I mean a global shocker that threw El Salvador into turmoil and then these El Sal people move in quickly and restore order. What do you think would happen then?"

Joe scratched the bald spot on the back of his head. "I guess that would depend on what happened. You have anything in mind?"

"My crystal ball didn't tell me," Cathy admitted, "but I know something is going to happen down there and we have less than a month to figure out what."

"If they come in from Honduras and Guatemala, it could work," Joe mused. "They could pull it off using your plan. Hey, the people in El Salvador have been fighting for twelve years; what's another war to them? Then, if their neighbors recognized the new regime, it would give them clout and put us in one hell of a bind. Have you tried this theory on your esteemed boss yet?" Joe asked, as he stood and moved toward the door.

"Not yet—you know how Art is. I just want to fill in a few blanks first."

"Right or wrong, you had better take it to him, and soon," Joe advised. "I'm flying back tomorrow and I will nose around some more, maybe even go out and see my new friend Captain Navero."

As Joe opened the door, Cathy looked up with obvious affection and a mock frown. "And what happened to that diet I gave you that you promised to try?"

Joe looked pained, "I'm trying it," he said. "And that Slim fast isn't so bad when you put ice cream in it."

"Funny," Cathy retorted. "Remember you're supposed to be taking pounds off, not putting them on."

Chapter 5

Atlanta, Georgia, Friday, February 18

Jack awoke from another troubled sleep and, in that first after-sleep haze, reached across the bed to touch her as he had so many times before. He couldn't find her and reached further, knocking a pillow to the floor, and became fully awake. He stared down at the empty place beside him. She wasn't there and never would be. He felt the knot in his stomach tighten. Walt had insisted that he rest before the memorial service and surprisingly he had fallen asleep. He wasn't sure if he felt better or worse, even though he knew he was sleep deprived.

The past week had been a kaleidoscope of faces, names, and words of condolence that he neither heard nor remembered. It was an out of body experience. His body was there, but his brain was not. He wondered if it would get any better after tonight's service.

Jack planned a memorial service for Nancy and Tim at Corpus Christi Catholic Church, where they were members, and Nancy was a dedicated volunteer. After the service, family and friends would leave to go back to their world and he would go back… to what, he wondered.

The search for the TACA flight had been abandoned three days ago and already the media had turned to other disasters and tragedies. The only piece of concrete information that had come from the Nicaraguan investigation was from a Panamanian freighter. A lookout had reported a flash or explosion in the sky that approximated the position of the

TACA flight. There was no warning, no radio message, and no trace of the plane, passengers or crew. They couldn't even find the black box. If it was a terrorist attack, no one was claiming responsibility for it. The Nicaraguan authorities were continuing their investigation, but their cooperation was noticeably lacking.

It was early evening, and Jack took a long hot shower and dressed in a dark pin-striped suit, white shirt and tie. He dreaded the approaching service and was glad that he had support from his two friends.

Walt Kutch was there, of course, but Gene Belden's appearance had been a real surprise. He and Jack had served together in Vietnam and becoming friends with Gene hadn't been easy. Gene was a West Point graduate who didn't have much use for weekend warriors. That changed as Jack completed each mission successfully and, when his medal count exceeded Gene's, Gene had, grudgingly, conceded that Jack might be an exception.

The years had treated his friend well, Jack thought, as he tied his tie. He had made Colonel at a relatively early age and was on track for his star. He appeared to be in great shape with the same bull-like neck, trim waist, and GI haircut, now beginning to gray. Jack joined Walt and Gene in the library, a bright airy room with high Hurd Windows and full patio doors that offered a great view of a thickly wooded ravine. The windows were draped with luminous custom woven silk that muted the light. Walt handed Jack an ice cold, Grey Goose martini.

"Drink it," Walt ordered, "I think you're going to need it."

Belden agreed. "The families said to let you sleep, that you needed it and they would meet you at the church. They are all packed, and will leave after the service. Are you OK?"

Jack shrugged, then nodded and took another swallow of the drink. Walt was right; it helped. The ringing of the chimes interrupted any further conversation and Jack motioned Walt to stay put as he got up to answer the door. He assumed everyone knew about the service tonight and was annoyed by the intrusion. He opened the door, trying to hide his annoyance and was confronted by a diminutive young woman dressed in a severely tailored light gray suit, a white blouse, and black low-heeled shoes. She was pretty, despite her austere dress, and carried a small package wrapped in brown paper. Jack noted a waiting taxi.

"Yes?" he inquired shortly, trying to mask his impatience.

The young lady leaned slightly forward, squinted up at him in the fading light, and smiled in relief. "Oh, I'm so glad that I caught you at home, Mr. Nordone," she blurted. "I know I should have called first, but my time is limited and I thought even if you weren't home I could leave the package with a neighbor."

"Package," Jack repeated in confusion and shook his head, "I'm sorry, this has been a trying week, and with meeting so many people, I'm afraid I don't remember…"

"Oh, you don't know me," the girl broke in. "I recognize you from the pictures and even feel that I know you because I've heard so much about you."

Now Jack was completely mystified and he opened the door, inviting her in. "What pictures?" He asked, shaking his head.

"The pictures Tim had," the girl answered and held out her hand. "I'm Linda Masters, Sister Linda Masters. Tim was a good friend of mine. We taught school together in Ocotal and he was always talking about you, bragging really."

For the first time since the accident, Jack showed a spark of emotion as he realized that this girl had lived, worked, and talked with his son for the last year and a half—time that was lost to him.

Linda, seeing Jack's emotion, reached up and touched his cheek. "I didn't mean to intrude on your grief," she said softly, "but I did want to stop by and express my sorrow and that of all the people at the school. Tim was special, genuinely loved, and will be greatly missed. He asked me, made me promise actually, to deliver this package to you. He said it was very important and that you would know what to do with it. He knew that I was going home to visit my parents in Minneapolis and would have a plane change in Atlanta."

Jack frowned, "I don't understand. If this package is so important, why didn't he bring it with him when he left with his mother?"

"I wondered the same thing," Linda admitted. "When his mom arrived and I found out they were flying back to Atlanta, I gave the package back to him. After Tim and his mother left, I found it back in my room."

"That is odd," Jack murmured, "do you know what it is?"

"It's a wood carving of a pope, or maybe a saint."

Jack examined the knotted cord around the package and started to untie it.

Walt Kutch and Gene, standing in the entrance to the foyer, had been listening to the conversation. "We don't mean to rush you," Belden said as he took the package from Jack's hand and placed it on the small wooden table next to the grandfather clock. "We have to move out. You can't be late for this one."

Jack glanced at the clock, told Sister Linda about the memorial service for Nancy and Tim and begged her to stay. "Maybe," he implored, "you could attend the service, spend the night here and tomorrow morning tell me about Tim's life in Ocotal. I will be glad to take you to the airport."

Linda shook her head helplessly, "I would really like to, except that my parents are expecting me and I have a taxi waiting."

Walt had watched Jack's reaction to Linda and he wasn't about to let her get away, so he took her arm and steered her toward the door. "Sister, it just happens that I have to fly to Chicago tomorrow on the company jet. It wouldn't be any trouble to drop you off in Minneapolis. I'm traveling alone and would welcome your company. I know you will enjoy it; the plane has all the comforts of home and then some. I'll take care of the taxi and your luggage while you call your parents."

Walt lowered his voice, "I'm really worried about Jack and I think your visit would be a big help. This is the first time he has shown any interest in anyone or anything since they died. Please, help him."

Walt pushed the right button and when Linda saw the expression on Jack's face, she sighed and agreed to stay. Walt went out to take care of the taxi while Linda made the call to her parents.

Sister Linda sat in the back of the Lincoln Town car with Jack and she could feel his tension and apprehension. She took his hand. "Remember," she said quietly, "other people have their grief, too. You're not alone. Your wife and son were loved by many people. Don't shut them out. They need you as much as you need them. Accept this for what it is, a tribute to two wonderful people from friends who care."

***

The recently crowded church had about emptied and Jack was still standing in the vestibule accepting condolences. Linda's words had helped and he realized he had been shutting out both friends and family because of his own feelings. He felt he had done a good job of handling the memorial until he turned and faced a large black man with wide shoulders that tapered to a narrow waist, frizzled gray hair, and a broad expansive face. The man just looked at Jack for a moment, shook his head in evident sorrow, and enfolded Jack in his long arms. Jack hugged him back in total surprise and the tears he had withheld for so long suddenly coursed down his cheeks and his body was racked in a long agonizing cry. The last of the mourners turned away, trying to provide some sort of privacy while their own tears flowed out of control. Walt raised his eyes upward, knowing that now his friend could began healing.

After Jack had regained his composure, he made the introductions. "This is TC Brown," Jack managed, one arm still around TC's shoulder, "the best top sergeant and friend that a brand new, not-too-bright lieutenant could have been blessed with."

Introductions and good-byes were intermingled, and hugs and kisses exchanged, as the out-of-town people headed for the airport. TC said he was staying at the Airport Holiday Inn and he would catch a ride with one of the relatives. Jack wouldn't hear of it.

"The least I can do is to take you there myself, if you're sure I can't talk you into staying over."

"You know I would if I could. I have to be back in Chicago tomorrow and I'm scheduled out on the early bird."

"Well then, why don't we all go down to the Holiday Inn with you and have a drink. I think we can all use one about now."

Walt and Linda nodded in agreement, but Belden shook his head and looked at his watch. "I can't," he said, "I did get in touch with an old buddy of mine and he should be here to pick me up any minute. I took a couple things for overnight and will see you back at your house tomorrow." A car drove slowly into the parking lot and Belden gave Jack a quick hug and left. "See you around noon," he called.

Nancy's father left her car in the parking lot, so Jack asked Walt to take the car and Linda and follow him to the Holiday Inn. Linda begged off at the last minute.

"I've been up since four this morning and travel really tires me out," she said. "Why don't you drop me off at your house? I can get good night's sleep and we will talk in the morning."

"And," Walt broke in, "I have to make preparations for tomorrow's flight, so I'll pass and take Linda to your house. We can talk over our plans for tomorrow and you guys can tell your war stories."

***

The Holiday Inn's lounge was about half full, and they found a quiet table in the corner and ordered drinks from the blond waitress in the too-tight dress. They talked of old friends, the war, and Chicago, where Jack had gotten his law degree and TC joined the police department after returning from Vietnam and retiring from the army. They were often together as couples and Jack and Nancy were godparents to TC's only daughter, Tessie. Then Jack and Nancy had moved to Atlanta and they lost touch.

"I really tried to get a hold of you about a year ago," Jack said. "Your telephone was unlisted. I couldn't get a forwarding address, so I tried your old precinct. They gave me the run around. I know Nancy wrote a couple times, and never got an answer. Where are you guys living now? How is Alretha? And I imagine Tessie has grown up to be quite a young lady."

A mask dropped over TC's face as he slugged down the last of his drink. He didn't look up, just kept staring at his empty glass as he told Jack the story of a black cop, working Chicago's South Side, playing it straight, working two jobs, and trying to make a better life for a wife with lupus and a daughter, who was running out of control. He finally made it, moving to a better neighborhood, but it was too late. The gang had a better hold on Tessie than he did and when he got tough, she ran away and died of a drug overdose. He blamed himself, too much work and not enough time at home. Then his voice broke. "Three days after Tessie's funeral, I came home to find Alretha dead. They said it was an accident, that she took too many pills, but...," His voice trailed off.

"My God," Jack exclaimed in anguish, "I, we didn't know, why didn't you...."

"Call you? I was going to after Tessie died. Then after Aretha, I was in shock. I think you understand now. I didn't want to talk to anyone."

Jack thought back to the trim attractive woman and the cute little girl in pigtails and shook his head, "I'm sorry as hell that I wasn't there for you."

"Don't fret it," TC said, "you had no way of knowing and now you have enough on your plate. Besides, I'm carrying enough guilt for half the world."

They were both locked in their own thoughts, their own hell, and Jack looked at his friend. "Tell me—is there any kind of life after this? I really can't find a good reason to get out of bed in the morning."

TC hesitated, "I guess each person has his own way of coping and for me it was a year in the bottle. Then one day I sobered up and decided to get even. I quit the force and went into a kind of freelance work. It was me against the drug dealers—the guys that kill our kids. I get a lot of help from the people I used to work with because they know I can and will do things they can't. I did it *pro bono* at first. Now it's beginning to pay pretty well."

Jack frowned at TC, wondering just what he meant, not sure he wanted to know.

"Hey," TC said, defensively, "it gave me a reason to get out of bed and stay sober and I'm doing a hell of a lot more good now than I did when I was on the force." TC looked Jack in the eye, "Tell me, what would you do if you got your hands on the people that blew up that plane?"

Jack shrugged. "First, no one knows if it was a bomb, and even if it was, do I go out and kill some misguided crazy who is trying to make his world right? No, nothing is going to bring them back. They were in the wrong place at the wrong time; I have had enough war for one lifetime."

"A call for Mr. Nordone, Mr. Jack Nordone," came over the speaker.

Puzzled, Jack stood up, and was directed to the nearest telephone.

When he returned, his face was ashen and he grabbed the top of his chair for support. "That was Walt. My house, it's gone. They think a fire bomb, and Sister Linda died in the fire."

Chapter 6

Lake Lanier, Cumming, Georgia

Saturday, February 19

"Damn it," Belden complained, echoing the thoughts of the other two, "where the fuck is he?"

The three men, Belden with coffee, Walt Kutch with a Jack Daniels, and TC with a Bud, sat on the padded seats of the breakfast nook in Walt's home on Lake Lanier. The kitchen had a high 13-foot ceiling, twin stainless-steel ovens, and a solid oak butcher's block island. The nook was surrounded by large bay windows that framed a great view of the lake, unnoticed by the men who were worrying and wondering about Jack.

"You were with him when he learned about the fire and then drove back with him," Belden said to TC. "What frame of mind was he in, what did you guys talk about?"

TC shrugged, "Personal things mostly, about Nancy and Tim. I was a little surprised. Jack wasn't interested in payback, or even finding out who did it. He said no one really knew what had happened and even if it was a bomb, he wasn't going to look for some crazy, trying to make his world right and then kill him. He said nothing would bring them back and he had enough war for one lifetime."

"Probably a good choice," Belden said, "they play pretty rough in those Central American countries."

TC looked up, "Rougher than Nam?"

Belden shrugged.

Walt drained the rest of his drink and moved toward the bar for a refill. "You guys have known him longer than I have, but I think what happened last night will change everything. After the fire, he gave me TC to take care of and took off without a word."

TC grabbed another beer, "I agree. I think that Tim got involved in something political down there and whatever it was, he and his mother were killed because of it. Now it's personal. The son of a bitch who is responsible for all this better watch his back, because he's a dead man walking."

"Knowing Jack though," the Colonel said, "he wouldn't do anything foolish. He's always been pretty much by-the-book."

TC took a long swallow, put the bottle down carefully, looked at the two men and made his decision. "There is a lot you don't know about Jack,"TC started. "Let me tell you a story of a by-the-book lieutenant. I knew right away that our new lieutenant was something special," TC said pensively. "I saw a bunch of them in my day and you never got a chance, or even wanted to know them because their life span was numbered in days. Most were carried out. You could see that this one was different. He learned their language, read their maps, and always had his nose in some book when we weren't fighting."

"Then he started to go out nights, alone. Sometimes he was gone a couple of days. I guess it was cool with the skipper, because he brought back good intel and got to know the territory as well as the Cong did. He made friends with a village not too far from our camp, and especially with a pretty, young, pregnant woman. She had a two or three-year-old daughter. We would stop there, either coming or going on a mission, and would bring food and medicine. They would tell Jack stuff. One time, going out on patrol, we stopped and found the village had been hit by the Cong. They completely destroyed it and Jack found his friend with her belly ripped open and her baby stuck with a bayonet. Her little girl was shot." TC stopped and shook his head.

"Jack didn't say a word, or even stop to bury them, just took off with us on their trail. He knew a few short cuts, and after a day and most of the night, we ambushed them the next morning. Jack ordered us not to kill the officer. We did kill the rest of them. I knew what Jack wanted to do, but his upbringing and morals wouldn't let him, so Jack and the gook stripped to their waist, each took a bayonet and they went at it. He even ordered me to let the gook go if he won." TC paused again. "I've never seen anything like it and will never forget it. Sure, Jack got cut, while he, literally, cut that bastard to pieces. He then pushed him against a tree, and pinned one of his hands to the tree with his bayonet, picked up the other bayonet and pinned the guy's other hand to the tree. His adrenalin was running because he drove those bayonets two or three inches into that tree." TC shook his head, "We took off, and you could hear the screams for the first mile or so."

"I never heard about that," Belden said skeptically, "and I was there at the time."

"That was because we all decided it never happened. We were afraid Jack might get into trouble. Last night, I saw the same anger I saw in Nam."

"What would have happened if the other guy had won?" Walt asked.

"I would have shot his balls off," TC answered, and the conversation stopped as Jack walked through the door.

He looked like hell and probably felt worse, as he slipped onto the padded seat and dropped a large brown envelope on the table. Walt handed him a mug of fresh coffee, laced with Jack Daniels, a little sugar, and Jack sipped it gratefully. It had been a long day. He explained how he had found Linda's parents and told them what happened. That part never got any easier.

He made arrangements to ship the body to Minneapolis. After that, he took care of some personal business and then stopped by his office. He talked with his partners, reassigned his active cases and took an indefinite leave of absence. He set up an answering service and a post office box in Stone Mountain, adding a new will, giving Walt his power of attorney.

"There are some instructions," Jack said to Walt, nodding toward the envelope, "day to day things that I would like you to take care of for me, because I'm not sure where I'll be for the next few months." Jack paused and looked around the table. "I talked with the police and fire chief, and they confirmed that it was a fire bomb. Now I know it wasn't a 'wrong place, wrong time' thing. My family was the target and that includes Sister Linda. Tim wasn't very political, but he got mixed up in something important and, knowing Tim, tried to help. I don't know who is responsible for this, or why, but I do know where. Right now, I have no family, no job, no home, and no life. I do have a mission though, which will keep me busy until I finish it."

Walt watched the change in the shade of Jack's eyes and gave an involuntary shudder.

Jack's head turned, and he looked puzzled. "What was that? It sounded like something scratching at your basement door."

Walt, almost smiling, walked to the door and opened it. Ralph bounded out and in two leaps landed on Jack who fell to his knees. Ralph put a paw on each shoulder, licking his face. Jack choked back the tears and buried his face in the soft fur.

"Your neighbor found him in his back yard," Walt explained. "He had a cut on his face and side. It looks like he jumped through a window. The guy took him to the vet and called the police. I left my number with one of the officers explaining that they should call me if they needed you. I would keep in touch with you. They did call so I went to the vet and picked him up this morning."

"You got a weird looking dog there," TC said. "What is it?"

"Jack thinks he is half Chow and half German Shepard," Walt answered.

TC shook his head. "I've never seen a red German Shepard with a big bushy tail before."

"I advise you to keep on his good side," Walt answered. "He is one tough dog and the neighborhood hero. Somehow, two big Dobermans got into the neighbor's yard and chased the neighbor's two kids, kids that played with Ralph every day. Ralph was out back doing his thing, must have heard the change in their voices and recognized the terror. He jumped over the fence, killed one of the Dobermans and messed up the other."

Jack stood up, wiped his eyes, and sat back down on the window seat.

"You have one hell of a problem," Belden said. "Where are you going to start?"

Jack rubbed his jaw and pushed his empty mug towards Walt for a refill. "I'll start where this all started, in Ocotal."

"I don't know," Belden said shaking his head, "unfamiliar territory, language barrier, and you can't identify the enemy." He paused, "I don't think that's a very good idea."

"Probably not," Jack agreed. "I have to start somewhere and Linda told me about a parish priest in Ocotal that was a friend of Tim's and might know why that statue was so important. Maybe he can tell me what this is all about and steer me in the right direction. One way or another, I will find out who is responsible and why they killed a plane-load of people.

They all started to talk at once when TC waved them to silence. "I have to fly home tomorrow. I re-booked my flight, and it will take me a couple days to get things in order. I should be back in about three or four days."

Jack started to protest.

"Hey," TC retorted, "I loved that wife and son of yours, and you can't keep me out. Besides, you're taking on one hell of a job and can use a good detective, someone to watch your back, just like the old days."

"You can count on me, too," Belden said, "anything you need."

Again, Jack started to protest but Walt cut him off.

"And I'm involved, not only because of my feelings for you and your family, but if I hadn't offered Linda a ride in our plane, she might still be alive. I feel responsible." Walt looked at each man around the table. "So with that said, I am declaring this," and he pounded on the kitchen table, "headquarters for the mission because it looks like we will all be in different places." Walt took out a small notebook, wrote a telephone number down, made three copies and passed them around.

"This is my private line, which is very secure. I will gather and dispense information, always keeping in touch with Jack. He knows I'm pretty good with a computer and have the best equipment in the world available to me. It's amazing the information you can get from a good computer, so use me."

There appeared to be a general agreement, then Belden said, "I know that nothing is going to stop you from going down there, even though I think it's a bad idea, so why don't you let me do a little checking first? I know something about that part of the world, because I spent two years in Honduras as an advisor, and two years in El Salvador as the military attaché."

"I remember the Christmas cards," Jack said.

"There were times when I worked with the CIA and I still have contacts there. Why don't I fly to Washington, see a friend of mine in the CIA, and see what I can find out. They should know something about that TACA flight going down, and you know what they say about moving too fast with too little intelligence."

Walt and TC agreed it made sense. Jack was too tired to argue.

"But I'm going with you. I just can't sit anymore. I can get a flight to Managua from Washington or New York," he lifted Ralph's head, "and one way or another, I'm taking Ralph with me. I know it's a dumb idea, but he is the only thing I have left. I don't even have a picture."

Walt wanted to confirm that it was a dumb idea, but watching the expression on Jack's face, decided not to.

Chapter 7

CIA HQ, Monday, February 21

CATHY STANFIL GLANCED AT THE clock, continued chewing on her pencil, and went over her notes one last time, dreading the approaching meeting. She had taken Joe's advice and told Art Clausen, the DDI, Deputy Director of Intelligence, about the information she had gathered and the projections she had made regarding the election in El Salvador. He wasn't impressed, but passed it on to the big boss. Now she was about to meet with Art, Richard Hightower, the Director of the CIA, and Senator Aaron Rucker from Georgia.

Rucker was an interesting man. He was a Vietnam War hero, self-made millionaire, and successful politician. He was the president's closest friend and advisor, head of the Senate Arms Committee and the second most powerful man in Washington. He had a reputation for honesty and loyalty, which was more than you could say about most of the people on Capitol Hill.

Cathy took out a small mirror, checked her makeup once more, then, with a sigh of resignation, gathered her notes.

She went up two floors, down the wide, red-carpeted hallway to the corner office and knocked on the partially opened door. The room was spacious, with two large windows overlooking the woods. The three men were already seated around the table and her appearance interrupted their conversation. Cathy was aware of Senator Rucker's appraisal. She wore a severely cut navy blue suit that was unable to hide her figure and Cathy felt the Senator's approval as their eyes met. Aaron Rucker, a widower, was often shown in the society pages escorting a beautiful lady to some function or other and although some years her senior, she was well aware of his energy and magnetism.

Art Clausen made the introductions as he waved Cathy to a seat.

"I was just explaining to the Director and Senator Rucker that you," emphasizing the word you, "believe we might have some problems in El Salvador regarding their upcoming election."

"I want to point out," Director Hightower interrupted, "that the Senator is the direct representative of the President and as such has the highest possible clearance. Anything that you can say to me, or Art, you can say to Senator Rucker." He paused. "Do I make myself clear?"

Cathy nodded, and couldn't help stealing a glance at her boss. Art thought that any information given to outsiders, no matter who they were, was close to treason.

"O.K.," Clausen said reluctantly, "Cathy, why don't you take it from here, and please, separate the facts from your suppositions."

Cathy thought the remark was uncalled for and started to retort, when she was interrupted by the Senator.

"As you know, the President has personally assured the people in San Salvador a fair election. We have enough problems at home and don't need any surprises in El Salvador. I believe that Miss Stanfil is an analyst, so let her analyze. I am interested in her theories as well as the facts."

Cathy suddenly had a warm feeling for the Senator, nodded, and tried to keep the smugness out of her voice as she basically repeated her conversation with Joe Ellison. When she finished, she could feel the Senator's interest, Clausen's displeasure, and the Director's neutrality.

Rucker pushed his chair away from the table and moved to the map of Central America on the far wall. Cathy joined him, pointing out the cities of San Marcos and Puerto de San Jose, which the Senator studied for some time before turning away.

"So you believe," he summarized, "that sometime, just prior to the election, the people training in Georgia will be flown to Honduras and join the group training in San Marcos. Then the ex-patriots from El Salvador will cause a major disruption that will give them an excuse for sending their mercenaries into El Salvador to restore order."

"Their kind of order," Cathy agreed.

Art Clausen made no effort to hide his skepticism. "You have projected one hell of a scenario, backed with very few facts," he said. "I still don't understand how the people in Miami will benefit. They are all members of ARENA, which is a big favorite to win the election." He threw up his hands.

"There might not be an election if they have their way," Rucker said. "I can see how they would benefit. They aren't just robbing a bank; they're trying to steal a country. Anyone know what a country is going for these days?" He looked at Clausen.

Clausen shrugged, "I know as much about that as I do about this horrible disruption that is supposed to happen in El Salvador. Miss Stanfil, do you even have a clue?"

Cathy shook her head, "I don't," she conceded. "I talked with Joe early this morning. Joe Ellison is our head of station in El Salvador," she explained to Senator Rucker. "He is also concerned. One of his most reliable informants told him about a statue that contained information regarding the election. Joe arranged to meet him. When he arrived at the meeting place, he found his informant with his throat slit, and his, ah… privates cut off, and stuffed in his mouth."

"And you think there is a connection?" Rucker asked.

"I do," Cathy said, "and Joe agrees. He thinks that someone on the inside got cold feet and gave information to an antique dealer in San Salvador who is known to be anti-government. Apparently the antique dealer had a religious statue with a secret compartment and he put a message in it and gave it to

Roberto Velado, a former teacher at the University of Central America. Roberto smuggled it out of the country."

"Who is this Velado?" Rucker asked.

"A patriot or terrorist, depending on who you ask," Cathy answered. "Two of San Salvador's infamous Security Police tried to arrest one of Roberto's students right in his classroom. Velado flipped, killed the two officers and helped the student escape. Then Roberto and his wife Maria fled to Ocotal, Nicaragua, a little town near the Honduran border. He has been fighting with the FMLN, a leftist guerilla group, ever since."

"A professor killed two police officers in his classroom?" Clausen questioned.

"He did," Cathy said. "The war in El Salvador lasted a long time and just about everyone there carries a weapon, even professors. Especially since their campus was invaded by the Security Force."

Rucker looked at Clausen. Clausen just shrugged and looked away.

"The Velado's," Cathy continued, "became friends with an American, Tim Nordone, from Georgia, who was teaching at a Catholic school in Ocotal. Joe thinks that Roberto got the statue to Tim. Soon after that, Tim's mother, Nancy, arrived in Ocotal and the two of them flew home on that TACA flight that went down in the Gulf."

"That name, Nordone, sounds familiar." Rucker said.

"They are from your state, Senator. Mr. Nordone, Jack, is a prominent attorney in Atlanta."

Rucker snapped his fingers. "I remember, I met them at a fund raiser in Atlanta—nice people. I was impressed with them both. God what a shame. I was out of the country at the time and didn't get many details."

"So you think that the Miami people blew up that TACA flight to get rid of Tim and the statue?" Hightower asked.

"I'm sure of it," Cathy said, "especially considering the new information I have. I now know that Tim did not have the statue with him when he boarded the flight home. He had given it to a fellow teacher, Sister Linda Masters. He knew that she was going home to visit her parents and had a plane change in Atlanta. Tim asked her to get the statue to his father. She arrived in Atlanta Friday."

"That doesn't make sense," Art Clausen interrupted, "if that statue was so damned important, why didn't Tim take it with him?"

Senator Rucker broke the silence. "Back-up maybe? Evidently he felt the information was so important he wanted backup. The best news is, we get a look at the statue and see if there is a message."

"I'm afraid not," Cathy said softly. "Friday night they had a memorial service for Tim and Nancy at Corpus Christi Catholic Church in Stone Mountain. Sister Linda attended. After the service, Jack took an army buddy to the airport and a friend took Sister Linda to Jack's house. While he was gone, his house was completely destroyed by fire. Sister Linda died in the fire and the statue burned. The fire department suspects arson, a fire bomb."

***

Art Clausen left the CIA complex soon after the meeting and by the time he turned onto the George Washington Parkway he was seething. Damn that girl, he thought, quickly admitting to himself it was more than just Cathy. She was just doing her job and, unfortunately, was too good at it. The whole thing was falling apart, turning into one fucking mess, with him right in the middle. And it wasn't his fault. If those idiot bureaucrats, including the President, realized they needed the people in Miami to take over that shit-hole down there, he wouldn't have had to get involved.

Clausen turned off the Parkway at King Street and made two quick turns, then a double back to make sure he wasn't being followed. He then drove to the apartment. He must be getting paranoid; who would follow the DDI? He parked the car, got out and made his way to the apartment on the second floor. It was never the same apartment or even the same building. He knocked on the door and it was opened by a dark-skinned man, who appeared as wide as he was tall. The man studied Clausen, then moved aside, letting him in.

The apartment was devoid of anything personal and he was led into the stark living room. Art stopped in surprise when he saw Nelson Martinez waiting. Martinez was the richest, smartest and the most vicious of the Miami people. He was a small, slender man, and dressed casually in a white sweater, dark slacks, and black alligator shoes.

Art took the offered hand and joked, trying to cover his nerves, "I didn't realize I was meeting the Head of State."

Martinez waved away the compliment, motioning Art to sit. "When you have serious problems, you send serious people," Martinez said with a smile that only reached his lips.

"We do have some problems," Clausen agreed, "but nothing I can't handle." He outlined what was said at the meeting he just attended.

Martinez listened with half closed eyes, without interruption and when the DDI had finished, he clasped his hands behind his head sitting back in his chair.

"So," he said softly, "you don't think it's serious when an obviously intelligent agent is tracking our every move and making accurate projections about our next one?" Martinez paused for effect. "It also appears that the President is now involved."

"I wouldn't worry about the President," Clausen said with more confidence than he felt. "He was just showing the flag because the director called him. Believe me, they have more important issues at home than El Salvador."

"And your agent," Martinez said, "she appears to be the catalyst here. Where would the investigation be without her?"

Art caught the implication and shook his head, "She's not even an agent," he protested, "just an analyst, and you can't…"

"Can't?" Martinez hissed.

"I mean," Clausen blurted, "no one is listening to her right now. But if something should happen to her after that TACA flight went down and that guy's house was burned, killing that nun, someone might put two and two together, giving credence to her theories."

Martinez frowned, "I don't understand what those two unfortunate accidents have to do with any of this?"

Clausen felt the sweat run down his neck and shifted uneasily in his seat. "Well, I just thought," he tried to explain.

"No!" Martinez snapped. "There are times when you don't think." He shrugged and in a softer tone said, "However, you might be right about the timing. I will hold you responsible for her."

"Don't worry," Clausen promised, "I will find a way to keep her out of it." He hesitated. "Is she right about some occurrence happening down there?"

Martinez stood up, obviously dismissing the DDI, leading him to the door and putting an arm around his shoulder. "The only event that will occur in El Salvador is our reclaiming our country from the Communists and the Liberals and becoming a better friend and ally to the United States. Go with God."

Long after Art left, Martinez sat watching the rain bounce off the asphalt below. With only two weeks left, this new information was very disturbing. He would get his people out of Georgia at the first opportunity. The extra time in San Marcos might even be beneficial to them, getting used to the climate and the country.

The girl was another matter. He turned to Manuel and handed him a folder. "All the information you need is in here. I want that lady dead, the sooner the better. Make it look like an accident."

Chapter 8

Ocotal, Nicaragua, Tuesday, February 22

WHAT A GLORIOUS DAY, FATHER Ernesto Esteban thought, as he listened to the birds while he walked down the hill to the children's playground. He would love to join the birds in their song, but that would only chase them away. The nuns in third grade had set him straight early in life. They said his voice would chase angels away and would he please just mouth the words? He sighed. How could they be so cruel to a nine-year old who wanted to be a great singer? Instead he became a great priest.

Some great priest, he thought, as he looked back at his church and shook his head in dismay. The cracked walls and peeling paint he could live with. The roof was another matter. His people should be able to pray in church without umbrellas. The good Lord knew he wanted to make the repairs. It was just that every time he got a little ahead, a child or a family needed the money more. He hoped God would understand because he knew the Archbishop wouldn't.

Father Esteban was in his mid-thirties. He was a tall, thin, wiry man with thick dark hair and a black, neatly trimmed beard that accentuated his dark, piercing, energy-filled eyes. He wasn't a popular priest with his superiors, because of his independence, but he was loved and admired by his parishioners. He stopped suddenly, finding his path blocked by a very small person. A pretty girl with braided hair, dressed in a clean, well-mended uniform, crying unconstrainedly as she rubbed her injured knee. Father Esteban scooped her up carefully, kissed the scraped knee, whispered a few words of endearment, hugged her, and set her back on the ground. Another miraculous cure, he thought, as he watched her scurry away. He wished that all his problems could be solved so easily. What to do with his poor church and people, a Peace Accord that didn't stop the killing, and his latest problem, Maria Velado.

Maria and her husband, Roberto, had moved into a farmhouse just outside Ocotal. The farm was owned by Maria's cousin, Victor.

Maria had golden brown skin, black silky hair that fell to her waist and shimmered in the light, and the face of a Madonna. She was the most beautiful, intelligent, caring woman that he had ever met.

He also admired Roberto, a former teacher at the University of Central America. He had a quiet manner that belied his strength and purpose. As a teacher, he had tried to keep to the middle of the road, politically. That changed in November of 1989 when the El Salvador army invaded the campus. Three Jesuit priests, the President, the Vice-President and the head of the Human Rights Department were killed along with their housekeeper and her daughter. They also killed three scholars, who were theology and human rights professors, along with fifty students. The administrators' only crime was caring for and helping the poor.

They were friends of Roberto's, and later, he killed two security officers trying to arrest a student. He and Maria fled to Ocotal. Roberto joined the FMLN, the *Farabundo Marti for National Liberation*, a leftist guerrilla group. Because of his passion and intelligence, he quickly rose to a position of importance and returned often to his country to help in their fight.

Roberto had been missing for over two weeks now and Father Esteban feared the worst. Maria was very active in church work, especially where the children were concerned, and they often worked together. He knew she liked and respected him as a priest, but he wondered about his true feelings for her. Stop, he didn't want to go there. The life of a priest was not easy.

Father Esteban's thoughts were interrupted as Pedro, his sometimes handyman, came running through the trees wildly waving his arms.

"Father, Father, come quick," he panted. "There is a jeep parked at Maria's house and there are soldiers. Not ours… from El Salvador, I think."

"How many, and what are they doing?" Father Esteban yelled over his shoulder as he ran toward his battered twenty-some year old Ford, praying that it would start.

"Four or five," Pedro yelled as he tried to keep up with the long-legged priest. "I don't know what they want. I sent Rodrigo for the men."

"You did well," Father Ernesto said and sighed with relief when the truck started on the first try and he headed out of the school-yard in a shower of dust.

***

Maria, trembling with fear and frustration, was backed into a corner of her bedroom trying to cover her bare breasts with the remnants of her blouse. Rafael Gomez slowly, very deliberately, unbuttoned his tunic and continued to torture her with his words as well as his actions.

"Your husband died well," Gomez said, as he took off his undershirt and laid it over his tunic. "It was only toward the end that he told us about the statue and the message he sent to you. Unfortunately, my men have very little patience and he died before he could tell us more." Rafael unzipped his pants very slowly, let them drop to his feet and kicked them away. He grabbed a handful of Maria's hair, forcing her to look at him.

"Now, after we have enjoyed ourselves, you will tell me about the message," Gomez said insolently. "Roberto thought he was so much smarter than we are, but he was wrong and paid the price."

Maria looked for a weapon, found she no longer had the will to fight, and felt his hardness as he pushed against her. He ripped the torn blouse from her fingers and dropped it to the floor. His right hand cupped her breast while his left slipped inside her skirt. She prayed that God would take her now and save her from this humiliation.

"Now you will have a real man," Rafael said, as he maneuvered her toward her bed and, as his desire intensified, tore off her skirt and threw her down on the bed. He put his hand on the top of his underwear, starting to pull it down. "Now you will see…."

Startled, Gomez turned toward the noise as the bedroom door burst open and he found himself staring into two intense dark eyes filled with loathing and hatred. The man was tall, thin, and dressed in priest's garb.

"Get out, priest," Gomez ordered hoarsely. "This is none of your affair. This woman is wanted for murder." He moved toward his gun that lay on the dresser. Father Esteban was quicker, grabbing Rafael's arm and the two men struggled. It was a test of strength and Rafael smiled confidently at the skinny bedraggled priest. Their arms were locked together and he bent Father Esteban's arm behind his back, trying to snap it. Then realized the priest's arm had stopped bending and was now moving back toward him. He grimaced in pain as the priest forced him to his knees and hit him on the side of his head, knocking him to the floor. Father Esteban moved to the dresser, picking up the gun. He told Gomez to stand and marched him to the outer door, ordering him to strip.

"Let's show everyone what you're so proud of."

Gomez started to refuse, saw the look on the priest's face and noticed the gun was pointed at his groin, with the safety off. His face filled with furry but he did what the priest ordered. As soon as he got outside he would get a gun from one of his men, and kill him.

"You will die for this," Gomez snarled, as Father Esteban pushed him through the front door into the bright sunshine. It was hard to see in the contrasting light and Gomez ran toward his jeep yelling for a weapon. He would take great pleasure in shooting the priest. Suddenly he became aware of jeers and laughter. He saw his men, grouped around the jeep with their hands on the top of their heads. They were guarded by eleven or twelve men, each carrying a weapon of sorts—an old rifle, several pistols, even a machete and ax. They were all mocking him. With as much dignity as he could muster, Gomez climbed into the jeep and motioned the driver to go.

"And don't come back," Father Esteban warned. "You have no business here. If you come back, we will kill you." He blessed himself as an afterthought, asking for forgiveness.

Maria came out of the house, having changed to another dress and watched the jeep drive off. She turned to Father Esteban, putting a hand on his arm. "Thank you, that was very brave of you."

Her hand felt like fire on his bare arm. "Why didn't you call for help?"

"I didn't think anyone was here. I knew Victor was gone for the day and I thought the others were in the fields. I'm glad Victor wasn't here; he would have killed that man."

Father Esteban removed his arm, reluctantly.

Maria's voice quivered. "He told me that Roberto was dead, and he wanted to know about some message that was in the statue, the one I gave to Tim. I don't know anything about a message; I didn't look. Now I feel responsible for Tim and his mother. I wish I would have never given the statue to him."

"You only did what you were asked to do, and you know Roberto had a good reason for sending it. You and Roberto are not responsible. Someone is, however, and one way or another, God will see that he is punished for his sins."

Chapter 9

Langley, Virginia, Thursday, February 24

THE CIA COMPLEX WAS EIGHT miles from downtown Washington. Belden turned off the George Washington Parkway at the Central Intelligence Agency sign and told Jack that it had been a public works sign in the fifties, but it didn't fool anyone except the tourists. They drove down the tree-lined road, came over a small rise, and arrived at the first check-point. The complex was built on one hundred and twenty-five acres of woods and rolling hills and surrounded by a chain-linked fence. They stopped and gave their credentials to the two uniformed guards who checked them, their license plate, and made a phone call. They were directed to the next check-point, going through the same procedure, and then to the parking lot near the main entrance.

"If you think this is bad, you should try getting in here without an appointment."

"You seem to know your way around," Jack commented.

Gene smiled, "Let's just say that I've been here before."

They were met at the entrance by two young men in dark suits and short hair, who again checked their credentials and led them to a bank of elevators. Jack was impressed with the huge sky-lit ceiling. Gene pointed out the north wall where stars were carved into a marble facade, honoring the CIA agents who were killed in the line of duty. The guards motioned them to a waiting elevator and pushed a button. Jack noted that there were no buttons in the interior. They were told they would be met at the elevator.

Cathy was still puzzled as she left her office. She was surprised when she received the call that Colonel Belden and Jack Nordone were on their way to see her. She recognized Jack's name and immediately called the DDI. He wasn't much help other than instructing her to tell them as little as possible. Art said he knew Belden and had authorized the visit. Belden worked with the CIA in Central America, and the DDI emphasized that she was not to mention her suppositions. Cathy wasn't comfortable with that. She had read Jack's file. He served two tours in Vietnam, earned a bunch of medals, including the Silver Star and the Purple Heart with cluster, and now was a respected lawyer in Atlanta. She figured he had earned the right to know about his family.

She met the two men at the elevator and after introductions led them back to her office. She studied them as they took their seats. The Colonel was in full dress uniform, complete with ribbons. Not that he needed the uniform—he exuded power. Jack was the opposite, dressed casually in a navy sports jacket, white opened neck shirt, and khaki slacks. When their eyes met she could almost feel his pain and had to resist the urge to give him a big hug, not at all CIA like.

Cathy folded her hands on the top of her desk. "I don't know how you were able to get here, or why you wanted to see me. That said, what can I do for you?"

"We need information," Belden demanded. "To be more specific, we need to know about the TACA flight that went down in the Gulf about two weeks ago."

"I'm sorry," Cathy apologized, "I think you've come to the wrong place. I'm just an analyst and not authorized to give out information. We do have a department that…"

"I know all your departments," Belden interrupted, "and I also know that you are an analyst for Central America and very much aware of what goes on down there."

How did he know that, Cathy wondered, or was it a shot in the dark?

Belden leaned toward her desk. "Look,'" he said in a less commanding voice, "I carry a top security clearance, and Jack is a Major in the reserves and also carries a clearance. If you're still not sure, call your boss, Art Clausen. I know he will tell you to cooperate with us. If he doesn't, I can always have someone from the National Security Council call your Director."

Cathy was wondering if he really had that kind of clout when Jack interrupted.

"Let me ask you something, Miss Stanfil," he said quietly, getting to the point. "Did you recognize my name when we arrived here, and do you know that my wife and son were on board that TACA flight that disappeared?"

She drew a quick breath, hesitated, looked into those blue eyes and admitted that she did.

"And do you know," Jack pressed on, "that last week my house was fire-bombed and that my guest, a teacher from Ocotal, was killed in the fire?"

Cathy wondered where this was leading, but couldn't help nodding.

"And do you know the name of my guest, Sister Linda Masters, and that she brought me a statue that was given to her by my son?"

Cathy didn't like being backed into a corner, "I do know about the fire," she evaded.

"And the statue," Jack pushed.

Cathy shrugged, feeling the pressure and figured she really didn't know much about it. Not really a lie, but close.

"What kind of statue was it?" Cathy asked, trying to mask her interest.

Jack shook his head, "I don't know. We were late for the memorial service and it was wrapped in brown paper. I never got a chance to look at it. It was about a foot high, and I do remember thinking that it was light for a wooden statue."

Maybe a hollow statue, Cathy thought as she glanced at her watch and stood up. "I'm sorry. This is all the time I can give you and all I can tell you. The government in Nicaragua has not been very cooperative, as you can well imagine. If you leave your card, I will keep you informed."

"That could be a problem," Jack answered, "I'm leaving for Nicaragua in the morning and have no idea where you could reach me."

"Nicaragua!" Cathy exclaimed. "You're going to Nicaragua? I, I don't think that's a good idea."

"Exactly what I've been trying to tell him," Belden agreed. "He won't listen though," and the Colonel handed Cathy his card. "If you do come up with new information, I would appreciate a call and I will relay it to Jack."

Cathy took his card and ushered them out of her office, stopping at the door. "Ah, you go ahead and I'll meet you at the elevator. I want to get some of my cards so you can reach me if you need to."

When Cathy arrived at the elevator, she handed Jack and Belden her card. Promising to keep in touch with Belden, she admonished Jack to be careful, and as she shook his hand, she pressed a book of matches into it. Jack tried not to show his surprise and thanked her for her time, slipping the matches into his pocket.

Belden watched her retreating figure and gave a low whistle of admiration, "If I knew that analysts looked like that, I might have joined the CIA myself."

Jack, surprised and puzzled, felt the matches in his pocket, and had the urge to tell Belden, but didn't. When the elevator stopped, they were met by the same blue-coated men. Jack had one of them escort him to the men's room. When he was alone he took out the matches, saw they were from a Mr. Smith's restaurant, read the address and saw 6:30 written on the inside cover, followed by the word "alone", which was underlined twice. He wondered what was going on and felt she made it clear she didn't want Gene there. Whatever it was, he intended to find out and learn why she excluded Belden.

"So, what do you think?" Gene asked as he drove back to the hotel.

"I'm not sure," Jack answered, "but I have a feeling that she knows more than she is telling us."

"I have the same feeling and will dig a little deeper. Also, I've kept in touch with some of the people I worked with when I was in Central America; one is in Nicaragua and I might be able to get him to help you out. I'll meet you tomorrow for breakfast so we can go over your plans and you can give me your flight information."

***

The bar at Mr. Smith's was crowded with a beehive of workers downing a quick one or two before heading home. Jack was lucky to find a newly vacated table, isolated from the others. The tables were covered with dark red tablecloths and the long, dark, highly-polished bar reminded him of the ones in Illinois. He ordered an Old Grand-Dad on the rocks with plenty of ice, wondering if he should even have the one drink. He still felt a little guilty about not including Belden.

It was just after 6:30 when Cathy walked through the door and paused, trying to adjust to the light. Jack stood up, caught her attention and waved her to his table. Even in the dim light he noticed the stares given her by the male population. When she reached the table they greeted each other warily and Cathy ordered a glass of Merlot. She glanced around the room, noted that their table was set apart from the others, and smiled her approval.

"I'm sorry for all the cloak and dagger stuff," Cathy apologized. "I'm not very good at it, but I didn't know what else to do."

Jack just raised an eyebrow.

Cathy sighed, "I'm afraid I'm breaking some kind of rule, or if not breaking, at least bending the heck out of it."

"What rule?" Jack asked.

"Maybe not rule," she amended, "and it's not like this is a State secret, however, I was told to give you as little information as possible."

"Well, I think you handled that part very well," Jack smiled. "Who told you that?"

"My boss, Art Clausen, and it's nothing personal. He doesn't think we should give information to the President."

Jack took a swallow of his drink. "So why am I here?"

Cathy toyed with her wine glass. "Well, after meeting you and going through your file, I decided you deserve to know what I think happened to your family. I wouldn't be doing this if you hadn't told me that you were going to Nicaragua. You could be in grave danger there and I thought you should be warned and be made aware of what you might be up against."

Jack frowned. "Why exclude Colonel Belden?"

Cathy tasted her wine. "I could give you the easy, need to know answer, though it's more than that. I know that the Colonel worked with the CIA and my boss when he was in Central America. Since I've been at the agency, I find these guys bond pretty tight. Also, I believe that sometimes they have their own agenda and I thought our one on one would be better. Did you tell him?"

Jack shook his head, "No, I got your message loud and clear."

Cathy took another sip of her wine and for the next thirty minutes told Jack all she knew about the TACA flight, the Miami Five, the training camps, the statue, and how she tied it into the coming election in El Salvador. Jack listened intently, interrupting only occasionally to clear a point. When she finished, he realized a terrible anger that now had direction. Cathy could feel this new intensity and wondered if she had done the right thing.

"Remember," she cautioned, "much of this is pure conjecture, although the pieces are starting to come together."

Jack nodded absently, "Don't worry; I won't shoot from the hip. I understand what you're saying. Do you think that this Roberto Velado or his wife, Maria, might have given the statue to Tim?"

"That's what Joe, our station chief in San Salvador, thinks. Roberto disappeared, so Joe can't verify it. He thinks the security people either have him in their custody or killed him."

"Is his wife still in Ocotal?"

Cathy nodded, "As far as we know she is."

Jack was quiet for a time, lost in thought, and then he looked at Cathy and forced a smile, "I really appreciate your leveling with me. I know it could cost you."

Cathy colored, "Hey, I think it stinks, allowing you to go down there without any warning or information," and she slid a card across the table to Jack. "If you're going to do a job, do it well," and she laughed. "This will probably break another rule. I think your search will lead you to El Salvador and if you need any help, give him a call." She motioned toward the card. "Joe Ellison is our station chief in San Salvador. Don't let his looks deceive you. Behind that baby face and the rumples, he is as tough as they come, and very competent. He is also a sweetheart. I'll tell him about you."

Jack had made quick decisions all his life and he made one now. "O.K., you leveled with me and I'll do the same," and he told her about Walt and TC, and gave her Walt's number. "If you ever need me or have information for me, let Walt know because we will always be in touch. If you're right about El Salvador, we might be able to help each other."

Cathy wrote down the number, put it in her purse, and stood up. She took Jack's hand and squeezed it, "And you be careful there, if those people did blow up that plane, they will have no problem taking out a tourist from Atlanta."

Jack beckoned for the waitress as he watched Cathy weave her way through the crowded room, and then she was gone. Lost in thought, Jack was still watching the door and noticed that a large, Hispanic looking man had followed Cathy out. The hairs on his arm stood up, his early warning system. Most of the men ogled Cathy at one time or another, but that one was different. It was like he was studying her, and Jack dropped some bills on the table and hurried out of the restaurant. Outside, Cathy was nowhere to be seen and his concern turned to worry. Most of the parking was to the right of the restaurant and he hurried in that direction, remembering one lot in particular that did not have an attendant.

Cathy took the keys out of her purse as she approached her car, and was about to open her door when she heard a noise behind her. When she turned, a large hand slid over her mouth and her body was slammed against the car. Some CIA agent, she thought, getting mugged in a damn parking lot. The man turned her around and when he didn't take her purse, her worry turned to fear. The man was big, very strong, and she felt completely helpless in his grasp. She jerked her head away from him and one of his fingers slid into her mouth. She bit down as hard as she could and was rewarded with a cry of pain and a vicious punch to her stomach that doubled her over. Then his hand closed over her throat and she began to feel the blackness.

Jack heard the man's cry, hurried toward the sound, and saw two people pressed against a dark blue automobile. The man's back was toward him but he could see that he was choking the woman. He moved in quickly, grabbed the man's coat collar, pulled him away, and hit him in the kidney. The man tried to bring his arms up and Jack hit him again. The man staggered back, kicking out as he fell. He caught Jack just below the knee. Jack also fell to the ground in serious pain. The man looked at Jack, saw Cathy fumbling in her purse, pushed himself to his feet, hurriedly stumbling away. Jack didn't think he could follow, not knowing the condition of his knee, and wasn't sure he wanted to. That guy was really big. He finally managed to stand up and limped over to Cathy to see if she was all right.

She coughed, rubbed her throat, and tried to dismiss the attack as just another Washington mugging.

"That was no mugging," Jack said flatly, "he was watching you. He probably followed you to the bar. I noticed him staring at you and when you left, he went after you."

Still rubbing her throat, Cathy smiled, "Well, I'm glad you noticed."

"The guy was Latino," Jack said, "and could be part of this El Sal thing. I think this proves you're on the right track. Someone wants you out of the way. By the way, were you looking for your gun?"

Cathy blushed, "I don't have it with me. I tried to make it look that way though."

Jack smiled, despite the circumstances. "Well, you fooled me, but most importantly, you fooled him. Do you carry a gun?"

"I'm supposed to."

"Well, you better start," Jack advised, "and be careful. It looks like Washington can be just as dangerous as Nicaragua." Jack glanced at his watch to see if he had time to visit Ralph at the kennel and decided against it. He would see him tomorrow. He watched Cathy drive away.

***

Martin's Tavern on Wisconsin Avenue, in Georgetown, was Belden's favorite watering hole and he nursed his drink, impatiently waiting for Art Clausen. When he saw him he had to stifle a laugh. Art looked like he was walking into the OK Corral where everyone had a gun but him.

"Jesus," Clausen complained as he sat down across from Belden and ordered a double martini, straight up. "I agreed to this mess because it was the right thing to do. We need those Miami people. However, I didn't count on all this crap," and he related his conversation with Nelson Martinez.

"I can't believe this has gotten so out of hand. Even if we got caught, I didn't think there would be a problem. It would be an Ollie North kind of thing. Us doing what those assholes in the White House don't have the balls to do. Now, after blowing up that TACA flight, burning that guy's house down and killing the nun, it's a different ballgame."

Belden toyed with his glass. "Hey, I know you're doing this for the right reason. The money Martinez is passing out is incidental, but you should have known that some eggs would be broken." Belden felt little sympathy for the man. "I wasn't happy about the TACA flight either and killing Sister Linda. It was an unfortunate accident."

"How could firebombing a house be an accident?"

"I said killing Sister Linda was an accident. I thought she was down at the Holiday Inn with Jack. I knew about the statue and was at Jack's house when Sister Linda brought it to him. I had to take it before he got his hands on it, or get rid of it. I got some help from one of Martinez's friends. He has people on his payroll all over the country. Anyway, we were trying to break in when some damn alarm went off. The guy panicked and threw the bomb. When I left the church, Sister Linda said she was going with Jack to the airport. That's a problem with every war, collateral damage."

Clausen threw down the last of his martini and signaled for another. "I almost had some collateral damage of my own to deal with. Would you believe, Martinez wanted to take out one of my own people?"

Gene raised an eyebrow

"You met her, Cathy Stanfil. He thinks she is getting too close. I told him she was off limits."

"You told Nelson Martinez?" Belden asked skeptically.

Well," Clausen vacillated, "maybe suggested, and gave him some good reasons."

"And he agreed?"

"He said he would leave it up to me, that I would be responsible for her."

"I wouldn't count on anything Martinez told you."

"God, you don't think…?" Clausen started and then snapped his fingers. "I have to send someone to Rome next week. It's only courier duty and Cathy will be mad as hell, but at least she will be out of the country. I'll assign the El Salvador operation to a more experienced analyst. Also, she's been saying that something weird is going to happen down there just before the election. Do you know anything about that?"

"I think it's a good move, sending her to Rome. She will be out of the way until this thing is over." Belden shook his head, "I haven't heard of anything happening in El Salvador. If it would help Martinez though, I wouldn't bet against it." Belden paused, "It's not all bad news. I'm playing those good old Georgia boys like a fiddle. I'm a trusted member of their inner circle now and will always be one jump ahead of them."

Chapter 10

Washington, D.C., Friday, February 25

THE MORNING WAS CRISP, CLEAR, and cold. It was too cold for Manuel as he drove across the Theodore Roosevelt Memorial Bridge, his thoughts on Cathy Stanfil. He was pissed that things got so screwed up yesterday. Where do these crazy want-to-be heroes come from? Still, he had mixed emotions. He hated failure, which didn't happen very often, but worse, Martinez didn't tolerate failure. On the other hand, he couldn't forget the feel of her under that silk blouse. Now he could have her as long as he wanted. He would make up for last night's humiliation before he killed the bitch. He would tie her, gag her, and take whatever he wanted.

He exited at New Hampshire, took a left on Massachusetts, passed the Naval Observatory and turned on to Butterworth. He pulled the Ford panel truck into a parking place that gave him a good view of Cathy's condo, cut the engine, and reached for his thermos of coffee mixed liberally with sugar and dark rum.

He had just finished his second cup when he saw Cathy come out of the parking garage. He pulled in behind her, giving her space. He followed her for a short distance. Making sure she was on her way to the CIA, he turned and retraced his way back to her condo. His space was still empty and he parked the truck. He was dressed as a TV repairman, complete with tool belt and bogus company logo on his shirt. He broke into the garage with little effort, elected to climb the stairs and once he reached Cathy's condo, rang the bell as a precaution. When no one answered, he took out his tools and quickly entered. He closed the door quietly, locked it, thinking how many people didn't have an alarm system when they lived in a so-called secure building.

He poured another cup of his brew and nearly spilled it when he entered the kitchen and was confronted by a large black cat. The cat snarled at him from its perch atop the refrigerator and Manuel snarled back. He hated cats.

The kitchen was bright and roomy, decorated in blue and white, and led to a cluttered dining room and a large living room with walls painted a luminous golden yellow. It was the bedroom he was interested in. He wasn't disappointed. A large four-poster bed dominated the room and the bed was covered with a white gold satin comforter and numerous pillows. He went through her dresser drawers and stopped when he found one filled with lingerie. He took off a glove, running his hand over the surface of a black silk slip. He felt the excitement as he imagined the things he would do to her. This job would definitely take longer than usual.

LANGLEY, VA

Cathy felt the urge to scream or throw something, and if it involved throwing, her first choice was Art Clausen out the window. She knew a hissy fit wouldn't help, so she clenched her teeth and reread the memo. Courier duty for God's sake, and she had to be in Rome on Monday. Ordinarily it would be a bonus; she loved Rome. What was Clausen thinking? Things were beginning to fall into place and there wasn't much time left, just over a week. She was sure she could do a lot more here than in Rome. She tried to reach him several times but his secretary, German Staff Officer Virginia Brassfield, blocked her. When she tried to explain, it was like talking to a brick wall, Cathy thought maliciously.

Her thoughts were interrupted by a tap on the door and her associate, Kim Roberts, entered carrying a large white mug and a blue folder. She placed the mug and the folder on Cathy's desk and the delicious aroma of hot chocolate permeated the office.

"I'm going to have to look for a new assistant," Cathy smiled, "one that doesn't know me so well."

"I just thought that you might need a little pick-me-up after you learned that you were being sent into exile by old what's-his-face."

Cathy sipped the drink in satisfaction. This definitely beat throwing things.

"And here," Kim continued, opening the folder on Cathy's desk, "is your itinerary, tickets and flight schedules."

Cathy heard the disapproval in her voice.

"This is the only copy and I printed it all out of office. If someone starts looking for a trail, they won't find it here."

Cathy started to say something but Kim held up her hand.

"The less I know the better. What I do know is that you had a doctor's appointment this afternoon and won't be back in the office until the end of next week. I'm going to call in sick Monday and take my telephone off the hook."

Cathy looked at Kim with real affection. "I wonder what would have happened to me if, when I came here, I wasn't lucky enough to get you and, God forbid, ended up with Virginia Brassfield?" She told Kim about trying to get through to Clausen.

"Maybe she didn't want to interrupt him," Kim answered. "He was in his office with one of those friends of yours."

Cathy frowned, "Friends of mine?"

"You know the guys that came to see you the other day. It wasn't the cute one, it was the army type."

"That's strange," Cathy mused, "why would he see Art instead of me?"

Kim shrugged, "I don't know, but I do know what you mean about Brassfield. I'd rather tackle that big Marine at the gate than go through her, and besides," Kim smiled impishly, "it would be a lot more fun."

Cathy laughed. "If you're talking about the Marine I'm thinking of, I would help. How long has Brassfield been with Art anyway?"

Kim shrugged, "It's been a long time. She keeps moving up with him."

"It must have been a match made in heaven because I couldn't stand either of them for long."

Kim giggled, "You don't suppose that the two of them are, you know, fooling around?"

Cathy snickered, imagining the very large Virginia Brassfield in bed with the diminutive Art Clausen. Kim read her thoughts and the two of them broke into uncontrolled laughter.

Kim wiped her eyes and then pointed to Cathy's itinerary. "I booked you into the Holiday Inn Airport in Atlanta and the, ah, bogus papers you wanted will be sent to you there by UPS. The CIA guy who did the work said you shouldn't try to get into Fort Knox, since it was a rush job and not up to their usual standards. It should be O.K. for your purpose though. I also reserved a car for you, a mid-size from National, and both the car and the room are in your new name, Jeanie King, a writer for *Woman's Adventure*. Here is the number for the Holiday Inn in Waycross. I didn't make a reservation there because you will probably be dead by then."

Cathy looked up in surprise and didn't know whether to laugh or cry. "Gee, thanks for the vote of confidence."

"Mata Hari you're not. Anyway, you are booked out of Atlanta at 8:20 Sunday night, on a Delta nonstop to Rome."

After Kim left, Cathy went to her closet and took out a small bag that contained an extra make up kit and a change of clothes. It would be sufficient for some places, certainly not Rome. Luckily she still had time to go home, pack some better things and feed the cat. Art could make her disappear but he couldn't stop her from getting a look at those guys playing soldier in Georgia. There should also be time for a quick visit with Jack's friend, and she searched through her notes…Walt Kutch.

If he knew as much about computers and international money as Jack intimated, he might be able to help her get more information on the El Sal Corporation. It was worth a shot, and with time so short she wouldn't have another chance to see him. She stuffed the notes into her purse and left to pick up her things before going to the airport. She glanced at the clock and thought she had better hurry.

Chapter 11

Miami, Florida, Friday, February 25

They were all there—Nelson Martinez, Jose Blanco, Miguel Castillo, Pablo Matus, and Jorge Lupe—to welcome their guests—Brad Loring, Gene Belden, and Rafael Gomez—who had just flown in from El Salvador. Their anticipation was evident. After all these years of waiting, it was almost over and they would go home and take back their country from the peasants and liberals. They were in a fiesta mood. Gomez watched and listened to their animated conversation as they bragged about all the things they would do when they returned to El Salvador. He tried not to show his disdain.

It was a beautiful day for late February and tables were set up around the pool and loaded with good things to eat and drink. The men gathered around a smaller table that held a map of Central America, marked in different colors. Martinez put a hand on Rafael's shoulder and patted Loring's back.

"I believe we have everything covered," Martinez said as he picked up a marker and pointed to a section of the map.

"Captain Loring will command the red group from San Marcos and split them into two units. One will cross the Honduran border at Nueva Ocotepeque and move quickly to Metapan where they will occupy the communications center. The other unit will enter here, just above San Francisco, take San Francisco and control of the South. The soldiers in Guatemala will also split into two units. The first, going by sea, will land at La Liberated securing the airport on their way to

San Salvador. The second group will move across the border here, take Santa Ana and then move to the capitol to help if you need them. The resistance should be minimal," and he looked pointedly at Gomez.

"An excellent plan," Gomez said, "and it will be over before America and the rest of the world recovers from their shock at the horrible crime committed by the FMLN."

"And I see no problem," Loring said, "my men are ready and will handle anything they throw at us."

Nelson nodded in satisfaction and took Rafael's arm, leading him away from the others.

"I hesitate to bring this up, but some of my friends have questioned your commitment."

Gomez snorted. "Where were these friends when the fighting started and where were they during the twelve years that I fought their war? They were warm and safe, basking in the luxury of Miami while I was fighting in the streets and hills of El Salvador. I was at El Mozote and also with the army when we fought the rebels in the streets of San Salvador."

"I appreciate your sacrifice," Martinez broke in.

Gomez smirked. "And I also helped stop the flow of liberals from the United States when we killed those four church women in the early eighties."

"You mean the ones that were raped and murdered?"

Gomez's eyes sparkled, "The one I had was young and pretty. It was too bad that we had to kill them. I think she enjoyed it."

Martinez masked his distaste, putting a hand on his shoulder. "Tell those old women not to worry; everything will go as planned. We are still holding the three top leaders of the FMLN. After they have committed that heinous crime against the world and the people of El Salvador, they will be shot and their bodies burned. The FMLN will die with them because we will have absolute proof that they were responsible. Our people will welcome your return with open arms."

The men toasted their coming success and Martinez extended an invitation to dinner. Gomez begged off, saying he had to get back as soon as possible. He had much to do.

Loring also declined for the same reason.

After they left, Miguel Castillo shook his head. "There must be another way. Haven't our countrymen suffered enough of war and haven't we killed enough innocent people?"

Martinez put his arm around the old man. "We have already talked about this. If we don't do this now, the casualty count will be much higher."

Miguel didn't say anything, just moved away when Belden sat down with Martinez. They sipped their drinks, looking out to sea.

"Gomez," Martinez began, "is a very ambitious man, arrogant and self-centered, a dangerous combination. He will not take orders for long and might already have his own agenda. Besides, he knows too much. No, he has been necessary and very useful and it would be a pity if he died in the line of duty on that terrible day."

Belden smiled.

"I'm sure there will be a substantial reward if this should happen," Martinez continued, "and it would also be good for your country. Also that friend of yours, Jack Nordone, his name keeps coming up, will he be a problem?"

"I don't think he will be able to accomplish much in such a short time. Besides, he trusts me and I can keep track of what his people are doing. I think he serves us better alive."

Martinez gave Belden a look, "All right, but if things change I expect you to take care of him." Belden felt the implied threat.

Washington, D.C.

The morning briefing over, only Senator Rucker remained in the Oval Office with the President. Michael Keane ran a hand through his thinning hair and turned the pages of *The New York Times*.

"Have you seen the latest polls?" the President asked.

Rucker shook his head, knowing they were good because of the President's attitude.

"Yes sir, we just might surprise a few of those so-called experts and this old corpse might rise out of that grave they put me in." Keane swung his chair around and looked out at the rose garden, his stress reliever. "Wouldn't that be an unpleasant surprise to a lot of people?" he said with a smile.

"Some on both sides of the aisle," Rucker agreed.

The President laced his fingers together. "Yes, we do have our own detractors, don't we?" He shook his head. "Sometimes they are like a bunch of children. If they don't get their way, they will take their ball and bat and go home."

"Just sometimes?" Rucker queried.

"You know there must have been a good reason why I wanted this job, but darned if I can think of it."

"Well, you might not have to worry about it if the election in El Salvador goes sour. I'm a little concerned. After all the money we poured into that country, we could have a problem if we don't get one free election out of it. We know Carter will be watching."

"Anything new?" the President asked.

"I don't know and that's another problem. When I tried to get in touch with that analyst at the CIA, I found out she was in Rome and I can't find out why."

"Are you talking about that very attractive analyst?" the President asked.

Senator Rucker smiled and shook his head. "Come on, Mike, she is almost young enough to be my daughter. And how in hell do you know what she looks like?"

"Well she's not your daughter is she? And I have my sources; after all, I'm President of the United States."

"I know the President of the United States should have more important things to do," Rucker retorted. "I am concerned though. I know Art Clausen doesn't agree with her scenario, but sending her to Rome a week or so before their election does not make sense."

"Do you really think the American people will remember El Salvador in November?"

"Probably not, but your opposition will. It's just another loose end for us that I would like to tie up before our election heats up."

"I'm sure Clausen had his reasons," the President said. "If you want her back, tell Hightower and keep me in the loop."

"If Cathy is right, you will be right in the middle of the loop and may need help from that Army and Navy of yours."

"Why don't we assume the worst and you get in touch with General Whalen. Tell him what you might need and when. He will take care of it. He's one of the good ones. We have the cooperation of the Hondurans, although Guatemala hasn't come around yet."

"I'll have a talk with Whalen," Rucker said as he headed for the door. "I have a pretty good handle on what is going on and have a few ideas on how we can stop it. Whalen can coordinate with the Navy."

Chapter 12

Washington, D.C., Friday, February 25

Cathy had just passed Washington National when the traffic slowed and then stopped. She vented her frustration on the various parts of the dashboard, gaining nothing but a sore hand. It took another fifteen minutes before traffic started to inch forward and Cathy knew she wouldn't have time to stop at her condo. She picked up her car phone and called her neighbor. Martha Hulsey was a sweet elderly lady who lived in the condo just down the hall. She was a good friend who had helped her out many times before.

"Martha," Cathy asked? "I hate to bother you at the last minute, but I really need a big favor. I'm on my way to the airport and was going to stop by to feed my cat and get some clothes. I'm on the expressway waiting for an accident to clear and afraid I won't have time. Would you mind terribly going over, feeding Cuddles and keeping an eye on her for a few days?"

"Of course not," Martha responded cheerily, "it will give me something to do, and I haven't seen that pretty girl of yours in over a week. We can renew our acquaintance. I still have your key."

"You're a doll," Cathy said. "I also need a couple of things. You know where all my clothes are and have great taste. I was hoping you could pack a small bag for me. I will have someone from the office pick it up and take it to the airport. I'm on my way to Atlanta and have to fly to Rome Sunday night. I need two dressy outfits and a couple of casual things."

"My, my, you young people certainly live exciting lives nowadays. I'm sure I can take care of that for you and will have it ready when your young man comes."

Parking at the airport was always a problem and elevated Cathy's stress. She finally found a space and made it to her gate with only minutes to spare. She was glad she had paid for the flight rather than the CIA. She always traveled first class, thanks to a substantial trust fund. She needed a little comfort and ordered a vodka and tonic as soon as she sat down and then took stock of her situation. Her new I.D. would be delivered to the Holiday Inn, identifying her as a feature writer for a woman's magazine. She would be researching an article on CAMA, the Central American Military Assistance Program, based in Alabama. This would be confirmed by the magazine if anyone checked. She hoped it would be enough to get her into their training camp and see what was going on. She also wanted to meet Jack's friend, Walt Kutch. He could be a big help to her.

The flight landed on time and Cathy took a shuttle to National and rented a car. She checked in at the Airport Holiday Inn and called Walt's office for an appointment. She got it and headed north on I-85. After pulling onto the expressway, she wondered if fifty-five was the minimum speed limit in Atlanta.

When Walt's secretary told him about Cathy's call, he groaned, accepted the appointment as a favor to Jack, but told her to keep it short by coming in to remind him about a meeting he had. It was a busy day.

Cathy was shown into Walt's office after a short wait, and was impressed. It appeared to be more like a living room than an office, with deep gray carpeting and artistic Norwalk furniture surrounding a heavy glass coffee table. There was a small conference table with four chairs at the back of the room and a large teakwood desk dominating the front. The floor to ceiling windows gave a magnificent view of Atlanta.

Cathy wasn't the only one who was impressed. As Walt watched her enter, the annoyance he felt at the interruption quickly vanished. She was about 5'6" he judged, couldn't be over a hundred and fifteen pounds, and moved with an unconscious grace and sensuality that sent his blood racing. The sunlight that filtered through the windows played tricks with her long brown hair, and when she offered a tentative smile, her green eyes crinkled. He was completely captivated.

Walt immediately abandoned his power position behind his mammoth desk and led her to one of the sofas. He ordered coffee and started to say something to his secretary, but she interrupted. "I suppose you want to cancel your next meeting?" she smirked.

"Yes, I do." Walt affirmed with a straight face and then to Cathy. "I don't mean to stare, but you don't look very CIA."

Cathy cocked her head. "And what do CIA people look like?" she countered.

Walt held up his hands and apologized. "To tell the truth, I don't really know. You are the first one I have ever met."

Cathy smiled her forgiveness. "I don't feel very CIA today. Please, call me Cathy."

"Walt and Cathy it is," he answered and then turned serious. "Jack filled me in on your conversation with him and your concerns and I promise that anything we talk about will remain with the three of us. Also, if you want an outside opinion, you did the right thing. I've known Jack for a number of years and he is a special kind of person. He was devastated by what happened to his family and even then, I don't think he would have gotten involved in this if it wasn't for Sister Linda. He feels responsible for her death and believes the two events are connected. He knows his wife and son were killed for a reason and he will find out who and why or die trying. He doesn't know what he is getting into, but don't sell him short. Like I said, he's a special kind of person."

Cathy nodded. "I read his file and if I felt he would go down there, bumble around for a few days, then come home, I wouldn't have told him anything. I know that's not the case. He won't give up until he finds what he's looking for and by then it could be too late. I felt I had to warn him about the Miami people and what he might be up against."

Walt stood up suddenly, moved to the window and said in a voice choked with emotion, "I'm sure it was a difficult decision for you and I won't forget it. If you should ever need my help, it's yours, unconditionally."

Cathy was surprised at Walt's show of emotion. She had done quite a bit of research on him and hadn't suspected he was the sentimental type. Somehow it made her feel more secure. She decided to ask for help.

"Ask and you shall receive," Cathy said, as she handed a file to Walt. "This is the file on the El Sal Corporation. I am sure it's a front for these people who are up to their necks in the deaths of Jack's family. I also think they are involved in other illegal activities but can't prove it. Jack said you know your way around money and a computer."

Walt flipped through the file and then paused at a list of companies.

"Their subsidiaries," Cathy explained, "and I've underlined the ones I think are involved."

Walt continued to read the file, slowly, and then nodded. "Interesting, every bank that they deal with is either in Panama or the Cayman Islands."

"It appears that way."

"Well," Walt said as he closed the folder, "most of this is about money and if there is anything I can do, it's follow the money trail. You would be surprised at the stories it tells."

Cathy smiled her appreciation, started to rise, and Walt held up his hand.

"Hey, you just don't rush in here, give me a job to do, and then rush off; it's not the Southern way. You said that you weren't flying to Rome until Sunday night, so why not let me show you the great city of Atlanta, starting with dinner tonight followed by brunch tomorrow morning?"

Cathy gathered her thoughts as she sat down. Now what? Then she realized it didn't matter. If she was wrong about involving these guys she was already in deep trouble. She had crossed too many bridges to change course now, so she told Walt the real reason she had come to Atlanta and about her going to Waycross before her trip to Rome.

Walt frowned, "You mean you are driving down to Waycross tomorrow, posing as some writer, and will try to get into the training camp?"

Cathy nodded.

"From what I surmise about the lunatics you're dealing with, I don't think that's a very smart move."

"That appears to be the consensus," Cathy laughed. "Time is running out though and I feel I have to try something. I think I will get some answers in Waycross."

Walt tried to talk her out of it and found her just as stubborn as Jack. He did get her promise to accept his invitation for dinner and told her he would pick her up at seven.

Cathy was surprised at how comfortable she felt around Walt and asked to use his telephone, explaining about her troubled ride to the airport and that she wanted to check with her neighbor. Walt moved away, trying to give her a little privacy. She was really something, he thought, and he was looking forward to tonight. He watched as she dialed the number, seeing her look of surprise, and then the blood drained from her face. She was crying when the call ended and Walt moved to her side.

"That was my friend from the CIA," Cathy explained between sobs, "he was going to pick up my suitcase and send it to me. He is in my condo now and told me that my neighbor, Martha, is dead."

Walt gently pulled the story from her. Cathy's co-worker had stopped by to pick up her suitcase, found Cathy's door open, and no Martha or suitcase. He went to Martha's condo, her door was open, but still no Martha. He decided to look around and found her body at the bottom of the stairwell. Her neck was broken.

"I'm so sorry," Walt said. "She must have fallen."

Cathy shook her head. "She didn't fall. Martha had a bad hip and never used the stairs. Someone threw her down those stairs. The man that attacked me must have broken into my place somehow, and when Martha went in to feed the cat, he, oh, my, God," and the tears flowed as she told Walt what happened to her in the parking lot in Washington and how Jack had saved her.

Walt held her and let her cry it out and then offered to drive her back to the airport. She declined.

"I'll manage," she sniffed. "I would still like to have dinner with you tonight. I'm going to need some company."

Walt made her drink a cup of coffee and then reluctantly let her go. As soon as she left, Walt dialed a number in Chicago.

"Hey," TC answered.

"Got your act together yet?" Walt asked.

"I guess you could say that."

"Well then, catch the next plane and get your butt down here. It looks like the trouble has started and it could be worse than we thought. Let me know your flight number. I'll pick you up and fill you in on what's happening."

***

Cathy sipped her frozen vodka and enjoyed the view of downtown Atlanta from the glass enclosed Nikolai's Roof restaurant. She tried one of the *les petits piroshkis* Walt had ordered and smiled.

"Not too bad, huh," Walt asked?

"That doesn't begin to describe them."

"I think you will find the rest of the dinner just as enjoyable," Walt continued and motioned for one of the red-coated, white-gloved staff.

The food was delightful, and the conversation was stimulating. Walt and Cathy—In spite of her sadness—enjoyed themselves. Over coffee, Walt couldn't help asking why Cathy had joined the CIA.

Cathy grimaced, folded her napkin and placed it on the table. "I guess it was a number of things. I was born into old money, lived the good life, and went to the best schools. My parents didn't make any of the money, just spent it. They traveled a lot, drank a lot, and I always felt that I was an unintended interruption to their party. I did my share of partying, too, and one day woke up knowing there had to be more. I was raised by a nanny from Central America and she would tell me stories about her country. Some weren't very pretty. Anyway I decided to go to Guatemala, against my parents' wishes, and see for myself. I spent a couple of years there and found I had a knack for languages. I came back here and returned to school.

"I went to Boston College and even opened a couple of books. I graduated with honors and was getting my Masters at Georgetown when I met Joe Ellison, a CIA agent. He's a sweetheart, intelligent, dedicated, and he talked me into giving it a try."

"So you have something going with this Joe?" Walt asked, trying to keep the concern out of his voice.

"I do," Cathy answered. "We work together and he is the father I never had."

"Oh, that kind of thing," Walt said happily.

Cathy pushed her chair away from the table. "Now I better get to bed because I have a big day tomorrow. I hope I didn't bore you with the family history. This restaurant and the vodka loosened me up. I didn't want to spend the night alone, so thanks, you helped a lot."

"I don't know when I have had a more enjoyable evening," Walt answered truthfully, "and I hope there will be more to come."

Chapter 13

Managua, Nicaragua, Saturday, February 26

As the plane glided down to the Cesar Augusto Sandino International Airport, Jack had his first look at Nicaragua and was surprised at the arid landscape. He thought the country would be all lush green forests. He couldn't help but wonder what had been on Nancy's mind at this point. He tried to push the thought away. If Cathy was right, he needed to focus on the job ahead.

He joined the line going through customs and was surprised at his reception. There were many soldiers carrying automatic weapons, but the people he dealt with were courteous and friendly. Nicaragua was desperate for US dollars and Jack changed the mandatory sixty US dollars for cordobas and looked for the ground transportation sign.

"Señor Nordone?"

Jack heard the voice, turned in surprise and was confronted by a heavy-set man with dark wavy hair and small dark eyes hidden under heavy brows. He appeared to be in his early forties and was holding out his hand.

"You're surprised," the man laughed. "The Colonel described you perfectly and we don't get that many gringos in my country anymore."

Jack shook the extended hand.

"My name is David Cordero," he said in almost perfect English. "I'm a good friend of Colonel Belden and I've come to help you through the pitfalls of Nicaragua."

"He mentioned that he had a friend here. I didn't expect you to meet me."

"Not to worry," Cordero said as he directed Jack out of the terminal to the parking area.

Jack held up a hand. "Hold it, I have to get Ralph."

"Ralph?" David questioned.

"I brought my dog, Ralph."

"*Perro*, you brought a dog here?"

"It's a long story," Jack answered. "The short version is yes, I did."

David shrugged, perplexed. "I don't think they take dogs where you are staying." Then he brightened. "I recall a dog place, a kennel, nearby. We will stop on the way."

"I have taken care of everything, a room for the night and dinner at one of our best restaurants. Tomorrow morning I will drive you to Ocotal. Our bus service is the worst in Central America but still better than our trains."

Jack started to protest, thought better of it, collected Ralph and followed Cordero who led the way to his car, a mid-1980's Volkswagen. Jack stowed his bag in the rear with Ralph and David forced his way into traffic driving out of the airport.

"I appreciate the offer," Jack said, "but I estimated it is only about a hundred and fifty miles to Ocotal and I thought I would drive there this afternoon."

David shook his head, "The Colonel said that you would be running in overdrive and that I should slow you down." He laughed. "Besides, travel in Nicaragua does not compare to travel in your country. Our driving is different and it takes time to get used to it. Do you see that driver in front of us?"

"You mean the one waving at someone?"

Cordero laughed again. "He is not waving at someone; he is just telling us that he is going to do something. He may turn right, or he might turn left, or he might stop. That is the only signal you get on our roads."

Jack smiled and shook his head.

"Besides, it will take you longer than you think. It can be very dangerous after dark, especially where you are going. The highlands north of Esteli have many banditos. I think it would be wise for you to enjoy our city tonight."

Gene was right, Jack thought. He was on fast-forward, tired, and an accident waiting to happen.

Managua was a city of disaster, desperation, and survival. A 1931 earthquake destroyed more than three quarters of the city. This was followed by a Chicago-like fire in 1936 that consumed the rest. A second earthquake in 1972 killed more than 12,000 people in the rebuilt city and devastated the area.

The rest of the city was destroyed by the revolution. The Bank of America building, the one remaining skyscraper, stood like a lonely sentinel in the middle of town, guarding the ruined buildings and open fields. The new house of government stood adjacent to the Bank while the rest of the city moved to the outskirts and now encircled the almost deserted old city.

David drove with practiced ease, pointing out the few remaining points of interest. He stopped at a group of one-story buildings with a sign that pictured a dog. Jack put Ralph on a leash and entered, noting that the lobby was neat and clean. As David talked with a gray-haired man in a white coat, a young boy in his teens came around the counter and knelt in front of Ralph.

That worried Jack and he started to pull on the leash when the man in the white coat said something in rapid Spanish. David turned to Jack. "He said not to worry. The boy has a mental problem that animals appear to know. They get along great with the boy."

Sure enough, Ralph gave a short whine and began licking the boy's extended hand. Jack felt more comfortable about leaving him.

When they left the parking area, David turned right at the next traffic light onto South highway. They hadn't gone more than a mile when David pulled into the Hotel Ticomo.

The rooms were little cottages in a park-like setting and were clean and cool. Jack was pleasantly surprised. David said that he would be back at 6:30 to pick him up for dinner.

Jack unpacked, using only the first drawer of the dresser, laid out his shaving gear, changed and went out for a quick run before David returned.

Cordero arrived on time and took him to the Lobster Inn where Jack was in for another pleasant surprise. The service was quick and efficient and the décor delightful, featuring a small pool that housed two undersized alligators and several inactive turtles. Jack let David order for him and listened as David continued to talk about his country, past and present.

The meal started with the best seafood cocktail Jack had ever tasted, followed by a delicious lobster and ended with strong black coffee and a shot of brandy. David expressed his sympathy for Jack's loss and offered to show Jack Managua at night. Jack begged off, admitting that he was completely exhausted. David drove him back to his hotel, promising to meet him at 7:30 for breakfast.

Jack closed the door to his room, thought about another quick run and decided he wasn't up to it. He could always find a good excuse not to run. He undressed and went to the bathroom to brush his teeth, noticing that his razor was laying blade down. It was a thing with him. He never laid a razor with the blade down. Someone had been in his room. He doubted that the Hotel Ticomo had a chocolate-on-the-pillow service. He went back to the bedroom, checked the one drawer he had used then looked in his bag. While he couldn't prove it, he knew someone had gone through his things. He double locked the door and went to bed, wondering if this was a random break-in, or did the wrong people already know he was in Nicaragua?

Breakfast the next morning was another culinary experience of freshly baked breads and tortillas, exotic fruit juices and a large assortment of fresh fruit. This was followed by a delicious rice and bean dish called speckled rooster and a spicy omelet.

It was all complimented with a strong black coffee and thick cream.

"I'm going to get fat," Jack said, "if you keep on feeding me like this."

Jack was dressed in jeans and a sport shirt, and Cordero wore sharply pressed slacks, a blue oxford shirt opened at the neck, and highly polished black shoes. Jack noticed the unusual bracelet he wore. It was silver and looked like two snakes entwined.

They talked, getting to know each other and Jack wondered if Belden's friend was always in such a good mood, until the end of the meal. The waitress slipped and spilled some coffee on David's shirt. He jumped up from his chair and berated her in Spanish. When he noticed Jack staring at him, he cut his tirade short, forced a smile and asked the waitress for a wet cloth. The change was too late. Jack had already seen the malevolent anger in his eyes and knew that he was not the happy-go-lucky person he portrayed.

They picked up Ralph from the kennel and he gave a low growl when David brushed against him. David quickly moved away.

They drove North through the city, around Lake Managua to Tipitapa and then due North to Sebaco. Jack noted the cultivated fields of cotton and rice, which were replaced by tobacco plantations and hardwood forests as they neared the highlands. They passed through Estile, here Cordero explained that it was the cigar capitol of Nicaragua. Once out of the city, they turned east toward Ocotal and the Las Manos crossing.

The landscape changed for the better as they passed thick pine forests, cultivated land, and cattle farms. In the distance they could see the coffee plantations.

Cordone told Jack that Ocotal was a pleasant compact town that suffered much, from both sides, during the war. When the Sandinistas held the town, they killed the people for helping the Contras, and when the Contras held it they killed the people for helping the Sandinistas.

"The city depends on the cattle, timber and coffee industries," David explained, "but unemployment is around seventy percent. Those lucky enough to work at the coffee plantations make about a hundred US dollars for the season. That has to last them until the next season."

The town was in a valley, completely surrounded by forested mountains. They entered the city on a broad boulevard and Jack was impressed with the lovely main square, a picturesque church, and colorful houses.

They checked in at the Frontera, a small hotel in the center of town with a pool. Jack took a swim while Cordero left to make inquiries. Jack had told him that he would like to meet with a priest, Father Ernesto Esteban, as soon as possible.

David returned in less than an hour and told Jack that he had found Father Esteban. They drove to the edge of town where Jack saw the church on a small hill. They turned onto a bumpy, pot-hole filled driveway and followed it to two buildings that sat below the church. One of the buildings appeared to be a dwelling with a thatched roof and a wide surrounding verandah. The other was larger, rectangular in shape, probably the office and classrooms.

They parked by the dwelling and, getting out, heard laughter coming from the other side of the building. As they turned the corner, they almost tripped over a tall thin man dressed in the robes of a priest. He was down on all fours and crabbing his way through the dust with two small boys on his back who were laughing uncontrollably. The priest slid to a halt at their feet, sat back on his heels, letting the children slide to the ground and squinted up into the bright sunshine. He glanced up at the two men, gave Jack a slower look and Jack saw recognition as their eyes met. Jack helped the priest to his feet while Father Esteban tried to brush himself off, laughed, and gave up the losing battle.

"I'm sorry you found me in these circumstances," he said in English, "but better you than the Archbishop," and he continued laughing.

"Father, I," Jack began.

"I know," Father Esteban interrupted. "You're Tim's father. You have his eyes." He took one of Jack's hands in both of his. "I have seen your picture many times and words cannot describe how sorry I am about Tim and your wife. You have been in my prayers. We all thought a lot of Tim and grew to love him as a friend."

Jack could feel the priest's empathy and began to choke up. Trying to hide his emotion, he introduced Father Esteban to David.

Father Esteban gave David a short nod and led them to three comfortable, well-worn chairs on the verandah. He nodded to a large woman dressed in a long shapeless dress who hovered protectively in the doorway. After the woman had served them a cold fruit drink she padded away and the priest began to talk about Tim. Jack was caught off guard because Father Esteban didn't talk about Tim with any trace of sadness. It was with joy in his voice. He painted the picture of an intelligent, caring young man who not only won the respect of the people he had come to help but also their love. He talked about the troubles that Tim, a young American big city boy, with a smattering of Spanish, ran into trying to fit into a small Nicaraguan town. Some of his escapades were embarrassing, most hilarious. This drew a small smile from Jack.

"He lived a good life," Father Esteban concluded, "helping others and doing what he was intended to do. His life was much too short, but what there was of it was filled with laughter, happiness, and love, for you, your wife, and those around him."

Jack stood up suddenly and stepped off the porch fighting to stop the flow of tears. It was a losing battle. Father Esteban followed him, turned him around and held him in a tight embrace.

"Don't be ashamed," the priest said. "There is no limit on the number of tears you can shed for your loved ones when their time is over. Just remember the good times and how lucky you were to have them as long as you did."

Jack could feel the man's goodness, his love and compassion, and he hugged him back, then stepped back and wiped away his tears. He told Father Esteban about Sister Linda. The priest was shocked to learn that she was dead. Jack asked about the statue.

Father Esteban started to reply, saw that Cordero had followed them down the steps and didn't say whatever he was going to. He rubbed his bearded jaw. "I don't recall Tim talking about a statue. You might try his school. He was quite close to one of the other teachers there, Bob Wood, if I remember."

Jack nodded, his disappointment evident, then asked about the Velados.

Again the priest hesitated before admitting he knew the family. He told Jack they lived on a small farm north of the city. He gave directions.

Jack thanked him and started to say goodbye.

"It may not be any of my business," Father Esteban said, then smiled and his eyes crinkled, "then again, I guess it is my business. Tim told me about the problems you were having with your religion and I would consider it a great honor if you would let me hear your confession tomorrow, around ten?"

Jack blinked in surprise. "My confession?" he repeated.

"I know it's been a long time," Father Esteban said hurriedly. "It might give you peace of mind."

Jack hesitated, shrugged, and agreed.

After leaving the church they drove through neighborhoods of small houses, shacks actually, with small dirt-filled yards. The children, he noticed, were all dressed in clean, neat, well-mended uniforms.

At the school they were directed to Bob Wood's classroom by a student. Jack hesitated at the door but was pushed aside by David who entered the room and spoke to the teacher in Spanish and then English.

As they talked, Jack watched the children. They appeared to be taking a test and Jack saw many of them spitting on their fingers. Their teacher was a tall gangling young man with thinning blond hair and thick wire-rimmed glasses. He looked at the two men, at Jack twice, and gave some instructions to his class while he walked to the back of the room.

Jack held out his hand, "I'm sorry to disrupt your class. I'm Tim's father and would like to ask you a question."

Bob took Jack's hand, expressed his sympathy and told him how much Tim was missed by the faculty and students. "And Sister Linda is gone too; I just can't believe it."

"I need some information about a statue that Sister Linda brought me, a statue that was given to her by Tim. I think their deaths might be connected and the statue could be part of it."

Bob shook his head. "We kidded Tim about his secret statue and the beautiful lady who delivered it, but he never talked about it. I saw it once. It was about a foot high and reminded me of a picture of St. Francis." Bob offered to show Jack Tim's room and told him it had been cleaned and everything personal sent home. "Although it did look like someone went through it before we did."

Jack declined, thanked him and seeing another boy spit on his finger couldn't help asking, "I see a lot of your pupils spitting on their fingers. Is that for luck on their test?"

Bob laughed. "Rubber is very expensive here and most children can't afford erasers. They use spit to rub out their mistakes."

That night Jack and David had dinner at the La Cabana and were seated in a pretty garden setting, surrounded by banana trees. Jack ordered what turned out to be a very good steak. After dinner, over a glass of brandy, David asked about Jack's trip to Nicaragua.

"Nothing special, I just wanted to see where my son spent the last two years of his life." They were quiet as they sipped their drinks and Jack asked Cordero if he was married.

Cordero shook his head, "I tried it once, but it didn't work out. I'm more the single type."

"Do you have any children?"

Again he shook his head, changed the subject and asked Jack if he wanted to see what little there was to see in Ocotal.

"I don't think so," Jack said. "I am going to take an early morning run tomorrow and see if I can find the Velado farm. Father Esteban said it wasn't far."

Back at the hotel, Jack couldn't get in touch with Walt so he called Belden, who was still in Washington. He brought him up to speed on his time in Nicaragua and then asked how well he knew David.

"Why," Belden queried, "what makes you ask?"

"Nothing really," Jack answered, "I just have this feeling that he's not all he appears to be."

"They all act a little strange down there," Gene assured him. "He is just trying to impress you. Anyway, you need him."

Jack agreed and told Gene that he was going to look for the Velados in the morning and then go back to see Father Esteban. "I'm sure the priest has something to tell me but didn't want to talk about in front of David. He said that Tim told him about the trouble I was having with my religion and asked to hear my confession."

"Hell, that's his job isn't it?"

"I know Tim would never tell him anything personal like that. Besides, I'm not having any problem with my religion. No, Father Esteban wants to see me alone."

Belden paused, "Well, I hope you find what you're looking for and can come home. Keep in touch and be careful."

A short time later, the incessant ringing of the telephone woke Cordero.

"David?" A voice inquired. "I think we have a problem," and Belden related Jack's call. "Jack has good instincts, and I think he's right on this. You better take care of the priest."

"Anyway I want to?"

"Anyway you want. Be careful though, I don't think Jack trusts you. If he looks for that lady in the morning, you might get into his room. Maybe a personal item of Jack's at the crime scene and a call to the police would slow him down."

David became fully awake, "Don't worry; I will take care of it, and I will make a call to the police, but I'm not going into that room as long as that damn dog is there. Jack slipped the room clerk some money so the dog could stay with him."

"Why don't you just shoot the damn thing?" Belden groused.

David replaced the telephone, lay against his pillow, and planned his day. He smiled. It might even be fun; he never had a priest before.

Chapter 14

Waycross, Georgia, Saturday, February 26

THE HOLIDAY INN WAS THEIR standard. Outdoor pool surrounded by rooms and a small iron fence, an adequate restaurant, and a lounge with a small bandstand and dance floor. Cathy's room was clean, with a queen-size bed, and a small desk. She sat in a chair by the window watching some children playing water polo, or at least a version of it, and having a great time. She tried to relax after her four-and-some-hour drive, wishing she could join the kids. She shuffled through the envelope containing her new identity and for the first time the thought struck her that she might be on shaky ground.

Walt had tried to talk her out of it during dinner last night, something that brought a smile to her lips. Walt was a neat guy, interesting, caring, and had a good sense of humor. You don't find many of those and she, too, hoped they would meet again. She replaced the identification cards in her wallet, showered, dressed, and headed for the training camp. She wore black high-heeled shoes, dark hose, a short gray skirt with matching jacket, and a white silk blouse. Sexy enough, she thought, to help get into the camp, yet business-like.

Cathy drove east out of Waycross, turning south on Highway One toward Jacksonville. It took less than an hour to reach Mattox where she stopped to look at the map Walt had given her. She found the back road leading out of Mattox. After about ten miles it turned onto a gravel road heading toward the Okefenokee Swamp. The road curved to the left, through a densely wooded area, then to a clearing, where it was blocked by a chain-linked fence, topped with barbed wire. There was a small guardhouse to the right. She watched as a man dressed in army fatigues, boots, and carrying a carbine walked to the gate. He made no move to open it so Cathy got out of the car and approached him with one of her best smiles.

"Miss?" He questioned.

"You look very military," Cathy answered, "so maybe I am at the right place. My name is Jeanie King, a feature writer, doing an article on adventuresome people like you. I have an appointment with your commanding officer."

"Captain Loring?" the sentry asked.

Cathy nodded in relief, "Yes, Captain Loring."

The sentry who was obviously uncomfortable scratched his head with his free hand, "I don't know about no visitor, so you wait right here. I'll check with headquarters."

The conversation was a little long and when the young man returned, he told her that Captain Loring would be down shortly.

Cathy saw the dust first, then a white Ford pickup as it sped to the gate and braked to a stop in a hail of dirt. A man with rugged good looks stepped out. He was wearing dark sunglasses, a green uniform with pants tucked into his boots, and a short-sleeved shirt. He had brown hair, about average height, weight, and carried a sidearm. He motioned for the sentry to open the gate.

"Now what in hell is this all about?" The man demanded as he strode through the gate.

Cathy saw that he was younger than she expected, maybe late thirties.

"Hi," Cathy offered, still with the big smile, and handed him her card. "I'm a feature writer for *Woman's Adventure*, doing a story on soldiers of fortune. Mercenaries if you want, and about their relations with the women in their lives. I heard about your camp, and thought I would check it out, maybe get an interview or two."

Loring, very slowly, looked Cathy up and down, as the suggestion of a smile pulled his lower lip, "And about that appointment?"

Cathy shrugged, "Hey, a girl's got to do her job."

The man studied her for another minute, let the smile come through and introduced himself. "I'm Captain Brad Loring." He held out his hand. "I would like to know how you heard about us."

Cathy took his hand. "I got a tip from one of my readers in Alabama, a member of CAMA. They all know I'm doing this story, and I get tips from all over."

"Interesting," Loring said. "Where was your last interview?"

"You know better than that, Captain, I don't kiss and tell."

Loring rubbed his chin speculatively, "A good habit, and tell me, what kind of information are you looking for?"

"The usual, what makes a man like you tick? How and why did you get into this business, the dangers you face, and especially about the women in your life."

Loring had been in camp for the last three weeks and was hooked. She was just what he needed. "We might be able to work something out but not now. We have a training exercise. Are you free for dinner?"

"Sure, that would be great, what time?"

"Where are you staying?"

"The Holiday Inn, in Waycross," Cathy answered with her best come-on smile.

Loring returned the smile. "Tell you what, I have to get back, but if you will have dinner with me, I will let you know then."

Cathy appeared to hesitate.

"Just dinner," Loring said, "I'm tired of eating with guys. We could even start your interview."

Cathy nodded, "It's a deal. I will meet you in the bar at 8:00."

Miami

Manuel sat on the straight-backed chair, sweating in the air-conditioned room, waiting for Nelson Martinez. He had never screwed up twice and he was worried. If that old broad hadn't come into Cathy's condo it would have been all over by now and he would be off the hook. He didn't have an option; she had seen him. He had to get rid of her. Nelson was really pissed. Manuel jumped when the door opened and Nelson Martinez came into the room, smiling. Manuel felt the tightness ease a little.

"I believe this is your lucky day," Martinez said as he took a seat. "I received a very interesting call from Captain Loring in Georgia. He told me about a writer from a woman's magazine who wanted to see the camp and interview some of the men. He asked if it would be all right."

Manuel shrugged, puzzled.

"From his description of the woman, I'm sure it's your friend from Washington. The good Lord is giving you one more chance. The Captain is having dinner with her at 8:00, which will give you plenty of time to get to Waycross. There will be no more excuses. Kill her when she returns, and with the Okefenokee so close, I'm sure you will have no trouble disposing of the body. Hopefully, with a little help from the alligators, it will never be found."

Manuel nodded.

"I booked you on a flight from Miami to Jacksonville, where you will rent a car. It's a short drive to Waycross. When you have finished come back here." Nelson stopped at the door. "Another failure will not be tolerated."

Manuel noted there was no trace of a smile.

Chapter 15

Atlanta, Georgia, Saturday, February 26

WALT TRIED TO CURB HIS impatience as he looked at his watch, wondering if any airline was on time anymore. He knew his irritation was brought on by his worry over Cathy. He waved when he saw TC come through the gate with one piece of luggage. TC acknowledged him with a short nod. They made small talk as Walt guided him down the escalator to the train and then to the parking deck. TC threw his bag in the back seat, admiring the new BMW and remarking that Atlanta was one busy airport.

Walt took I-85 to I-285 east and turned south on I-75. He told TC about his meeting with Cathy, her being assaulted in the parking lot, and the death of her neighbor.

"She was lucky it was Jack with her in Washington," TC said. "That sixth sense of his saved my ass more than once. What's this CIA lady like? She must have guts to go down there to that training camp after what she's been through."

"She's hard to describe," Walt answered. "You will have to see for yourself. She really went out on a limb to help Jack and give him the information he needed. She's quite a lady and really broke down when she found out about her neighbor. She feels responsible. You know how that goes."

"I do, and why do I have the feeling that she's not hard to look at either."

Walt glanced at TC and smiled, "That doesn't begin to describe her."

"So, tell me, where are we going and why?"

"I know where, not sure why. I'm just worried about her. She did call to give me her room number and told me she had a dinner date with the Captain in charge of training those guys. His name is Brad Loring. I checked him out on the computer and didn't find anything bad. He spent ten years with the US Commandos, honorable discharge, and the last six or seven freelancing it. Like you said, someone wants to get rid of her and I thought you might come up with something. Hell, you're the cop or detective. I thought you would know."

"Well, first we will get a room with a good view of her room. And then use the cop's best, most boring friend, surveillance."

***

Cathy wore a short black sheath, high-heeled shoes and the sheerest hosiery she could find. She wanted to lead him on, but not too far. She didn't have a lot of choices without her suitcase. Cathy had stopped at a mall near the airport and bought the black dress and a few other things. It was difficult shopping because her mind kept going back to Martha. She glanced at the clock and knew it was time to go.

Manuel watched her leave the room from his post across the pool. Even with all the problems he had, he knew he still couldn't kill her right away, not dressed like that. He would disable her and make her pay for his humiliation in Washington. After he had his fill, he would kill her. He licked his lips in anticipation.

Walt and TC also watched her leave from their room, and TC whistled in appreciation and, looking at his watch, asked about dinner.

"You go ahead," Walt said, "I had a big lunch."

TC shrugged and ordered two hamburgers, fries, coffee, and a Coke from room service. After he had eaten they pulled two chairs to the window and sat in their darkened room. Walt wasn't sure how long it had been since Cathy left when TC grabbed his arm and wondered if he had fallen asleep.

"See that guy by the pool, near Cathy's room?"

Walt nodded. The light was dim, but he could still see a big man walk slowly past Cathy's room.

"That is the third time he has walked by. He's not just walking by; he's casing the place."

Walt leaned closer to the window, and as he did, the man hurried up the steps to Cathy's room, did something to the lock, and then entered her room.

"Damn!" Walt exclaimed.

"You said a big dark-skinned guy assaulted her in the parking lot. That guy fits the bill." TC glanced at the luminous clock. "It's still early, and I don't want to be hanging around the parking area too long so I'll wait until about 11:30, and then go over to the lounge and try to talk to her. You stay here in case I miss her. Just make damn sure she doesn't go into that room."

Cathy met Brad in the lounge where they had a couple of drinks before going to a nice restaurant. Then it was back to the lounge where it was too crowded and noisy. Brad, red faced and demanding, finally found a table, ordered drinks and shoved his chair closer to Cathy. He ran his hand along her bare arm, to her shoulder. Cathy smiled and then excused herself to the ladies room. She took the tape recorder out of her purse and turned it off. Brad had a big mouth when drinking and he had told her everything she wanted to know. Heck, she thought, this field operations stuff wasn't so tough, and then wondered how to get rid of the Captain.

"Lord," Cathy exclaimed when she returned to the table and stood by Brad's chair, "I had no idea it was so late and I have a big day tomorrow."

Brad leered up at her and ran a hand down her thigh and then against the silk of her leg. Cathy moved away and sat down.

She shook a finger at him. "Not tonight. I will be at your camp early tomorrow, write my story in the afternoon, and tomorrow night, I'm all yours."

"How about a little preview," Brad slurred.

Cathy shook her head, "I'm really tired. Besides," she chided, "I'm not sure you could handle me right now, the shape you're in."

"Wanna bet?" He said, as he grabbed her hand under the table and pushed it between his legs.

Cathy felt his hardness and jerked her hand away as he laughed. "My mistake," she blushed, "it will still have to wait until tomorrow."

Brad started to argue and then shrugged, signaling the waitress for another drink. Cathy waved her off and asked for the bill.

"I want you in good shape tomorrow. You have a long drive back to camp, so no more to drink, and drive carefully."

Cathy walked him to his car, not wanting to, but figuring it was the lesser of two evils. She didn't want him anywhere near her room. When they reached his car he pulled her close and ran his fingers down her back. She let him kiss her until she felt his tongue and then tried to pull away. He held her in a firm grip and she started to struggle. Then suddenly she was free.

A large black man pushed Brad up against his car, flashed a badge, and identified himself as security. "What is going on here," TC demanded.

"None of your God-damned business," Brad answered belligerently.

"Sir, I am security here. This is my business. You were attacking this woman and if you would like to go downtown to discuss it, I would be happy to oblige."

"I wasn't attacking her," Brad protested, starting to worry, "ask her."

TC turned to Cathy with a frown.

"That's right, officer, we were just saying goodnight," Cathy confirmed.

TC turned back to Brad, stared at him for a minute, and put his badge away. "I want you out of here right now, and a word of advice. If I were you, I would stop for coffee before heading home."

A subdued Brad nodded, telling Cathy that he would see her in the morning.

Cathy smiled, "Thank you, officer. I really appreciate the help."

TC returned the smile, "You're welcome, Miss Stanfil, but I'm afraid this business isn't over with yet."

Cathy shook her head, "I don't understand," she said, wondering how he knew her name.

"I'm TC," he introduced himself holding out his hand. "I'm a good friend of Jack Nordone's and came down here with Walt Kutch who was worried about you. I'm on your side, TC Brown."

"Walt's down here?" Cathy asked in surprise. She took TC's hand, not knowing if she was glad or miffed. "I could have handled him," she said defensively. "You didn't have to drive all the way down here for this."

"I'm sure you could have," TC answered. "It's the next problem that you might need a little help with."

"What next problem?" Cathy asked, puzzled.

"We arrived here about six," TC explained, "and have been keeping an eye on your room. About an hour after you left for dinner, a big heavy-set guy cased your room and then broke in. He's still there, waiting for you."

"My God," Cathy said, "it could be the same one that attacked me in the parking lot and killed Martha."

"I would say that's a good guess, so here is what I want you to do. Give me about five minutes to get Walt. We will go around to the corner of your building. He won't be able to see us from there. I want you to open the door, reach in, switch on the light and then back out as fast as you can. I will be right behind you and I think I know where he will be hiding."

Cathy nodded. "Maybe we should just leave it."

TC shook his head. "No, I heard he tried this before. If we don't stop him here, he will just try again."

She squeezed TC's hand, nodding her acceptance.

Cathy had second thoughts as to her spying ability as she inserted her key in the door and pushed it open. She reached in, found the light switch, and turned it on. She immediately backed out and TC rushed into the room, didn't see anyone, and slammed the partially opened door against the wall. He was rewarded with the sound of the door hitting flesh and bone, a curse of pain, and a man stumbled out from behind the door. He was carrying a white cloth in his right hand. TC didn't take any chances, immediately hitting the man over the head with his Heckler & Koch. The big man fell to the floor. TC bent down to cuff him and smelled the cloth. "Chloroform," he confirmed.

Cathy looked down at the fallen man, "That's him, the one in the parking lot. I won't ever forget that face."

TC turned the man over. "O.K. Miss Stanfil, get your things together while Walt and I get this character out to our car. Walt will drive you back to Atlanta in your car. I will follow in Walt's car after I take care of our friend."

Cathy started to ask a question about the 'taking care of' and decided she didn't want to know. "Please, call me Cathy. I like to be on a first name basis with all the people that save my life. Unfortunately, or maybe fortunately for me, the list is growing."

TC looked at Cathy in surprise, grinned, and shook his head. He pulled the man to his feet and with Walt's help, half carried, half dragged him out. They threw him in the back seat of Walt's car and Walt gave TC the keys and told him he would meet him at his house at the lake.

"I really want to thank you for the help," Walt said.

"No need to and you were right. She is hard to explain. Anyone with a sense of humor under these circumstances is a keeper. Also, you know that when she helped Jack, she became my friend too, and I will see to it that this scumbag doesn't bother her again.

Chapter 16
Ocotal, Nicaragua, Sunday, February 27

JACK WOKE UP EARLY, BRUSHED his teeth, showered, and gave Ralph a quick run. He was jogging toward the Velados' house when the sun crested the mountains. The run felt good; the fresh air and beauty of the country was just what he needed to blow the cobwebs away. He followed Father Esteban's directions and found the house set back from the road and surrounded by trees. A stone fence followed the driveway to an old, freshly painted farmhouse. Not seeing any activity, Jack wondered if he was too early. He approached the house cautiously, trying to see in the large window. As he got closer he heard the unmistakable click of an automatic weapon. He stopped, raised his hands and turned toward the sound. He saw a small, wiry man with a black, neatly-trimmed mustache, standing behind the fence. He was carrying an AK-47 with practiced ease.

Jack was wondering how to explain and thinking maybe he should have brought David along, when the front door opened and a petite, dark-haired woman stepped out, speaking to the man in rapid Spanish. The man shrugged and lowered his weapon. As the woman turned toward Jack, he caught his breath at her beauty. She was dressed in tan slacks and a bright yellow peasant blouse. Her jet-black hair hung loose, falling to her waist.

"I," Jack began, again wishing he had David with him, "am Americano, and, ah, no hablar, Espanol." Jack's further efforts were interrupted by a melodious laugh from the woman who motioned him into the house.

"Certainly," she said looking at Jack's running outfit—an indigo shirt, expensive shorts, and white Nikes—"no one would ever suspect you were an American unless you told them."

Jack flushed at her words.

"You did come to the right house and I was expecting you. Father Esteban called. Would you like coffee?"

"Very much, just black, and your English is very good, thank goodness."

After she served the coffee, Maria turned serious. "I did want to meet you because I heard so much about you from Tim." Jack, surprised, saw that she was close to tears. "I feel partly responsible for the death of your wife and son."

Jack, shocked, stared at her.

"My husband and I were professors at the University of Central America in San Salvador," she explained. "We had to leave the country for political reasons and came here. My husband met your son at the school and we became close friends. Roberto, my husband, joined the FMLN, an anti-government organization when we left El Salvador. He is away much of the time. Although he has never been away this long," and Jack could sense her worry. "A friend of his brought me a statue, wrapped in brown paper. He said Roberto told him to get it to Tim, that he would know what to do with it." Maria's eyes filled with tears, "I did what he wanted, but have wished a thousand times that I hadn't."

"You think the statue had something to do with the death of my family?"

She nodded. "A police officer from San Salvador came here a short time ago. He questioned me about the statue and told me my husband was dead, that before he died he told him there was a message hidden in the statue."

"Did you read the message?" Jack asked.

Maria shook her head, "I never opened the package. I think part of me didn't want to know. I am so sorry."

"Don't be," Jack said, "I know how you feel. I feel the same way about Sister Linda," and he told her what happened. Jack reached out and took her chin in his hand. "Remember, you and I are not responsible and that's why I'm here, to find out who is responsible and make them pay for it."

Looking into his eyes, Maria believed him. They both sat with their own thoughts, until Jack told her about his meeting Father Esteban. "I was with another man and thought that Father Esteban didn't want to talk about the statue in front of him."

"I'm sure you're right. Father Esteban was close to Tim and Roberto. He might know about the message. Down here, you trust no one." She stood up. "I will drive you there after we have breakfast."

Jack thought about calling David to let him know he would be late and then reconsidered. They drove to the church in Maria's car while Maria told Jack how much good Father Esteban had done for his parish. Father Esteban wasn't in the yard with the children, so they knocked on the door. It was opened immediately by a distraught housekeeper. She recognized Maria, unleashing a torrent of words while twisting a worn towel in her hands.

"That's odd," Maria said. "Josepha said that Father Esteban received a call early this morning about a terrible accident south of here. Someone said that he was urgently needed. Of course, he went."

"Is that so unusual?" Jack asked.

"Well, Josepha felt that he should have been back by now to say mass. He has never missed mass before, so she questioned several parishioners. One from the south didn't know anything about an accident. News travels fast in a town like this and people would know about a bad accident. She is right to be concerned".

"Do you want to look for him?" Jack asked.

Maria nodded, hurrying toward her car. She drove out of the parking area, turning south. They hadn't gone over three or four miles, when Jack told her to stop. She pulled over to the side of the road and looked at him quizzically.

Jack pointed. "I thought I saw something hidden in the underbrush back there, it was a vehicle, maybe a truck. Let me check it out. I'll be back in a minute."

Jack walked back about thirty yards and followed a track into the woods. It was a vehicle and as Jack got closer he thought it looked like the old truck he saw in the churchyard yesterday. He grew wary as he circled the truck and saw a foot. It was bare, not moving. Jack inched his way forward. He almost gagged when he saw Father Esteban. The priest was completely naked and tied face down over the right front fender. His legs were spread apart and his lower body was covered with cigarette burns. There was no doubt that he had been raped and tortured. It made Jack sick to his stomach. He thought he had seen it all. He heard Marie coming, and tried to stop her, but she pushed past him.

Maria gave an agonizing cry when she saw the body, the color draining from her face as she fell to her knees. Jack tried to shield the body when she regained her feet but she brushed him away.

"Did you tell anyone that you were coming back to see Father Esteban?" she demanded.

Jack shook his head. "No, I haven't spoken to anyone."

"Someone knew, or saw you together, and I think you are right. He did have more to tell you." Her eyes softened as she moved toward the priest. "His people have so little, nothing but their faith. Then God sent Father Esteban to them. Now what will they do? He never had a thought for himself, the most totally good person I have ever known." She grabbed his torn clothing and started to cover him.

"Wait," Jack said, "maybe we shouldn't touch anything until the police get here."

"The police," Maria spat. "We are not in your country. There are no police or at least any that care. Death is an everyday occurrence here. They are corrupt and work for the highest bidder. Our duty is to Father Esteban. He would not want anyone to see him like this, or know what happened to him."

Jack saw the anger and determination in Maria and agreed. He untied Father Esteban. Maria gathered up his clothing, dressed him as best they could and placed the body in the truck.

"Look," Marie said as she held up a silver bracelet, "I found this under his clothes."

Jack took it and examined it. It was a silver bracelet with entwined snakes, much like the one David had. He doubted that there would be two such distinctive bracelets in this town. He put it in his pocket, feeling a great anger. There was one person that did know he was meeting Father Esteban.

Jack drove the truck, following Maria back to the churchyard where he parked it and carried Father Esteban into the house. He laid him on the bed, giving the bedroom a quick search. He found nothing, and returned to the front room where the two women were engaged in animated conversation.

"I have to go back to the hotel," Jack interrupted. Maria stood and told him that she would drive him, then come back to help Josepha.

"Now what will you do?" Maria asked as she started the car.

"First, I'm going back to the hotel and talk to David, the man that drove me up here. Then I will see. Probably go to San Salvador. I was given the name of a man there, an American who might be able to help."

"My Uncle Andrea owns an antique store in San Salvador," Maria explained. "He is also involved in the FLMN and I think the statue might have come from him."

Jack looked up with interest, "Give me his name and I will check it out."

"There is no need, because early tomorrow morning, my cousin, Victor, and I will drive you to San Salvador."

"No," Jack protested, "from what you've told me, it's too dangerous for you to go back to your country."

"I've lived with danger most of my life. Now, since the peace accord was signed and amnesty granted, we are supposed to have immunity. I am also going to search for my husband. Besides, you will need my help crossing the borders."

Jack hesitated, he didn't want anyone else hurt or killed because of him.

Maria saw his hesitation. "I am going with or without you."

Jack knew she would be a great help and reluctantly agreed.

Chapter 17

Atlanta, Georgia, Sunday, February 27

Walt jumped when he heard the car door slam and realized he had fallen asleep. Considering the amount of sleep that he had in the last forty-eight hours, it was no wonder. He opened the door for TC, led him back to the kitchen and poured coffee. He put cream and sugar on the table, and then sat down, looking at TC expectantly.

TC took a sip of the hot coffee, grinned and then shook his head, "No, I didn't kill the son of a bitch, if that's what you are wondering."

Walt sighed, "Hell, he tried to kill Cathy at least twice; I would have been tempted."

"I was, then I decided that a little conversation might be in order," and TC reached into his pocket and dropped a tape recorder on the table. "It's all here. He sang like a canary, a canary with a gun stuck in its mouth in the middle of a big swamp. He gave names and addresses. I'm sure the information will be a big help to both Jack and Cathy. Some guy in Florida, Nelson Martinez and his friends, run everything through the El Sal Corporation and some other companies."

"Cathy figured out most of that, so what did you do with our boy?"

"We made a little deal when I turned him over to the Waycross police. He pleaded guilty to attempted robbery and assault. For him, it beats kidnapping and attempted murder, and for us, it puts him away until this is over."

"That's all?" Walt questioned, disappointed.

TC smiled, "Not all," he answered. "I will make sure that Martinez finds out what he told me. When he gets out of prison his problems will be just starting."

Walt nodded his satisfaction and told TC he had talked to Jack and what had happened in Ocotal. "That Cordero character was recommended by Colonel Belden. What's your read on Belden?"

TC stirred his coffee, "A good soldier, goes by the book and gets the job done. That said, I wouldn't trust him as far as I could throw him."

"I agree," Walt said. "I know he spent some time in Central America and I wonder whose side he's on. The Cordero thing bothers me. Also, I was there when Linda brought that statue to Jack. As I remember it, Belden took a real interest in it. Jack was just starting to untie the package when Belden practically snatched the statue out of Jack's hands and put it on the table. It was time to leave, but then he disappears, supposedly to see a friend, and Jack's house burns down.

"Hey," TC said, "I don't like the guy either, but I can't see him killing Sister Linda."

"Remember," Walt pointed out, "at the time he left us at the church, we were all going down to the Holiday Inn. He didn't know she was in the house."

TC rubbed the stubble of his beard. "It's all circumstantial, but you make a case."

"It would also answer some questions as to how those people knew Sister Linda was at Jack's house and had the statue. I just don't know," Walt continued, "I think he has more in common with the people in Miami than he does with us. I think we should cut him out of the loop. Cathy already has."

TC agreed. "I could go along with that, but I wouldn't tell Jack until we get more information." TC finished his coffee and stood up. "Right now I'm going to cut me some sack time before this old body falls apart. I suggest you do the same and when we wake up, you can check the flights to San Salvador?"

"I already have. I figured you would be heading that way. I want to go with you but think it would be better if I stay here and take care of business on this end."

"And keep an eye on that girl."

Walt broke into a big smile, "And keep an eye on that girl."

TC returned the smile. "From what I've seen, she's worth it. I do have to go back to Chicago once more and will be back Tuesday or Wednesday."

SAN SALVADOR, EL SALVADOR

When Joe Ellison heard the news, he slammed the telephone down, shaking his head. What was that son of a bitch doing, he wondered. It just didn't make sense to send Cathy to Rome at a time like this. Courier duty, hell, even if Clausen did have doubts about her scenario, she could be doing something a lot more important than courier duty. A more experienced agent, bull. Something is rotten up there, he could smell it, and he was damn well going to find out what it was.

He looked back at the map of El Salvador on his desk, with Cathy's notes written in the margin and the more he looked at it, the more convinced he was that she was right. He leaned back in his chair and rubbed his jaw. It's too bad she didn't get her hands on that statue or at least a look at it. Maybe it would have explained things. Like why Jack's house was bombed and the nun killed. No, something is going down, and time is running out. But what dreadful thing, he wondered, could happen in a country where murder and mayhem are an everyday occurrence? Maybe he should shake the tree and see if anything falls. Gomez was a creature of habit and Joe knew where he had his Sunday dinner. If he stopped by, they just might bump into one another.

***

David Cordero ate with obvious relish, mopping up the rest of the thick red sauce with the last piece of bread and sitting back in satisfaction. The La Hola Betos served the best food in Central America and always made a trip to El Salvador a rewarding experience. Rafael had already finished his meal and took out two cigars, offering one to David.

"And now to business," Rafael said as the waiter cleared the table and moved to a discrete distance. "You killed the priest?"

Cordero shrugged, "I felt it was necessary. I'm sure he didn't know anything about the statue. I used my best persuasion and he never said a word."

Rafael remembered the scene at Maria's house, and smiled in satisfaction, trying to imagine the pain that David had inflicted. "Did he cry out, or beg?"

David shook his head.

A pity, Gomez thought, then asked, "This Nordone, what is he like?"

"From what I learned from Colonel Belden and what I observed, I would say, dangerous. He is smart, competent, and worse, on a crusade."

"Does he suspect you killed the priest?"

"I left a note that I had to return to Managua on business, but like I said, he's smart. I did set him up with the local police but don't know how that turned out."

"Well, maybe it won't matter. With the priest gone, maybe he will go home."

"I doubt that. He is not the kind to quit. My bet is that after talking to that Velado lady he will follow the trail of the statue. That could lead him here."

Gomez was about to answer when Joe Ellison passed by their table and appeared to slip, falling on to the table. Gomez spilled his drink, leaped up angrily, and then tried to control his temper when he recognized Joe. He waved his bodyguards away.

Joe regained his balance and offered an apology. Gomez reluctantly invited him to sit down for a drink.

Joe shook his head, "I think I've had enough, but it's good to see you back."

"Back?" Gomez queried, knowing his trip to Miami was a well-guarded secret.

"From Ocotal," Joe answered more loudly than necessary, and noticed Rafael stiffen. "Rumor has it you were looking for religious objects, a statue of some kind. I didn't even know you were a collector. Also, there was something about a woman and a priest."

Gomez glared at Joe, ready to explode. Joe just smiled, patted him on the shoulder, and ambled toward the exit, wondering if his words would have the desired effect.

Chapter 18

Ocotal, Nicaragua, Monday, February 28

Jack had trouble sleeping. He couldn't get the picture of Father Esteban out of his mind. Everyone that tried to help him was either dead or in danger. He added David Cordero's name to the list of things to do and strengthened his resolve to find the people responsible for all this, no matter what. He wasn't sure how long he had slept or if he had slept at all when his door crashed open and the lights turned on. Two uniformed police officers rushed into the room. One of them, a heavy-set man with a drawn gun, ordered Jack to get up. Jack staggered out of bed and started to raise his hands.

"What in hell is going on?" he managed.

"You know what is going on, American pig," the fat officer sneered, "you killed our priest and you will die for it." The officer moved closer to Jack, pulling back his gun like he was going to shoot him when he was hit by a ball of flying fur that knocked him off his feet. The other officer, seeing the dog, tried to draw his gun but Jack was on him before he could clear it, landing a solid right to the jaw, followed by a left to the gut. Another right dropped him.

The fat officer was on the floor, face down, and when he tried to roll over, Ralph's snapping jaws stopped him. The man whimpered, and Jack picked up the officer's gun and called Ralph off. He cuffed the officers with their handcuffs and gagged them. Jack was considering what to do next when another man appeared at the door. Jack automatically raised the gun in his hand.

The man looked at the two policemen, showing no surprise, and didn't appear to be carrying a weapon. Then Jack recognized him as the man behind the fence at Maria's and assumed he was a friend.

The man did show some surprise at Ralph and told Jack to get his things together and follow him.

"Maria is waiting with her car and will explain, so hurry."

Jack and Ralph followed the man down the back stairs, out a service entrance. Jack saw a dark blue Toyota Corolla.

The man put Jack's bag in the trunk and Maria directed Jack into the back seat with her. She was surprised when Ralph jumped in first.

"What a pretty dog," Maria said as she patted his head.

Jack started to warn her to be careful, but was too late. Ralph, with a contented purr, shifted his body and put his head in Maria's lap.

"And he is friendly, too." She smiled at Jack and introduced her cousin, Victor Trerado.

Victor gave Jack a barely perceptible nod. Jack noted the unfriendly eyes.

"What happened back there?" Jack asked. "And how did you know to come to my rescue?"

Maria shrugged, "Victor has many friends, some Policia. One of them told him that a man called the station and said you were involved in Father Esteban's death. He thinks the man paid one of the officers to see that you were arrested in the morning. Did you get a chance to talk to your friend?"

Jack shook his head. "No, he was gone and left a note that he had urgent business in Managua. I still don't understand, aren't you putting yourselves in danger? If they want me here, won't I have trouble at the border?"

"No," Victor answered from the front seat. "The local police have their thing going and don't mess with the border police.

Besides, our communications are not the best. The Border Police won't hear about this for days, if at all."

"We are going to take the Pan-American highway," Maria explained, "go through Somota to El Espino, where we will cross into Honduras, then to Choluteca and El Amatillo, where we will enter El Salvador. Sit back and enjoy, it is a long ride."

Maria was dressed in brown hand-tooled boots, blue denims that hugged her lithe figure and a dark blue blouse, opened at the throat. She sat back in the seat, eyes closed and Jack thought she looked even lovelier then he remembered. They passed through the dusty town of Somota, with its cobbled streets and red tiled roofs.

Victor broke the silence. "Are you carrying a weapon, or do you have one in your bag?"

"No, but I'm beginning to wish that I did."

"Time enough for that when we get to San Salvador," Victor answered. "Now is not a good time to have one. The Hondurans do not trust their neighbors, especially the Nicaraguans. They will search you and every piece of your luggage. If you have anything to get rid of, now is the time to do it."

Victor was right on the money. Three surly guards, carrying automatic weapons, searched them, the car, and then fumigated the car. They started to fumigate Ralph and changed their minds after a low growl and the baring of teeth. They opened every piece of luggage and checked their visas, passports, and driver's license before reluctantly waving them through. There were a few jokes directed Maria's way. One of the guards tried to rub up against her, but Ralph moved protectively between them and the guard quickly backed off.

They drove by parched landscapes and treeless hills covered with thorny shrubs. Maria told Jack that El Salvador was much prettier, and as she told him about her country, the good as well as the bad, Jack heard the longing in her voice.

"Are you sure it's all right for you to go back?"

Maria shrugged, and Victor made a noise of derision from the front seat.

"All the violence is supposed to be behind us," Maria said. "That ended when the Peace Accord was signed and amnesty granted, but in all honesty, I don't know. It's hard to end a twelve year war which killed over 75,000 of our people with a signed piece of paper."

"That's how all wars end," Jack answered.

They passed through Choluteca, one of the oldest colonial towns in Honduras and continued to the border town of El Amatilla. The crossing into El Salvador was relatively easy. Maria promised a treat at Santa Rosa de Lima where they would have lunch. It was another red-roofed town, but this one had a large, busy market that attracted traders from throughout El Salvador and Honduras. They stopped at an unmarked building that housed the La Pema restaurant. Jack had a heavenly fish soup, washed down with a cold Pilsner. It was the perfect meal.

Maria told Jack that the owner, Senora Maria Eutemia, had a secret recipe and would give it to no one.

Maria was right about El Salvador; the countryside was more colorful and beautiful, though marred by the trash alongside the road. The landscape had changed to undulating hills covered with trees and rivers that flowed between fields of rice, cotton, and sugarcane. A light rain began to fall soon after they renewed their trip. Jack was lulled to sleep by the lush countryside, the noise of the rain, and too much soup and beer.

It was dark by the time they reached their hotel, the Camino Real, on the southern end of the Boulevard de Heroes. It was one of the finest hotels in the city.

Maria explained that he could not take his dog in the hotel. "Victor will take him to a friend who lives close. His friend has a walled-in area. Your dog will be fine."

Victor turned to look at Ralph, remembered him helping Maria out of a tight spot, almost smiled, and nodded his acceptance.

Maria had reserved a large, airy, two-bedroom suite. Jack found that his room overlooked the Metro Center, El Salvador's largest shopping mall, while her room overlooked a garden.

Victor put the luggage in the rooms, surprising Jack when he kissed Maria on the cheek, gave him a curt nod, and left.

"I thought he would take Ralph to his friends and then come back."

Maria explained that he had family in the city, which he hadn't seen in a long time. He would be back in the morning to take them to her uncle's antique shop.

"Victor doesn't talk much," Jack said as the door closed." Does he have trouble with his English?"

"He both speaks and understands English very well. He speaks it as little as he can to protest the Americans funding a regime that kills dissenters and steals from the poor."

"I'm sorry about that. We really knew nothing of your troubles down here. After Nicaragua fell to the Communists, our government became paranoid about Central America and thought Russia would move all the way to Mexico. They backed any government they thought would stop it."

"Maybe if your government spent their millions on feeding the poor and creating jobs, instead of a corrupt government, they wouldn't have to worry."

Both Jack and Maria were drained from the trip and ordered chicken salad sandwiches from room service. As an afterthought, Jack, feeling depressed, ordered a bottle of Jack Daniels, Black Label.

When the food and drinks arrived, Jack tipped the server who put the food on a small table overlooking a garden. They ate, drank and talked, with Jack doing more drinking than eating and consequently most of the talking. Maria was a good listener, both attentive and sympathetic. She even tried to keep up with Jack's drinking, but couldn't. Jack told her about his life, the war, and about Tim and Nancy. His voice started to choke up when he talked about them and he poured himself another drink from the half-empty bottle. They were out of ice and Jack tried to stand, slipped and Maria grabbed him, saving him from a fall. Jack shook his head, apologized, and made it to his room and closed the door. Maria cleared the table, changed into a nightgown and went to bed.

    Maria didn't know how long she had been asleep when she heard a cry of anguish, then unconstrained sobbing coming from Jack's room. She hesitated, and then went to his room. Sitting on the edge of his bed, she softly stroked his hair, watching his strong and vulnerable face. Jack came awake slowly, still in a stupor and reached for her, pulling her down beside him. Maria fought him in a half-hearted way as Jack buried his face between her breasts. His crying subsided and his body relaxed. Maria could feel the heat of his body through her thin gown and knew she should move away, but Jack's hand slid down to her breast. He rubbed the nipple slowly and his other hand moved down to the hem of her gown, pulling it up to her waist. Marie knew it should stop now, was surprised at her own response, and when he touched her tenderly and kissed her, she became a willing participant.

Chapter 19

San Salvador, Tuesday, March 1

THE VOICES ROSE TO A deafening crescendo before Rafael Gomez took control. He clapped his hands once and then raised them for quiet. He glared at the group, giving them a message.

"You all have your responsibilities," he opened, "and we have one more week to make sure there will be no problems. If you find one, no matter how small, I want to know. We will meet again early Monday morning, on the day it happens. Remember gentleman, there will be no excuses."

The meeting started to break up when one of the men asked a question. "Why are we having this big parade the day before our election?"

"That is not your concern," Gomez said without looking up, "you will know next week."

All but four of the officers filed out of the room and as Gomez moved to join them, he motioned for one of them to make sure that the door was secured and no one was loitering.

"And now to the real business," Rafael said, as he nodded toward a small light-skinned man with a razor-sharp mustache, wearing a well-creased uniform. "How are our guests doing?"

The man smiled thinly. "They are quite comfortable, and will be ready to make their contribution to our cause. We will bring them up just before the crime is committed, where they will be shot and killed during the gun battle. We will have absolute proof that they are responsible."

Gomez continued, "The crowd will be so incensed with this atrocity that they will take their bodies and burn them.

You will see to that," and Gomez nodded to Colonel Umanzor. "Remember," Gomez stressed, "the key to the plan is to make sure that the guilt is laid on the FMLN. Their credibility will be destroyed and we will be heroes."

***

Jack awoke slowly, head in a vice, and wondered if anyone got the number of the truck that hit him. He couldn't remember when he had gotten so smashed. It was probably in Nam, a lifetime ago. He tried to sit up but fell back on the pillow as he heard a tapping at his door. What in hell did he do last night? Flashes of his memory started to filter through and he wondered if his night with Maria was a dream or reality.

There was a louder knock on the door then Maria entered, carrying a tray with coffee, a large orange juice, and a bowl of fresh fruit. She was dressed in jeans, a green blouse, and her hair was tied in a ponytail.

Jack sat up trying to cover himself as Maria sat down on the edge of the bed, putting the tray in his lap and smiling at him with tenderness and some amusement. Jack started to say something, but Maria placed one of her fingers on his lips, taking one of his hands in hers.

"Don't say it. I couldn't ignore your cry for help. Like you, I was not ready for what happened. It had nothing to do with my love for my husband or your love for your wife. It was just a beautiful, passionate meeting between two lost souls and it will never happen again." She kissed him on the cheek. "Now hurry, Victor will be here soon to take us to see my uncle."

The hot shower was almost as good as the food, and Jack felt a lot better. Now he was afraid he would die: a little while ago he welcomed it. He dressed in khaki slacks and yellow sports shirt. He tried to get in touch with Joe Ellison, who wasn't in, and he left a message that he was going to the antique shop and would call later. He heard the outer door open, ran a comb through his hair, and went out to meet Victor.

As soon as he entered the room, Victor gave him a brown paper bag. From the weight of it Jack knew it was a gun. He reached in and pulled out a Russian made 7.26mm Tokarev with two extra clips. The gun was already loaded, and each of the clips carried eight rounds. He hefted it, sighted at a picture on the wall, nodding in satisfaction.

When the three of them left the hotel, Jack noticed that the Metro Center was already active with young matrons in tight Sergio Valenti jeans, walking with purpose, and trailing maids and babies behind them.

Maria noticed Jack's attention. ""Oh yes," she said, as she gestured toward the mall. "We do have the very rich here in San Salvador. Unfortunately, they are few, and the poor are many."

Victor drove down the Boulevard de Los Heroes to Avenida Franklin Delano Roosevelt. After turning on to Calle Arce, Maria cried out, putting a hand to her mouth. Jack saw a burned out shell of a building and guessed that it had once been her uncle's store. The stores on either side appeared to have suffered some damage but were open for business.

Victor found a parking space and Maria asked if they would go to the Pharmacia across the street to find out if he knew what happened. She would go to the grocer next to the burned-out building because she knew him. He might tell her more if she was alone.

Jack bought toothpaste and aspirin and took them to the counter where Victor was questioning a frail gray-haired man who was answering in animated Spanish. Jack paid for his purchases, following Victor out. "He didn't know much, except that Maria's uncle died in the fire."

As they stepped out of the door, Jack stopped, adjusting to the bright sunlight, while Victor raced across the street. Jack, squinting against the glare, saw a black Jeep Cherokee parked in front of the burned-out store. There was a struggle going on. A big man in uniform was holding Maria against the vehicle. When Victor reached them he tried to grab the man's arm. Another uniformed man got out of the vehicle, came up behind Victor and clubbed him over the head.

"What the hell's going on here?" Jack demanded, as he ran across the street.

"Not your concern," the man with the club said, as he moved toward Jack, pounding the club into the palm of his hand.

"It is my concern," Jack said, and pointing to the man holding Maria, "you, let that woman go."

The man with the club smiled in anticipation as he drew the club back and moved closer. Jack anticipated the move and was one step ahead, kicking the man in the groin and grabbing the arm with the club. He gave the arm a vicious twist. The man screamed as a bone snapped, dropped the club, and Jack threw him headfirst into the jeep, where he fell whimpering, holding his broken arm.

The man holding Maria let her go and reached for his holstered gun, but Jack slashed at his wrist, knocking the gun to the ground. Jack asked Maria if she was all right while the big man with the slightly pox-marked face shuffled to Jack, shoes almost touching.

"You made a serious mistake, señor," Rafael Gomez said. "You have interfered in a State Security matter and injured one of my officers. You are under arrest. Any further display will be dealt with severely."

Another Jeep Cherokee pulled up with a screech of tires and Jack found himself surrounded by four armed officers.

Gomez backed away and looked from Jack to Maria. "So, my little one, you have a new protector. An American, I think." He bent to pick up the fallen club, moving back towards Jack. "Just what did you give this man to make him so impetuous, your body perhaps?"

Maria colored, moving to Jack's side. "Leave him alone," she demanded, "he has nothing to do with this."

"He does now," Gomez said. "Take a good look at him because you will not recognize him the next time you see him," and Gomez brought the club back.

Jack braced himself for the blow and then heard the click of a camera. It came from a short, fat, balding man in a rumpled suit who stepped into the circle of soldiers.

"Boy, that sure was exciting," the man said as he slung the camera over his shoulder, mopping his face with a soiled handkerchief. "If I didn't know you better, Colonel, I would have thought that you were going to strike an unarmed American citizen with that club."

Gomez lowered the club in frustration. "This person assaulted and injured one of my officers and is under arrest."

"I'm sure sorry to hear that," Joe Ellison drawled.

"I know you are," Gomez answered smugly, "but like in your own great country, justice will be served."

"You sure got me there," Joe said as he continued to mop his brow. "I just thought that we might just clear up this little misunderstanding before you get into all that paperwork."

"There is no misunderstanding," Rafael snarled.

"There is always room for misunderstanding and Captain Nordone here is one of my country's war heroes and a personal friend of the President's chief advisor."

"I don't care who he is or who he knows. He is in my country now and he will obey our laws and pay the price for the ones he breaks."

Joe nodded and scratched behind his ear. "I guess I don't blame you, but the timing is so bad, I mean with the election and all."

Gomez had started to direct his men to cuff Jack and Maria and put them in the Jeep. Puzzled he stopped and turned to Joe. "And what does this incident have to do with our election?"

"Probably nothing," Joe answered. "I just know they will send some people from Washington down here to look into this. I don't think you need all that attention right now. I mean so close to the election and all."

Gomez still wasn't sure what Joe was getting at, however, he held up a hand, stopping his officers from cuffing Jack.

"I guess it probably doesn't make any difference to you; however, I know some people in Miami who might care. I just might give Nelson Martinez a call to see if he can help straighten this out and save those people from Washington a trip."

Gomez knew he couldn't let that happen and forced a smile. "You might be right, Mr. Ellison. And in the interest of bettering the relationship between our two countries, I will give him a warning and put him in your custody." He turned, desperately trying to hold his temper in check and led Maria to the Jeep. "At least this one will dress up our jail," Gomez leered. "I have a special cell for her."

Jack started moving toward Gomez but was grabbed by Joe and ordered to stop, all semblance of the-good-old boy gone.

Gomez climbed into his vehicle, took a long look at Jack, nodded, and drove off.

They helped Victor up and Joe introduced himself. "Cathy said to keep an eye on you. I didn't know you would need me so soon. I know you wanted to help that lady, but we played all our cards and you got to know when to walk away, and when to run. You are one lucky Gringo to win a fight with that bastard. He doesn't lose many."

Chapter 20

Rome, Tuesday, March 1

CATHY RETURNED TO HER ROOM at the Sheraton Roma Hotel and Conference Center, kicked off her shoes, dropped her jacket on a chair and fell on the bed. She was bushed. If they were trying to wear her out, they were doing a good job of it. Her kingdom for a nap, and she rolled over to look at the clock. Just a little over an hour until she had to meet Chris in the lobby.

Rome, there was so much of it, even if she wasn't enjoying it like she should. El Salvador kept getting in the way. She had talked to Walt, learning he found a definite connection between the leased C-130's and the El Sal Corporation. The biggest problem was time. You lost track of it when you traveled. Suddenly it was March first. Just one week before the election and she still didn't have all the pieces. If only Clausen hadn't sent her here. It still didn't make sense. She glanced at the clock again and forced herself to put her feet on the floor and start getting ready.

Cathy wore a long sleeved V-necked flax colored cardigan with a long black linen skirt. The lounge occupied about half the lobby, offering large overstuffed chairs or divans and a great piano bar. The lounge was crowded and Chris stood up, in obvious pleasure, waving her over to the empty chair he had been saving. Cathy ordered a glass of Merlot while she listened to Chris's favorite subject, the sights and sounds of Rome.

Chris worked at the US embassy and had been assigned to keep her busy. He was very nice, intelligent, and a great guide.

"And tomorrow," Chris was saying, "we will see the Catacombs and the Vatican. Maybe we will climb St. Peter's Basilica, if you're up to it. If you're any kind of claustrophobic I don't recommend it; it's a long stifling climb."

"No, nothing like that," Cathy answered. "I am disappointed that I won't get a chance to see Pope John Paul. I so admire that man."

"You will have to wait until your next trip. I have a friend with the Vatican security and he told me the Pope wouldn't be back until Tuesday."

"Darn," Cathy said. "I was sure that I read somewhere that he was going to be here this week."

"He was supposed to come back here after a meeting in San Jose, Costa Rica. He changed his plans to include a stop in Buenos Aries. Then he's going to one of those banana countries to give a speech backing some election."

"That's too bad," Cathy said, and as Chris watched, the color drained from her face. "Oh no," she moaned, shaking her head in denial, "they wouldn't, not the Pope." She turned to Chris, "That election, where is it?"

Chris shrugged, "I don't know," he answered, "I wasn't really paying that much attention. Central America I think. What's wrong with you? You're white as a sheet."

"That friend of yours," Cathy said. "Can you find out which country?" She wanted confirmation, but knew it was El Salvador.

Chris shook his head. "No, when he found out about Pope John Paul he took a couple of days off to go skiing. I don't know where."

"See if you can find out," Cathy said, "it's important. I'm sorry about dinner. I have to catch the next plane to Washington."

Chris was surprised and disappointed. "Is this one of those, 'you will have to kill me if you tell me,' kind of things?"

Cathy nodded, "It's something like that. Now I have to call a taxi and go up to my room and pack."

"I'm sorry," Chris apologized, "this is serious, isn't it? And forget the taxi, you go up and pack. I will call the airlines and get you on the next flight out of here. Then I'll drive you to the airport."

"You're a doll," Cathy smiled. "I need to make a short stop at the office. I have to send a fax to Joe Ellison, our agent in El Salvador."

Cathy was exhausted when they touched down at Kennedy. It was hard to push a 747 all the way across the Atlantic. She rushed off the plane and was lucky to catch a flight to Washington with less than an hour's wait. The flight was quick and uneventful. She debated about going to her condo for a quick shower or going straight to the office. Thinking of Martha, she realized she wasn't quite ready for the condo, so she opted for the CIA building.

When Kim Roberts saw Cathy come through the door, she jumped up in surprise. "I didn't think you would be back until the weekend," she said.

"Something important came up and I had to come back early. Do you know if Art is in the building?"

"I'm sure I saw him earlier," Kim answered as she picked up the telephone, "I assume you want to see him ASAP."

Cathy nodded and disappeared into her office, hearing Kim yell that he would see her right away.

Clausen, as usual, made her wait as he shuffled through his endless papers. When he looked up it was with a full-blown frown. "Tell me, Miss Stanfil, why are you in Washington, in my office, and not in Rome?"

Cathy hesitated, not knowing where to start.

"As long as you are here and not in Rome, you might as well sit," he said, nodding to a chair.

"Last night, I found out something that I thought you should know…"

"I believe they still have telephones in Italy," Clausen interrupted dryly.

Cathy ignored the sarcasm. "This needed more than a telephone call. I found out that Pope John Paul is in San Jose, Costa Rica, meeting with the clergy from Central and South America. After the meeting he will make a stop in Buenos Aries and then give a speech Monday in a Central American country, encouraging voters to vote."

"So?" Clausen asked.

"Don't you see?" Cathy answered, "The only election down there is in El Salvador. This is the missing piece."

The DDI frowned and then comprehension set in. He started to sweat. "No, they wouldn't, not the Pope."

"Those Miami people are capable of anything," Cathy retorted. "Also, the FBI informed us that the Georgia mercenaries have flown to Honduras. I know this is the final piece. We have to do something and we have to do it now."

Clausen suddenly stood up, paced around the room nervously. "Have you told anyone about this," Clausen asked, "anyone at all?"

Cathy hesitated and shook her head. She hadn't actually talked to Joe, she reasoned.

Clausen returned to his seat. "I'm still not sold on your scenario, but this is too important not to pass on to the Director and to Senator Rucker. You did the right thing coming to me. This is top secret and I don't want you talking to anyone about it, understand?"

When Cathy nodded, Clausen stood up and led her to the door. "Another thing, I'm ordering you to go home and get some rest. You won't be much good to anybody if you don't sleep. I'll see you in the morning."

As soon as Cathy left the room, Clausen called Belden, arranging to meet him at their bench near the Lincoln Memorial. The DDI was already there when Belden arrived and when Belden started to sit, Clausen stood up.

"Let's walk," he said.

"So who ruffled your feathers today?" Belden asked.

"The usual one, she also scared the hell out of me."

"I thought she was in Rome?"

"She was," Clausen answered, "She flew back last night and thinks she knows what is going to happen in El Salvador."

"What?" Belden prodded, now all interest.

The DDI let out a long breath. "She thinks they are going to assassinate Pope John Paul."

"My God," Belden exclaimed, "that sure as hell would cause the chaos that Cathy has been talking about."

"She found out that he will be in El Salvador on Monday, giving a speech backing the election. Of course he is against the present regime since they killed his Jesuits and nuns, and wants the people to vote them out."

"Damn," Belden exclaimed. "If they assassinate the Pope and can blame it on the FMLN, it would be the perfect answer for Martinez."

"The Pope for Christ sake," the DDI blurted: "I don't want any part of it."

"If it is true, and I have no reason to doubt it, you are part of it," Belden answered. "And so am I." He rubbed his jaw. "Do you know if she told anyone else about this?"

Clausen shook his head, "She said no."

"Well," Belden mused, "if she just found out about it last night, took a flight out of Rome, reporting to you this morning, she probably didn't have time."

"I'm sure she didn't. I told her to go right home and get some sleep. I told her not to mention it to anyone, that I would inform the Director and Senator Rucker."

"We know you can't do that unless you want to sign your death warrant. If you screw this up now, Martinez will kill you as sure as we stand here. He has a long arm."

"What the hell can we do?" Clausen asked hopelessly.

"Well, we have to get her out of Washington as soon as possible. Book her on the first and longest flight to San Salvador. Let her sleep a couple of hours, the less sleep the better. Then go to her place, wake her up and tell her that Joe needs her. Take her to the airport and stay with her until she boards that plane. Tell her Joe will meet her at the airport."

"Christ," Clausen groaned, "I can't do this. There must be another way."

"Well, you better do it because there is no other way. This is about survival, yours and mine. When you confirm her flight information let me know. I will take it from there."

Chapter 21

San Salvador, El Salvador, Wednesday, March 2

Jack sat across the desk from Joe in his cramped office, remembering what Cathy had said about him. She knew her man. Jack found that out yesterday. Joe didn't look the part, but he got him out of one tight spot and didn't even mention the stupid things Jack had done. That was class.

Joe asked the questions and Jack told him everything that had happened to him since he had landed in Managua. They were interrupted by a knock at the door and a heavy set, gray-haired lady, in a long shapeless dress entered.

"Excuse please, Señor Joe. Did you receive a fax this morning?"

Joe rifled through his basket, moved several papers on his desk and shook his head, "Don't see it," he answered.

Jack wondered how he could find anything on that desk of his.

"That's strange," the woman said, "you know I try to keep track of all our correspondence, numbering them, and one is missing."

"Do you know where it came from?"

"I already checked. It was from Italy, Rome I think."

Joe frowned. "Has there been anyone in the office earlier today?"

The woman chewed her lip in thought, "No, no one, except for señor Lemus, of course. He always comes in early to clean up."

"Tell him that I would like to see him."

"That could be a problem," the woman answered. "I found a note from him on my desk. He said one of his daughters was sick. He wouldn't be in for the next two or three days."

"Damn," Joe exclaimed and asked for his address and telephone number.

"What's the problem?" Jack asked.

"I guess you don't know that Cathy is in Rome."

"Rome!" Jack exclaimed. "What in the world is she doing there?"

"It beats the hell out of me. I know her boss, Art Clausen, doesn't really believe her theory, but to send her to Rome is bullshit."

"Why would he do that?"

"I don't have the foggiest," Joe shrugged. "It doesn't add up. I do know that when this thing is over I'm going to find out why."

"So you think the fax could be from Cathy,"

"I don't know anyone else in Rome and with Lemus taking off, which he rarely does, I don't like it."

"You think your handyman took your fax? That he's a spy or something?"

Joe sat back in his chair and sighed. "Everyone down here is a spy or something, for money or survival. They have been fighting each other for ten or twelve years and you have to have a scorecard to know the good guys from the bad. Hell, I have a scorecard and still can't figure it out."

He motioned out the window to some distant hills. "You ought to go up there sometime, to a place called El Playon. It's a lava filled field of dead and rotting bodies, dumped there at night by the men in the black Cherokees with the smoky windows. Most of the bodies are maimed or disfigured. The human rights people reported a hundred missing persons a month. They even go up there and take pictures of the dead and put them in a spiral notebook for people to look at. At least the relatives know what happened to their husband or brother." Joe sighed in exasperation. "Of course, the guys in the black cars are our friends, the good guys, or so I'm told by the people in our Embassy. It's a little better now since the peace accord was signed."

"Speaking of the Embassy," Jack said, "I think I will go over there tomorrow and see if I can get any help for Maria."

"From my experience of dealing with those bureaucrats over there, I don't think you will get much help. I was thinking of going to see this radio guy I know, maybe he will help. He owns a radio station. He is anti-government and for the past ten years had to operate in the hills. He was able to come back to San Salvador when the peace was signed. He has softened his stance some and his station has become the most popular station in the country."

"You don't think I'll get much help from our Embassy?"

"No, but it's worth a try. Those people don't think the way we do."

The silence was broken when Joe's secretary returned to the room and put a piece of paper on Joe's desk. "Here is his address. He doesn't have a telephone."

Joe read the address, stuffed it in his pocket, then looked for and found his car keys under a mustard-colored napkin. "I'm going to pay Mr. Lemus a visit. I want to see how that daughter of his is coming along. You're welcome to come and I've noticed that you won't need any artillery."

"I would like to, and it's a 7.26 Tokarev."

"Nice weapon," Joe acknowledged. "I don't expect any problems, but in this town you never know."

Joe muttered a curse as he turned south on Avida Cuscatlon.

"What?" Jack asked.

"Notice anything different?"

Jack shook his head. "No, except I don't see any people."

"See that black Cherokee parked up ahead?"

Jack nodded.

"That's one of those cars I've been telling you about. When they stop, no one comes out of their house."

Joe drove about half a block past the Cherokee and parked. "I don't like it," he said as he stepped out of his Audi. "I'm glad you decided to come." Joe had read Jack's service record in Cathy's office and felt he couldn't have better backup.

"The Lemus' house is on that back street, right behind the meat market. I might be getting paranoid, but humor me. Why don't you go around to the left of the store and I'll take the right. Remember, all the good people are tucked in their little houses. If you meet anyone, it's probably one of the guys from the black car and they have little regard for human life. They shoot first and ask questions after."

Jack nodded. "I'm acquainted with people like that."

"O.K., I'll meet you at the back door of his house."

There was another building next to the market and the space between them was dark, narrow, and filled with junk. Jack made his way through the obstacles and when he came around the corner, into the light, he stopped in shock. David Cordero was walking toward him, carrying a gun in his right hand. Cordero also stopped in surprise and recovered first, firing three shots.

Jack's instincts saved him as he threw himself back into the dark passageway, hit the ground and rolled around the corner just before the first shot. The shots went high, but Jack gave a grunt of pain.

Cordero didn't know if he hit Jack and wasn't even sure if Jack was armed, but he wasn't going to take any chances. He ran to the other side of the building and then to the street. He looked both ways and, not seeing anyone, sprinted to his vehicle.

Jack guessed that Cordero would try and reach his vehicle and made his way quickly back to the street through the dark passageway. He got there just as Cordero was approaching the Cherokee and Jack pulled his weapon and ordered Cordero to drop his gun.

Cordero turned at the call and took a wild shot and missed. Jack returned the fire and hit Cordero three times, twice in his groin and once in the stomach. Cordero dropped his gun, sinking to his knees in agony.

Jack walked over to him, kicked the gun away and reached into his pocket and pulled out the bracelet he had been keeping. He threw it at Cordero. "I knew I would be able to give this back to you someday. You know I could have put any one of those shots in your brain or heart. I just wanted you to share some of the pain you inflicted on Father Esteban."

Fear filled Cordero's eyes and he whimpered as he tried to raise an arm to say something, but blood flowed from his mouth and he fell back onto the pavement.

Joe puffed his way around the corner of the store, took in the scene with a glance and told Jack to get in his car. He did a quick search of Cordero and then joined Jack.

As soon as the door closed, Joe pulled away with a screech of tires. After what he considered a safe distance, he slowed down and looked at Jack. "Boy, I don't think my heart can take much more of having you around."

Jack explained about Cordero and Father Esteban.

Joe rubbed his jaw thoughtfully. "Wasn't it your friend, the Colonel, that fixed you up with that guy?"

Jack nodded.

"Well, remind me never to ask him for help."

"Hey, it's been a few years," Jack retorted defensively, "and you said yourself that these people are always changing sides. What about Lemus, did he tell you anything?"

"Too late," Ellison answered. "I found him with a bullet in his head—probably killed by your friend. I searched the place and didn't find anything. I have seen that guy before. He has dinner every once in a while with Gomez. The good news for you is that no one around here sees or hears anything and shootings are a daily occurrence. The bad news is if he is one of Raphael's goons, you could be in big trouble. I think, if I were you, I would catch the first plane out of here."

"I'm sure that is good advice."

"But not taken?"

"Don't worry, as soon as I take care of business, I will be out of here."

Chapter 22

Washington, DC, Wednesday, March 2

Cathy sat back in the soft leather seat, wondering if she needed sleep more than a drink or a drink more than sleep. The hell with what she needed, she wanted a drink. Her boss was hard to figure. She knew she was not one of Art's favorite people, and to find him on her doorstep at four in the morning was unbelievable. And here she was, on another flight, headed to Los Angeles, then to San Salvador. Cathy decided on a Bloody Mary. At least he had booked her in first class, even that was a surprise.

Art said Joe needed her in San Salvador, and that he would meet her at the airport. She couldn't help thinking it was strange. What could she do in San Salvador that she couldn't do better in her office? If Joe asked for her though, he must have a good reason. She took another swallow of her drink and hoped that she would be able to sleep when she finished it.

The flight ran into a little weather and still arrived in LA on time. She had tried, but hadn't been able to get any sleep or shut her brain down. She wasn't in love with LAX, especially when she was so tired. It seemed so, so sprawling. She made all the right turns because she arrived at the International concourse and found her flight to San Salvador with time to spare. She hoped her luggage did, too.

She boarded the plane and again, sat back in her seat and tried to relax. She was surprised when she was jolted awake by a hard touchdown in San Salvador. She was surprised but happy; she needed that sleep.

She joined the passengers leaving the flight and found the airport passageways roomy and clean. She didn't worry about reading the signs; Spanish was her second language. It really didn't matter because every sign was in English and Spanish. She claimed her baggage and went to immigration where a tall, trim man in uniform blocked her way.

He smiled at her. "Señorita Stanfil?" he asked.

Cathy stopped in surprise and nodded.

"I am Captain Alejandro, at your service. Our mutual friend, señor Ellison, was involved in a slight accident and asked me to meet you." The Captain saw the concern on Cathy's face and reassured her. "It was very minor and he is fine. Unfortunately it will take some time. The paperwork in our country…" and he shrugged.

Cathy was disappointed and cautious, but the man was in uniform and if Joe hadn't sent him, how would he know what plane she was on? She shrugged, allowing the man to take her bag. He ushered her to a special booth in customs. They were through in minutes. They entered the bright, airy atrium, crowded like all airports. He held the door for her as she walked into the hot humid air that almost took her breath away after the air-conditioned airport. Cars lined the curb and they walked between them, crossed a small boulevard, and went to a special parking lot with many trees and flowers.

The roads were in good shape and well marked. They said little as Cathy became absorbed in the scenery. There were many small fruit and vegetable stands and one ram-shackled, one-room building that looked like a police station. Most of the houses were stucco, walled, and topped with razor sharp wire.

They made a turn and Cathy noticed that traffic was thinning rather than increasing.

"Are we still heading for San Salvador?" she asked.

Alejandro shook his head. "It's a surprise, and you will like it. It is a very nice home, not far from San Salvador on Lake Ilopango, very quiet. Señor Ellison thought it would be a better place to work. He might even be there by the time we arrive."

Cathy wasn't sure why, but she felt a little uneasy, wishing that she had taken her revolver with her. It was always such a hassle though, going through airports, especially in a foreign country.

They finally turned into a long narrow driveway that wound its way through a dense wood. She noted two people walking near the road carrying automatic weapons. The house was a large, two-storied house and faced the lake.

The Captain took her bag and led her to the front door, which opened as they approached. They were greeted by two men, each holding a weapon.

Instinctively Cathy started to back away but was grabbed by Alejandro and pushed through the door.

"Where's Joe?" she demanded.

A large dark-haired man at the door laughed, as he looked Cathy up and down. "I'm Joe," he said, "or anyone else you want me to be," and all three men joined in the laughter.

Cathy felt her skin crawl at the way they looked at her. She knew she was in serious trouble. The men searched her luggage and purse and then took her upstairs to a bedroom at the back of the house. There were bars on the windows and the balcony door was locked. She gave a shudder; she had a feeling she might not come out of this in one piece. She just didn't understand. Thank God she had sent that fax to Joe. At least he would know about the assassination plot. She knew that Clausen must have betrayed her and must be working with the people in Miami. He had set her up and she was shocked, but held back her tears.

SAN SALVADOR

Jack picked at his breakfast of freshly baked tortillas, beans, eggs, and fresh fruit. It had been a rough night. He hadn't slept much, worrying about Maria and wondering if he would be arrested for killing Cordero.

Joe Ellison arrived, slumped into the chair across from Jack and declined Jack's offer for breakfast, then reconsidered after looking at Jack's plate of food.

"Still pissed about Maria?" Joe asked.

"No, you were right. I don't like her being with that bastard though. Isn't there anything we can do to get her out of there?"

Joe mopped up his plate with his last tortilla, wiped his mouth and sat back in satisfaction. "Things have changed a little since they signed the treaty, but make no mistake—the boys in the black vans are still in control, just wearing different uniforms. The new government closed down some of the most notorious government units and started some new ones. Unfortunately, it is the same people with a different name. I don't think Gomez will try anything, this close to the election. Victor and I arranged for Maria to get a bunch of visitors. They will come all day—some even at night—and it will give Gomez something to think about. Today we are going to see my friend that owns that radio station. He might be able to give us some help.

Once in the car, Joe explained that they were going to see Francisco Marroquin, a tough old bird that backed the FMLN during the war and suffered for it.

The building was small and compact. When they entered, Jack noticed that every desk was covered with papers. Everyone looked busy. Sound booths surrounded the room, and a tall gray-haired woman sat at the front desk. She confirmed their appointment and led them into Francisco's office. Joe shook hands with him, introducing Jack, who listened to them as the two discussed El Salvador and the coming election.

"I keep hearing rumors and innuendoes," Marroquin said, "about our coming election and they will not go away. Have you heard anything?"

Joe shrugged, "There is a saying in my country, that if you find a lot of smoke, you will usually find a fire."

"That is the problem with my poor country, as soon as we put out one fire, another starts. However, you didn't come here to discuss politics."

Joe told Francisco about Maria and the trouble she was having with Gomez, and about her arrest.

"Colonel Rafael Gomez," the editor mused, "one example of our slime that crawls under rocks. The peace people did a good job, getting rid of the Security Force and the National Guard but no one is perfect. Gomez slipped through the cracks. Enough of that, how can I help?"

"If you aired this story, questioning the arrest of Maria in the light of the amnesty, I think it would deter the Colonel for a time. Possibly save her much pain and maybe her life."

Francisco sat in thought.

"I know we might be putting you at risk," Joe apologized.

The editor waved it aside. "I've been at risk since the first time I criticized our government. My station and I have the scars to prove it. I have always admired the Velados, so I will help you. I will visit her personally and take a photographer with me to take her picture."

"Will Gomez let you see her?" Joe questioned.

"I still have some friends in the judiciary and I will take one with me. I am a man of some importance now. I don't think Gomez will do anything foolish; he is not stupid."

Joe told him about the visitors that he and Victor had been sending, adding that it was driving the guards crazy.

Francisco looked up in surprise. "I did not know that Victor Trerado was her cousin."

"Do you know Victor?" Joe asked.

"Not personally, I only know of him. He has a reputation as a fair, hard man and a scholar. While not a patron of the government, he had withheld his criticism. That changed three years ago when the army invaded the campus of the University of Central America. They killed the top three administrators, Jesuits, three human rights workers, their housekeeper, and her daughter. One of the human rights workers was Victor's brother. Apparently, that was the last straw. Victor disappeared for a while and a strange thing happened. All the officers that were involved in the invasion died under mysterious circumstances. Victor was rumored to be fighting with the FMLN in the North, but I believe he went back to Nicaragua."

Jack had always been impressed by Victor and now started to understand him.

Joe stood up and shook Francisco's hand. "I know you have work to do, so we will be on our way, and thank you."

They were lost in their own thoughts on the drive back to the hotel, but as Joe pulled into the parking lot, he exclaimed, "Oh, shit!"

"Now what," Jack asked

"Did you see that black Cherokee parked in front?"

Jack shook his head. "I didn't notice."

"I think we might have a visit from the Colonel."

They had just stepped into the lobby when they were accosted by two armed men in uniform who directed them to Rafael Gomez, who was sitting in a small hotel office.

"Ah, my American friends, I see you were up and away early to see the sights of our fair city."

They didn't answer.

"I'm sure you had an exciting day, but surely not as eventful as yesterday perhaps?"

Jack shrugged.

"We found a friend of yours yesterday, David Cordero. He was shot down in our streets."

"You seem to have a lot of that going on down here," Jack answered. "I'm sure it is not the David Cordero that I know; he is in Managua on business. He was my guide, not my friend."

"What is this all about?" Joe interrupted. "Jack was with me all day yesterday."

Gomez nodded. "I'm sure he was with you yesterday. I would strongly advise you to tell this close friend of the President's to leave my country as soon as possible."

After he left, Jack raised an eyebrow. "It's beginning to look like I'm not wanted in San Salvador."

"Hey, it turned out better than I thought. So how does it feel to be my country's most unpopular tourist?"

"I'll get used to it. Now I'm going to visit my dog and then try to get some help from the people at our Embassy. Maybe you can give me a name."

Joe sat back trying to organize his thoughts. "You will probably do better on your own. I'm not a big fan of the Embassy people here, and the feeling is mutual. I have been working for this country for more years than I want to remember and it's the best country in the world. There are times, though, that we do things that make me wonder, and this is one of them. So go over there without me dragging you down. By the way, who did you say you're going to visit?"

"My dog, Ralph," Jack answered.

"You brought a dog down here?"

Jack looked at Joe and sighed. "He's the only thing I have left in the world."

Joe looked into Jack's eyes, got up, went around the table and gave him a big hug.

Chapter 23

Atlanta, Georgia, Thursday, March 3

Walt was starting to wear holes in the floor from his pacing, when finally, in exasperation,

TC asked, "Go where?"

Walt shrugged, "Damned if I know. I'm just tired of waiting."

T.C. smiled, "She really got to you, huh?"

Walt looked up in surprise and then returned the smile, "That obvious?"

"More," T.C. replied, "and if I were a little younger, I might give you a run for your money."

"I think the word is, a lot younger," Walt said as he poured himself another cup of coffee. He returned to the alcove and stared at Lake Lanier. "She would have called if she could. I know she is in big trouble; I'll bet on it."

"Well, let's start from the beginning. You last talked to her when?"

"Tuesday, and I brought her up to date on all the El Sal stuff I found. She was still pretty ticked at being sent to Rome." Walt smiled, "I even offered to fly over and cheer her up. I also told her that Jack was in San Salvador."

"And then you got a call from her on Wednesday?"

"Yes, it was on the machine. I could tell she was really excited and said she flew back to Washington and would call me Thursday. She also told me to tell Jack to get in touch with Joe Ellison. That she found out what is going to happen in San

Salvador and faxed the information to Joe. God, if only I had been here Wednesday."

"Now don't go beating yourself up," T.C. said. "You just can't stay here 24/7. What did Ellison have to say?"

"I couldn't reach him either. I did find out that Cathy checked out of her hotel Tuesday evening, caught a flight to Kennedy, and a shuttle to Washington. There the track ends. She didn't call like she said, and I got zilch when I tried the CIA except that her assistant was also worried."

T.C. rubbed his jaw. "Don't you know that Georgia Senator who is always hanging around the President?"

"Rucker? Sure, I met him a few times, even helped him raise a little money."

"He has always impressed me as one of the good guys up there, a man that gets things done. I vote we fly to Washington, see the man, and ask him for his help."

Walt agreed. "Good thinking. I'm sure he can get information out of the CIA that I can't. And he is one of the good guys. I liked him and so did Jack and Nancy. I can't say that about many politicians. You grab your stuff. I'll call him for an appointment, then call our pilot and see if the plane is available."

"You own that plane?" TC asked.

Walt laughed, "No, but I have to go to New York and Washington quite a lot and have priority. Besides, I've made enough money for the bank to buy a fleet of them."

Walt called the pilot and made an arrangement for a quick flight to Washington. He said they would be in the terminal in about ninety minutes. Next, he called Senator Rucker's office and tried to make an appointment with him, regarding Cathy Stanfil. Rucker was out of the office so he told his assistant that they were flying to Washington this afternoon and would meet him in the bar at the Four Seasons at six. If he couldn't make it, they would understand and call him in the morning.

Once in the air, Walt poured drinks and put his briefcase on the table.

"Bank work?" TC asked.

Walt shook his head. "I'm sure that Cathy's disappearance is tied to those people in Miami and the El Sal Corporation. My computer and I found all the properties owned by them in or near San Salvador. I think Cathy flew to San Salvador, and somehow, those people grabbed her and are holding her at one of their properties. I even found two houses they own, one in La Libertad and another near San Salvador."

"La Libertad?"

"It's a small coastal town about fifty miles from San Salvador. It has a black sand beach and is known for its surfing."

"Well, I don't own a surfboard, but you know I'm going down there to help Jack, and now, it sounds like you might be coming with me."

"I am. Jack met some guy down there who has a bunch of friends. I'm going to bring my information to them and help in the search."

"It sure beats sitting on our heels."

The flight to Washington DC was uneventful and they took a cab to the Four Seasons.

As they walked through the opulent lobby of the Georgetown's Four Seasons Hotel, a pianist played muted melodies for their affluent customers that crowded the well-spaced tables. TC's head didn't stop bobbing. "Hey," he said, "this reminds me a lot of that place in Chicago where the cops hang out. Where are the doughnuts?"

Walt shook his head, but couldn't help a smile. "Well, when this is over, maybe Jack and I will back you on the comedy trail."

They found the Senator in the Grill Room next to the bar. Walt made the introductions. "Senator, this is T.C. Brown, a friend of Jack Nordone's who served with him in Vietnam. I want to thank you for coming."

The Senator rose and shook TC's hand. "It's always a pleasure to meet a comrade in arms," and to Walt, "I remember you from the campaign. I'm glad you came because the President is very concerned about the problem in El Salvador."

"A pleasure to meet you, sir," T.C. answered, "I've read some of your war stories."

"Please," Rucker said as he motioned them to take a seat, "it's Aaron. Like all war stories, some are true, some not so true. I did my best and like you, made it home."

T.C. nodded, "Which is the best story of them all."

They ordered drinks—a Grey Goose martini for Walt, a beer for TC, and a Wild Turkey on the rocks for Senator Rucker.

Walt told Rucker what he had found out about the El Sal Corporation and that Cathy had called him on Wednesday and he missed her call. "She sounded very excited, like she found some of her answers. I haven't heard a word since, and I'm worried. I think she might be in San Salvador."

"The election is next Tuesday so you have my complete attention," Rucker said. "I talked with Kim, Cathy's assistant, and she is also concerned. She said it wasn't like Cathy not to keep in touch. I called Art Clausen, couldn't reach him, but did talk to his secretary. You're right, she told me that Cathy left a message saying she was flying to San Salvador."

Walt shook his head, "It's still weird, why would she go to San Salvador now?" Walt told the Senator about the two attempts on Cathy's life.

Rucker shook his head in amazement. "I hadn't heard that and I can't think of any reason why anyone would want to kill her, unless she was right on her projections."

Walt and T.C. agreed.

"Well," Rucker continued, "things are getting complex, and there isn't much time left. I'll call the station chief in El Salvador, Joe Ellison, and see what he knows. Meanwhile, we have to find Cathy and talk to Jack. You see what you can learn. We will meet tomorrow for breakfast in the White House. An agent will pick you up at seven thirty in front of your hotel."

"The White House?" They both echoed.

"I think the President will be interested in what you have to say. He likes to meet people like you and get away from the politicians. And don't worry; it is not as scary as it sounds."

SAN SALVADOR, U.S. EMBASSY

"U.S. Embassy," the operator said, "hold please." She immediately contacted Bill Thomas. "Bill, it's that guy again, the one that wants to talk about that woman who was arrested."

"Tell him I'm out."

"I'm sorry but Mr. Thomas is out and I don't know when he will return," the operator told Jack.

"Miss," Jack replied, "this is the sixth time I've called and I am going to call back in fifteen minutes. If I am unable to talk with Mr. Thomas, I will call a friend of mine in Washington, Senator Aaron Rucker. I will ask why we are spending millions here and don't have people in our Embassy." Jack hung up without waiting for an answer.

Fifteen minutes later Jack called back and was put through to Thomas. Jack told him about Maria. Thomas agreed to meet him in Beethoven Park and gave directions.

Thomas was wearing a gray sports coat, white shirt and tie, with black slacks. He was just over six feet, solid build, and greeted Jack with a smile. The meeting place was near a small lake with a fountain that gave off a rainbow effect.

Jack told him about Nancy and Tim, the El Sal Corporation, and the people in Miami. He told about Nicaragua and how Maria helped him get to San Salvador.

"I know we give these people a ton of money every month and thought you might have enough influence to help get her out of jail."

Thomas shook his head. "You have to understand the situation down here. The election is a week away and the United States cannot be involved in anything political and the Velado woman is political. We can't even be thought to do anything that would influence the election. If the wrong people win,

El Salvador will be in deep trouble, which will cause a lot of problems for us.

"Well, thanks for all the help," Jack said sarcastically.

"I'm sorry," Thomas said, not looking at all sorry. "Tell me, is Joe Ellison mixed up in this?"

"Why do you ask?"

"It's my job to ask. He is a representative of the United States and as such, cannot be involved in situations like this."

Jack stood up, not offering to shake hands. "I think you should ask Joe that."

Chapter 24

San Salvador, Friday, March 4

It was a pretty day, light fluffy clouds drifting across a deep blue sky with a soft warm wind gently blowing. Jack hardly noticed as he crossed the hotel parking lot. His mind was far away. He crossed the street and had to jump to the curb to avoid getting hit by one of their multi-colored buses. He knew he had to get his act together. With all the problems he had right now, he had to sort them out. First Maria was arrested, and now Cathy was missing. What in hell was she even doing in San Salvador? He could also feel Gomez breathing down his neck.

He crossed another street and found the walled house on Calle Managua. It was just a few blocks from the hotel. He rang the bell next to the gate. The gate was opened by a balding, heavy-set man who patted him down and then motioned him in.

As soon as Jack entered, he was almost knocked down by Ralph who leaped on him, wagging his tail. Jack smiled as he got down on his knees, took a good licking, and gave Ralph a big hug.

Jack was led into a small kitchen and introduced to three men dressed in jeans, boots, and heavy shirts. Victor and Joe Ellison came into the room and Victor told Jack that the men were his cousins. Jack smiled and said that Victor must have the biggest family in El Salvador.

Victor returned the smile. He was finding it harder and harder to hate this gringo, especially after what he did to that policeman who arrested Maria. He could still remember the satisfying sound of the breaking arm.

Jack asked Victor about Maria and told him of their visit to Marroquin at his radio station.

"I have heard of him," Victor answered. "He is well respected, even among his enemies. I'm sure he will help. Our visiting program is working, mixing ordinary people with prominent people, and we are driving the guards crazy. They would like to turn them all away, but are afraid to. I'm sure it is helping to keep her safe."

"That should cause Gomez some concern," Jack said, "and I hope that problem is solved, because now I have another."

Victor raised an eyebrow.

"I just learned from my two friends, who are flying here today, that the lady from the CIA who is helping us, has gone missing. She flew to San Salvador on Wednesday and hasn't been heard from since. Naturally I can't go to the police, so I called all the hotels and got nothing." Jack looked at Joe. "Do you know about this?"

"I got the same message this morning from Senator Rucker and I'm worried sick," Joe answered. "I know she would call me if she could, so I drove out to the airport this morning. I checked with some TACA people and found she arrived all right and several people remember her. One of them is sure she left with a police officer or soldier."

"Damn," Jack exclaimed. "Gomez must have her."

"I don't know," Joe answered and shook his head in dismay. "I wouldn't bet against it."

"Anything that we can do?" Victor asked.

"I told you that two of my friends are flying down here this morning and one of them is a computer whiz," Jack said. "He thinks that Cathy found out what was going to happen here next week, sent a fax to Joe, and flew to Washington. Then, for some reason, she flew down here. He thinks that somehow the Miami people found out about it, grabbed her at the airport and are holding her somewhere. He is bringing a list of properties owned by the Miami people and the El Sal Corporation. He is sure she is being held in one of them."

Joe snapped his fingers. "I couldn't figure out why anyone would kill someone over a fax. Now I can. She found what she was looking for and sent me the information and Lemus took it."

Jack told Victor about the missing fax and finding the dead employee.

"We need to find that lady in a hurry," Victor said. "While you're gone, I will line up more help."

As Jack and Joe Ellison walked to the hotel parking lot, Jack asked Joe if he wanted to ride out to the airport with him.

"I would," Joe answered, "but just before I left, I got a call from this Captain Navero. He works with Gomez and said he wanted to see me, that he had information about Cathy."

Jack stopped in his tracks. "You're not going to see someone that works for that dirt bag without backup are you?"

"He said to come alone or no deal. I can handle Navero."

"Can you handle him and his backup?"

Joe shrugged. "This isn't my first time around you know," and he sounded a little miffed. "I arranged to meet him at a restaurant I know on the other side of town. They always have a good lunch crowd around one o'clock. What can he do to an American diplomat in a crowded restaurant?"

"You have a point," Jack conceded. "I still don't like it."

"I don't either, but I'll do anything to get Cathy back. I think it's worth a try. If it doesn't work out we will start the search."

Not much of a crowd, Joe thought, as he pulled into a parking space. There were only eight cars and a pickup. He opened the door to the restaurant and saw Navero at a far table. He let the door close and noted that there were about thirteen people in the room—all men, which was strange—and he stopped. He didn't hear the usual busy clatter of dishes and he started to edge back towards the door. Two men sitting in a booth close to the door stood up with drawn guns, motioning Joe to Navero's table. Joe noted the Carswell silencers, weighed his chances, shrugged and moved to the table and sat down.

Gomez came out of the kitchen and sat down across from him.

Gomez waved a hand around the restaurant. "See how respectful we are," he said, "we reserved the whole place just for you."

Joe smiled, "I really appreciate it, how about a menu?"

"Oh, I know all the specials," Gomez said as another man came out of the kitchen carrying a meat cleaver, "and for each selection that you won't talk about, you will lose a finger."

Joe sat back and forced another smile. He knew he was in real trouble. In his diplomatic position, if they hurt him, even a little, they would have to kill him. He glanced around the room. His chances didn't look good. He wished he had listened to Jack.

"I," Gomez went on, "would like to know what you know about our event next Monday."

Joe shook his head. "I have no idea what you're talking about."

"You should, because I heard from one of my friends at your embassy that you received a fax concerning it."

"My secretary did say something about a missing fax, but I didn't see it and don't know what you're talking about."

"I'm sorry to hear about your fax, but perhaps you received a telephone call?"

Joe spread his hands. "A telephone call," he repeated, "what, you are going to have a fiesta and wanted to invite me?"

"It will be a real fiesta for me," Gomez smirked. "I just thought that you might want to save the little CIA agent we have in custody some pain."

Joe fought for control. He needed all his facilities. Once they admitted to him that they had Cathy, he knew he was a dead man. It had been a good life, but he had to save Cathy. He wasn't going down without a fight. He leaned across the table, knocking over a glass of water with his left hand and covered a fork from the place setting with his right.

"O.K.," Joe whispered, as he leaned across the table. Gomez instinctively leaned closer and Joe jammed the fork into his neck. Gomez raised his shoulder, taking the brunt of it and screamed in pain and anger. Before Gomez could draw his gun, two of his men shot and killed Joe. Joe's body slid under the table.

Chapter 25

Washington, D.C., Friday, March 4

Washington was not Atlanta and Walt was freezing, wishing that he had brought warmer clothes. It didn't appear to be bothering TC. "Aren't you cold?" Walt complained.

TC looked at Walt and laughed. "Back home this is golf weather."

Walt shook his head and thought about going back into the hotel to get warm when a black Lincoln Town Car stopped at the curb. A young man in a navy blue coat, grey slacks, and tie, exited the vehicle, opened the back door, and motioned them in.

The drive to the White House was quiet. Walt was never a morning person, and T.C. was awestruck. "I just can't believe that this black kid from the hood is going to the White House to see the President of the United States," he said.

Walt shrugged, "Hey, we got the right. We own it or at least part of it, and Keane is just our present tenant." Traffic was light, and they soon entered through the gate to the White House grounds and the driver spoke for the first time.

"I'm going to let you off at the West Wing. You will be met at the entrance and escorted to the Oval Office."

They entered through the ground floor entrance on West Executive Avenue where an agent checked their credentials and led them to the North West door of the Oval office. Both T.C. and Walt were impressed with the protocol; it was both cordial and efficient. When the agent tapped lightly on the closed door, it was opened by Senator Rucker.

As they crossed the room, President Michael Keane came around his desk and shook their hands as the Senator made the introductions. Walt and TC were speechless. The President greeted them warmly and laughed. "Impressive, isn't it? Aaron told me about you two and your friend, Jack, and I wanted to meet you. The election in El Salvador is important to me and I wanted to thank you for your help. Actually, I really enjoy talking to people once in a while, instead of politicians."

Walt smiled. "This is impressive; you can almost feel the power."

TC's eyes continued to survey the room and he shook his head in wonder.

"You will have time for a tour after breakfast, but right now I'm hungry," the President said, steering T.C. and Walt to a cloth-covered table, laden with food and drink.

After they were finished and the table cleared, Walt and T.C. sat on a small sofa behind a coffee table that held a vase of fresh roses. Senator Rucker and the President sat across from them in matching chairs.

"I explained to the President how you two became involved in all this after the death of Jack Nordone's wife and son."

"God," the President said sincerely, "I am so sorry. I can't think of anything more devastating."

"We all feel that way," Senator Rucker said, "and we are convinced that it is connected to the election in El Salvador." The Senator looked up. "You know the President promised them a free election there, so he is interested. I want you to tell him everything you know."

T.C. deferred to Walt, "You were there from the beginning, so you start."

Walt told it all, from the disappearance of the TACA flight to their arrival in Washington, adding what he found out about the El Sal Corporation.

"I take it that you concur with what Miss Stanfil projected, that some terrible thing will happen in El Salvador and that we will have problems with the election?" Rucker asked.

Both men nodded. "And," Walt said," I'm worried about her. I talked with Jack last night; he is staying at the Camino Real in San Salvador. I told him about the call I missed from Cathy. He told me that neither he nor Joe has heard from her and they, too, are concerned. They think she sent Joe a fax when she was in Rome and that the fax was taken by an employee of the embassy. They went to the man's house to check it out, found the employee murdered, and no sign of the fax."

"I'm thinking," Rucker mused, "that Miss Stanfil found her missing piece, sent the information to Joe Ellison, and then flew back to Washington. She apparently met with Clausen, flew to San Salvador for some reason, and has gone missing."

"I'm with you," Walt said. "She found the answer she was looking for and flew back to tell us. I tried to confirm it with Clausen, but like I said, he is never around and doesn't return my calls."

"That Clausen is beginning to piss me off," TC said. "Oops, sorry, Mr. President."

"He is beginning to piss me off, too," the President said with a smile.

"I think we should implement our plan as soon as possible," Rucker said, "and help Walt and TC in any way we can."

"Implement what plan?" Walt asked.

The President sighed reflectively, looking at the two men across from him.

"Hell, it's no state secret. You people seem to be ahead of us anyway so here is where we stand. We already have troops in Honduras, involved in a joint exercise with their people on the Nicaraguan border. There are only a few places you can bring troops and equipment from Honduras into El Salvador and they will be covered by the Hondurans and us by tomorrow. The Navy sent a gunboat to El Salvador and it should arrive on station sometime tonight to block any sea assault. The only problem is with Guatemala. We are still working with their government and might have to come up with an alternative, if needed."

"It sounds like you have everything under control," Walt said, "except for Cathy. I've checked my calls every two hours, still no word."

"We don't have the answer for that either," Rucker admitted. "I too have tried to get in touch with Clausen, and can't locate him. I'm seeing the director this afternoon."

"That guy Clausen hasn't been much help to anyone," TC added. "We left a bunch of unreturned calls." Rucker flashed the President a look that confirmed his agreement.

"We're going to fly to San Salvador later today," Walt said. "I have a list of the properties that Martinez and the El Sal Corporation own, in or around San Salvador, and we're going to help look for her. Jack has some locals lined up and we will search all those locations and see if we can find her. We'll keep in touch."

"Good," the President said, and stood up. "I think it would be beneficial to everyone if you keep our CIA agent down there in the loop."

Walt and TC agreed and were ushered out of the Oval Office.

SAN SALVADOR

Walt and TC passed through customs with ease after an uneventful flight and were met by Jack at baggage claim.

"Nice airport," Walt commented.

"It's pretty new," Jack answered. "The military took over the old field."

On the ride to the hotel Jack brought them up to date on what they were doing regarding Cathy. He told them that Joe Ellison might have a lead and would catch up with them later.

"So how is it going, working with the people you met here?" TC asked.

"They sure have the experience," Jack answered. "Their war has been going on for twelve years and they are all veterans. I'm working with Victor Trerado, a Salvadoran I met in Nicaragua. He can back me any place or any time.

"You don't find many of those," TC said.

"No you don't."

They stopped at the hotel, Jack always on the lookout for a black car, stowed Walt and TC's gear, and returned to Victor's house.

"Cool," TC exclaimed when they reached the house and he noted the concrete walls topped with sharp wire. "They all look like small forts."

Jack introduced Walt and TC to Victor and his men and glanced around the room.

"Isn't Joe here yet?" Jack asked and told Victor about Joe's meeting.

Victor shrugged, "I know he puts a lot of store in that lady. I wouldn't worry; he can take care of himself. I'm sure that he will show up soon. Now, let's see what your friends brought."

Walt laid a stack of papers on the table explaining that they were lists of all the properties that the El Sal Corporation and its owners controlled or owned, in or near San Salvador. Most of the properties were commercial, but what interested Walt most were two residential properties, one on Lake Ilopango and the other on the Pacific Ocean, near La Libertad.

"I just think that dragging a kidnapped victim into a busy commercial building would be a big risk. They would want more privacy, like a private home, or one of their warehouses."

They all agreed and Victor continued studying the stack of papers. He looked up. "You really did a great job. We will pay special attention to the two houses and three warehouses. I think we can cover all of them by noon tomorrow. I'll arrange our search by location."

"Can we help?" Jack asked.

Victor nodded, "I was counting on you and your friends. We will go out in pairs. I will assign each of you to one of my men so you won't get lost. I will give each pair a list and we will cover as much as we can today and finish tomorrow morning. We will meet back here at noon."

***

Colonel Gene Belden was ushered into Rafael's office and his eyes widened at the large bandage on Gomez's neck and shoulder.

"What the hell happened to you?" he asked.

"Nothing of consequence," Gomez shrugged it off. "What brings my good friend down to my poor country?"

Gene crossed his legs. "The people in Miami are getting a little restless and thought I might be of some help, so I took some time off. Of course it's always good to be where the action is."

Rafael laughed. "I don't know how you can help, but a friend is always welcomed. We already have our FMLN leaders secured and they will commit that cowardly act on Monday. Naturally they will be shot and killed by my heroic troops. It will go as planned."

"Sounds good," Belden replied, "I checked with our people in Honduras and Guatemala. They will be moving out soon. Tell me, General, how does it feel to be the almost head of the El Salvador military?"

Gomez smiled. "There will be some changes, a few accidents perhaps, but the transition will go smoothly."

Belden stood up. "Nelson will be glad to hear that everything is in order. I will check in at my hotel. Maybe we can have dinner together, around nine?"

"I'm sure that can be arranged," Rafael replied, as he stood up and took Belden's hand. "Let me know if you would like any company tonight," and he winked, "to help you celebrate."

Belden declined.

Rafael watched as one of his men drove off with Colonel Belden. He wondered about Belden's sudden appearance. Something didn't feel right but he shook it off. They were getting close now and this was no time for nerves.

Chapter 26

San Salvador, Friday, March 4

ONE OF VICTOR'S MEN DROVE them back to their hotel and Jack asked for a quick drive by before stopping. TC and Walt looked at him quizzically.

"I think we all need a drink before we go to our room," Jack said. He invited their driver, who declined.

The bar wasn't very crowded and they found an isolated table. Jack explained, "I was looking for black Cherokees," Jack said. "I learned from both Joe and Victor that they are bad news. When they show up there is always trouble and their Colonel wants me the worst way. The drivers of the cars are the new police force, many former members of the death squads just wearing different uniforms."

"No wonder they need the walls with barbed wire," TC said, "to keep out the good guys as well as the bad."

Jack told them about breaking the arm of one of Gomez's officers. "And would you believe, Gomez thinks I had something to do with killing Cordero."

"I'm sure glad you got that scum bag," TC said. "After what he did to that priest," and he shook his head.

"Well, if it weren't for Joe Ellison I'm sure I would be in the slammer right now."

"We haven't met Joe yet, but I have the feeling that you were right on with Victor. He is a no nonsense guy, well organized, and even in the short time I've known him, I trust him."

"Agreed," Walt added. "I'm glad he is running the search. He has a lot of help, knows exactly what he's doing, and is confident we will find her tomorrow. God, I hope so, I'm really scared."

Jack studied Walt thoughtfully and realized Cathy had made quite an impression on his friend.

"Also," Jack said, "when we get up to our room, be careful what you say. Say nothing about what we've done or are going to do. Victor thinks every one of our rooms is bugged, and they are being monitored 24/7. Now, because of our advanced age, TC and I will take the bedrooms and Walt can sack out on the couch."

Walt complained all the way up to the room.

Jack had always been a light sleeper, and when something woke him, he noticed it was still dark. He sat up and grabbed his Tokarev 7.66, listening. Then he heard it again, a light tapping on the door. He padded to the door and opened it cautiously, leaving the chain on. Victor peeked through the crack and put his finger to his lips, motioning for quiet. When Jack unchained and opened the door, Victor pulled him into the hallway.

"Hurry," he whispered. "Get your friends out of there as soon as possible. Remember, someone is probably listening, absolutely no noise. I will be holding the service elevator at the end of the hall."

Jack was puzzled, but he had learned to trust Victor, not question him, and he nodded. He returned to the room, flushed the toilet to create a little noise, and cautioned Walt and T.C. to get dressed and gather up their things. He wanted them out of there like right now. They were out in less than fifteen minutes and followed Jack to the waiting elevator.

Victor took them down to the basement. They went through the boiler room and out a back door where a panel truck was waiting. Victor motioned them into the back and closed the door. He joined the driver in front. They drove for about thirty minutes before pulling in the driveway of a different house, also protected by a six-foot high concrete fence topped with barbed wire. Victor led them into the house while the driver closed the gate.

Jack smiled as they entered the house. "Do you have a thing about waking people up in the middle of the night?"

Victor nodded but didn't return the smile, directing them to the living room where hot rolls and coffee were waiting for them.

"Another cousin?" Jack asked.

Again Victor didn't return the smile and Jack knew something was wrong.

After they had coffee and rolls, Victor sighed and looked at Jack. "I hate to tell you this, but your friend, Joe Ellison, was killed last night."

"Oh God," Jack groaned, and put his head in his hands. "I warned him not to go there alone. I should have been with him."

"The police reported that the body was found in one of our worst neighborhoods, a robbery gone bad. They said Joe was probably looking for drugs or sex."

"We all know that Joe was not looking for drugs or sex and that there was no robbery," Jack said quietly. "Gomez, or one of his men, killed him."

"I know how you feel," Victor said. "After twelve years of civil war and the loss of thousands of lives, we have all lost family and friends. We also understand that 'ifs' won't help. You had to pick up your friends at the airport, and Joe had his job to do."

"When will it stop?" Jack asked angrily.

"It will stop," Victor answered, "When we find the missing lady and the people who are responsible for this."

"Joe Ellison," TC asked, "is he the CIA agent down here you became friends with?"

"He was more than just a friend, he is a great guy," Jack said.

The telephone startled them and Victor picked it up, listened, and then replaced it.

"That was a call from a friend at the hotel. About fifteen minutes ago two black Cherokees arrived there. Gomez and seven of his men went directly to your room."

Victor smiled, "Imagine their surprise. They know you were in your room, they heard you come in, and they didn't hear you leave."

"T.C and I would have been a part of that package, so thank you," Walt said.

One of the men walked over to the window and pulled up the shade, letting the light in.

Victor rubbed his hands together. "Well, this will give us an early start. We must try to finish by noon today and will meet back here.

Chapter 27

San Salvador, Saturday, March 5

Jack left with his assigned partner, Edgardo Rodenzo. He was a short, moon-faced man, with a good sense of humor. He also spoke fluent English. They were assigned to one of the more interesting properties. It was a large house on the Pacific Ocean in La Libertad, about twenty miles west of San Salvador, on the Pacific Ocean.

Jack asked Edgardo if he would mind if he brought Ralph along, that his dog needed a good run on the beach.

Edgardo was surprised, but reluctantly agreed, and pointed out the points of interest along the way and told Jack about La Libertad. The beauty of this countryside was also marred by the trash along the highway. There was enough to start a new dump every twenty miles, Jack surmised.

"La Libertad is a great fishing and surfing town," Edgardo explained, "but not much for swimming because of all the rocks. It gets very crowded on the weekends and you have to be careful. Many kinds of people come here making the town notorious for its thieves. They watch everyone, taking advantage of every opportunity, especially gringos. I know; I used to live here."

The property they were interested in was next to a resort hotel. As they passed the house they noted that the gate to the driveway of the house was closed and locked. Edgardo found an empty space in the hotel parking lot. They got out and blended in with the vacationers. The property had a concrete wall, which ran from the road to the beach, segregating it from the hotel. They still had a good view of a large white, two-story house. Jack and Edgardo walked to the beach, skirting the palm trees, deep green bushes, and some small picnic tables, which were set in alcoves, covered with thatched roofs. Many people were enjoying their lunch and a lovely ocean view.

The beach was not too crowded and Jack was surprised at the blackness of the volcanic sand. The property they were interested in was protected on the beach side by another concrete wall. This wall was much lower, offering the homeowners a better view of the water. The wall had two thatched roofed guard towers at each end. They could see that both towers were unoccupied. They walked to the water's edge, where Edgardo stopped to talk with the sunbathers while Jack threw sticks for Ralph to chase. After studying the layout once more, they returned to the car, questioning some of the hotel people on the way.

Edgardo shook his head. "I don't think there is anything here. From what I learned, there has been no unusual activity at the house. I can't believe that they would keep their captive here without some guards around."

"They could have her under tight security in the house," Jack answered. "I agree though; it doesn't look promising."

"La Libertad is a small town, and I have many friends here. We will stop on the way back and I will check out the grocers to see if any of their customers had an unusual increase in their food order."

"Good idea," Jack said, "can I help?"

"No, you and the dog better stay with the car so we have transportation back."

Jack remained with the Renault while Edgardo went in search of information. It was hot in the car, so Jack got out with Ralph and gave him some water. Jack stood by a vacant building next to an alley while Ralph found a little shade under the car. There was a nice breeze blowing and Jack sucked in the fresh air. This part of the town was a little dilapidated and Jack watched as three men crossed the street, walking in his direction. One was about six feet tall with wide shoulders and dark curly hair, one of medium height, while the third was short and fat. When they got to Jack they looked both ways and the larger one held out his hand. "Hey gringo, we want *dinero*—your money and your automobile."

Jack, still angry and frustrated about Joe, saw an outlet for his frustration. "I really don't think that you want to do this," he said.

The big man sneered and pointed to Jack's wrist, "And we want your watch and ring," he said as he reached into his pocket and pulled out a knife. Ralph leaped up at the man with a snarl and his closing jaws just missed the man's hand. The man fell back in surprise and panic.

"If you make one move, my dog will rip your throat out," Jack promised.

The other man also reached for a knife, but before he could get it clear Jack grabbed him and twisted the man's arm upward as he smashed his hand against the stucco building. The man whimpered, dropped his knife, and Jack hit him in the gut. The man bent over in pain, tried to pick up his knife, but Jack stomped on his hand and smashed his head against the wall. The smaller man turned and fled down the alley. The man with the knife kept edging away from Ralph, then turned and ran. The last would-be thief staggered to his feet, mumbling obscenities, and followed his friends.

When Edgardo returned, Jack told him about his little episode and Edgardo laughed. "Well, I did warn you. Maybe Ralph needed a little more exercise. I do have some news though. I found the store that does business with the owners of the house and he said they haven't had an order from that house in over a month. He thinks that no one was there except the caretakers."

"Short of breaking in and searching the place, I think we have done all we can." Jack said.

"I think so," Edgardo confirmed. "If no one has found her, we can always come back," he looked down at Ralph, "and you can bring your dog with us."

"Everyone told me I was crazy to bring Ralph down here and they were probably right but he saved my rear end twice now."

They didn't get back to the house until after two, and it was after four when the last of the searchers arrived.

They all crammed into the dining room and told of their experiences. Most, including Jack, TC, and Walt enjoyed a much-welcomed Pilsner. Victor was talking with the last group and came into the dining room with a big smile.

"I'm sure that we have found our missing lady." The group cheered, erupting in self-congratulations.

"How sure?" Walt asked.

Victor shrugged, "Very close to one hundred percent. There is a large volcanic lake about twelve miles south of here, Lago de Ilogano. Along the lake is a very private section, Amatitan, with extravagant houses, one of which is owned by the El Sal Corporation. Apparently there has been a lot of activity around the house in the past couple of days. Armed guards have been seen patrolling the grounds. The house is on the lake, surrounded by a wooded area with a paved driveway leading from the road to the house. One of our people drove a TV repair truck down that road and was stopped by guards carrying automatic weapons. He pretended to be lost and asked directions."

"They must be protecting something or someone," TC said.

"And there is more," Victor said, winking at Jack. "I have a cousin that does landscape work in that area and he talked to one of the cooks. She told him that a woman arrived at the house last Thursday. She has cooked some meals for her but has never seen her. She said that one of the men always takes a tray to her. The lady is in the back bedroom on the second floor, facing the woods. The cook was kind enough to draw a rough map of the interior of the house."

"That should help," Walt said, and hesitantly, "is Cathy all right?"

"As of last night," Victor acknowledged. He thanked Walt and TC, "This was only possible because of your work. It made our job easy." He turned to the people in the room. "I'm sorry that we cannot use all of you tomorrow and I want to thank you for your help. It was very important. You will know why in a few days. The rest of you, including Pablo, who knows the area, get some rest. We will attack the house at first light tomorrow."

After some of the searchers left, Victor placed a map of the area on the table, along with the crude map of the house. The men drew close. They discussed the operation and agreed on a three-sided attack, coming from the lake, the driveway, and the woods.

Victor explained how busy the lake was every weekend, with people coming from San Salvador. Some came to fish, some to relax, and many just to drink. "Two of my men will be in a boat. They will be noisy, pretend to be drunk, have engine trouble, and row to the dock. This will draw the guards in front, and my people will take care of them. Two more of our men will come up the beach in case they are needed."

"Walt and I, along with two others, will approach from the road in a stolen security van. This should get us close enough to the guards to disarm them. Jack and TC will be dropped off before we get to the house. They will come through the woods and dispose of anyone in back. Their main objective will be to get to and secure the lady before the fighting starts."

"There is a climbable trellis next to the balcony of her room and that should help. All the weapons have silencers, except for Jack's and TC's. They will probably have to force their way into that room, so once you hear their shots you will know our cover is blown and we will all rush to the house to help."

"It sounds like a plan to me," Jack said.

"One more thing," Victor said, "we will all be wearing black with a yellow patch on our right shoulder." He paused. "Hopefully this will help us from killing each other. Now let's get what sleep we can."

Chapter 28

San Salvador, Sunday, March 6

When Jack awoke it was still dark. He knew his inner alarm clock was still working. His pride took a hit though as he slid out of bed and saw TC standing by the door, fully dressed. "Damn," Jack exclaimed, "I was sure I would be up before you."

TC smiled, "You were never up before me. Old habits are hard to break."

There were eggs, the ever-present beans, tortillas, and coffee waiting for them. After the meal they loaded their gear in Victor's car. Jack and TC would ride with Walt, Victor, and his two friends. The men that were going by boat and the two assigned to the beach had already left.

Their weapons were a mismatch, but all were well oiled and in top condition. Walt was given a Heckler & Koch VP-70 with eighteen rounds in the grip. TC went over the parts of Walt's weapon with him and helped attach his suppressor. He suggested that if he had to use it to go for a body shot. Jack carried his Russian 7.66 Tokarev and TC, a Beretta Model 12 Italian sub machinegun that fired 550 rounds a minute. They weren't sure what they would run into, but Jack felt assured they had the necessary firepower.

They left the house in darkness, but light was breaking when they reached the drop-off point for Jack and TC. Victor pulled off the road to let them out.

"You shouldn't have any trouble finding the house," Victor said.

Jack nodded, and TC said, "I've steered him through tougher places than this."

Victor laughed and Jack reached across the seat and took his hand. "I've served with worse," Jack said, "and if I find another war, I know who to call. And please, take care of this useless friend of mine," and he nodded toward Walt.

Victor squeezed Jack's hand. "I thought Maria was wrong to bring you into this, but as usual, she was right. And who knows, this useless friend of yours might be the one that saves us all."

"Then God help us," TC interjected.

As Jack watched the car disappear, he felt as if he had been dropped back in time. He mentioned it to TC.

"I know," TC responded, "for the first time in a long time I get the feeling I'm home," and he checked his compass.

The going was easier now that the sun was rising and TC asked, "Do you think she is still alive?"

"I would bet on it," Jack answered. "They went to a lot of trouble to get her, so they must want something from her. If she was still alive last night, then they haven't gotten what they wanted, so I think her chances are good."

They slowed when they caught a glimpse of the house and took what cover they could. They hunched down, moving from tree to tree, scanning the property for any activity. A row of bushes encircled the back yard. They crawled the last few feet, using them as cover. Jack pointed to an upper bedroom with a small balcony, which had a trellis next to it. He started to stand up, but TC pulled him down, mouthing the word, "smoke". Jack nodded, looked through the foliage and saw a man with an automatic weapon standing near the garage, having a cigarette. The man took one last drag, threw it away, stepped on it, scratched his belly, and started walking to the front.

Jack waited a few minutes, looked at TC and shrugged. "I'm going to test that trellis," he said. "You cover me."

There were two windows on the first floor, probably the kitchen, Jack thought, and he moved to his right, trying to avoid them as much as possible. He saw a break in the bushes and stopped. After looking both ways and seeing nothing, he signaled TC and ran across the yard to the house. He stood with his back against the house, gun ready, waited, and when nothing occurred, edged his way around the house to the trellis.

He tested it and it felt secure so he shoved his gun in his belt and started to climb. He felt a sense of accomplishment when he was able to grab the rain gutter. He tried to peer through the glass door. He couldn't see much because of the railing, so he took a deep breath and pulled himself over the railing on to the balcony. He really felt exposed and hugged the floor as he drew his gun. He waited a few seconds before moving to the door. The room looked empty, except for what looked like a person lying in a bed. He checked once more before motioning TC to come up. TC followed Jack's path and soon joined him.

"The door is locked," Jack whispered, "and the room is empty except for someone, Cathy I hope, in bed."

TC saw that the bed wouldn't be in the line of fire and told Jack that he would fire one burst at the lock before they kicked the door open.

"You cover the room, just in case, and I'll watch the door," TC finished.

Jack nodded and TC blasted the door and lock. They kicked it in easily. Cathy sat up, emitting a sharp cry, and tried to pull the sheets around her. At the same time the bedroom door flew open and a man rushed in carrying a weapon. TC killed him with another burst.

Cathy, recognizing Jack and TC, shook her head in disbelief. Jack gave her thumbs up, told her to get dressed and watch the back and see if anyone came from the garage and to let them know right away. Jack followed TC into the hallway where another armed man was coming up the stairs. He raised his weapon, but was cut down by a hail of bullets from TC, knocking the man through the banister to the floor below.

Now they heard gunshots from the Lake Front and woods. Jack motioned TC to the next room. TC pushed the door open, quickly stepping aside as several shots were fired from the room. TC nodded to Jack, moved to the doorway, and fired three quick bursts. Jack ran into the room, keeping low and saw a disoriented man with a gun kneeling behind a bed. Jack shot him twice. They used the same method on the next bedroom, but it was empty, as were the two bathrooms.

Keeping one eye on the staircase, they approached the last room, the master bedroom, with caution. They took their positions—ready to go in—when the door opened and a scantily clad, very attractive lady came out in tears, her hands over her head. She was followed by a tall dark man with his hands on top of his head. They directed the two down the stairs, Jack and TC following closely, using them as shields. There was no one downstairs except for the body of the man TC shot, and Jack called to Cathy. He gave her his gun and told her to guard the two prisoners.

"Can I tell you how happy I am to see you?" Cathy asked.

Jack shook his head and smiled. "Not until this is over."

He moved to the front picture window, watching three of Victor's friends, dressed in black, walking up the front lawn with drawn guns. He noted at least two bodies, one on the dock and the other on the front lawn. Jack opened the door slowly, waving a white handkerchief, signaling that they were in control. The men crossed the lawn, joining Victor, Walt, and the others. When they entered the house, Walt saw Cathy and rushed across the room, giving her a relieved hug.

Now Cathy was really surprised and blurted out, "What are you doing here?" She returned the hug.

"Everything in control out there?" Jack asked.

Victor nodded. "There were two men guarding the road and two in the garage. Our attack was a complete surprise. I do have two wounded, neither seriously."

The two captives sat quietly on the couch and Cathy gave the gun back to Jack. "I'm really surprised Joe isn't here," she said.

Jack started to say something but Walt waved him to silence, took Cathy's arm, and led her down to the lakefront. Jack watched as Walt talked to her and when she burst into tears, Walt took her in his arms. She was still drying her eyes when they reentered the house and she went to Jack.

"I just can't believe he's dead," she said. "He, he, was so sweet, like a father to me, the one I never had. Did the fax I sent him have anything to do with his murder?"

"Joe never saw the fax," Jack answered. "An embassy employee took it. When we went to his house we found him dead and no sign of the fax."

"I've been so worried, wondering, what you were doing about Pope John Paul." They all looked at her blankly.

"Pope John Paul?" Jack questioned.

Cathy looked dismayed. "You don't know about the assassination?" she said.

Everyone stared at her blankly.

Cathy's color drained and she put a hand to her mouth. "Then what are all you people doing here?"

"Looking for you," Walt said. "We don't understand why you came down here, but we were sure Gomez grabbed you."

Cathy sank down into an upholstered chair. "Oh my God," she exclaimed. "Then you don't know."

"Know what?" The men asked in unison.

Cathy gathered her composure. "Pope John Paul is in San Salvador right now and will be giving a speech tomorrow." She paused. "They are going to assassinate him."

"They wouldn't," one of the men blurted, "not the Pope."

They all looked at the two prisoners.

The man paled. "I don't know anything about that, I swear. I have done some pretty rotten things in my time, but I would never be a part of killing that holy man."

The woman was terrified, and Victor, looking at the two of them felt they were telling the truth. They decided to hold them until things were sorted out.

"I believe you, but we will hold you until Tuesday. Now," he said to the group, "I think that we should leave this place as quickly as possible. I don't think it will be too long before the black Cherokees arrive. We will talk about this back at the house. The Pope's visit is no longer a secret. There was a story about in today's paper and the parade route will be published in tomorrow morning's paper, but I never considered…" and his voice trailed off.

Chapter 29

Washington, D.C., Sunday, March 6

It was a beautiful day for Washington DC in March. The sun was bright, clear sky, crisp, but not freezing. Senator Rucker wasn't enjoying it, though, as he drove down Pennsylvania Avenue, passing a slow moving Buick. His mind whirled. He looked at his watch for the third time, knowing that looks wouldn't stop it but he couldn't help it. Time would just keep on ticking; the problem was there weren't many ticks left.

The telephone call had really shaken him, the Pope for God's sake. There was no denying that it would be the perfect hit for the Miami people. The Pope, assassinated in El Salvador on Monday, a country of what, seventy, seventy-five per cent Catholic? El Salvador would go to pieces. Then those ex-patriots, living in Miami, could bring their mercenaries in, restore order, and kill the perpetrators, or so the El Salvadorans would be led to believe. That would pretty much destroy the FMLN. Wow! After hearing from Jack and Walt about Pope John Paul, he knew he had to call this meeting immediately. Tomorrow would be too late.

Senator Rucker entered the West Wing of the White House and was immediately escorted to the Situation Room on the lower level. The meeting was held in the conference room inside the Situation Room.

They were all there: the President, Secretary of State, Chairman of the National Security Council, Joint Chiefs of

Staff, and Richard Hightower, the Director of the CIA. He knew he heard some grumbling.

Rucker took a seat opposite the President, put his papers on the table and cleared his throat. "First, I want to apologize for taking you away from family and friends on a Sunday but this couldn't wait."

The grumbling stopped and they looked at Rucker with interest.

"It had better be important," the President said, "I had to break a date with my granddaughter. You are not on her good people list right now."

The Senator smiled, "Knowing Abby, I don't think I will be there very long," and the President smiled his agreement.

Rucker turned serious. "Early this morning I received a telephone call from Jack Nordone and Walt Kutch. Most of you are aware of Jack's involvement in our El Salvador problem regarding their Tuesday election. Walt Kutch is an Atlanta banking friend of Jack's. Friday, the President and I met with Mr. Kutch and TC Brown. Mr. Brown is former military and a retired Chicago Police Officer who served with Jack in Vietnam."

This caused a stir and a few raised eyebrows, especially those of the CIA Director, who wondered why he hadn't been informed.

"They had information," he glanced at Hightower, "the CIA does not have and shared it with us. Some of the information has to do with our missing CIA agent, and after our meeting, they flew to San Salvador.

"Mr. Kutch is somewhat of a computer expert and was able to find all the properties owned by the El Sal Corporation and their officers, in or near San Salvador. They brought this information to Jack and are staying to help search for Miss Stanfil.

"Wait a minute," Hightower scoffed, "you mean three of them hope to search San Salvador, in what, a day?"

"Please," Rucker said shortly, "let me finish. Jack became friends with a man there who has a similar interest to Jack's. He is a competent, intelligent person who fought with the FMLN during the civil war. He has many friends and they have agreed to help find Miss Stanfil."

"I believe we are getting entirely too many people involved in this," Hightower muttered, "and if this guy fought with the FMLN, he is certainly not our friend."

Rucker gave him a look that clearly told him to shut up.

"Jack, Walt, and TC met with Victor and his friends and started the search for Miss Stanfil late Friday afternoon." Now he had all their attention and Rucker paused. "They located her late Saturday. She was being held in a private residence, owned by the El Sal Corporation, on a lake a few miles south of San Salvador. The house is in a very affluent area." They all looked at Rucker, waiting for the rest.

"Did I hear the words, was held?" the President questioned.

Rucker grinned for the first time. "Jack, Walt, TC, and their friends hit the place at dawn this morning and freed Miss Stanfil. She is alive and well."

The senator was interrupted by cheers and smiles.

"Unfortunately," Rucker continued, "it is not all good news. As in most operations, there are casualties. Our CIA station chief in San Salvador, Joe Ellison, was killed."

"Damn," Hightower exclaimed, "how did that happen, and again, why am I not getting all this information?"

"I don't have an answer for that, but I would check with your Mr. Clausen," Rucker said shortly. "Our friends believe that Joe was killed by a Colonel in the PNC, their new police force, Rafael Gomez. Jack thinks he is next on the list and he and his two friends narrowly escaped being arrested by Gomez early Saturday morning. The police broke into their hotel room. They were only able to escape because of the help from his new friend in San Salvador. The police are now looking for him."

"Can't we put a stop to that sort of thing?" Admiral Cabe asked. "Damn we're pouring a million a day into that rat hole. Doesn't that give us some leverage?"

"It sure as hell should," Rucker answered, "but hold that thought because I'm not through yet. This is the real shocker. You know Miss Stanfil has been predicting an event in El Salvador for some time. It would be an event that would create chaos there and give the mercenaries a reason to cross into El Salvador. For some reason, Art Clausen, the DDI, sent her to Rome where she found her answer."

Rucker paused for emphasis. The interest was intense.

"While she was in Rome she found out that Pope John Paul would be in San Salvador on Monday, giving a speech, urging people to vote in their first free election in years. It's no secret that he would like to see the present regime out of there after they invaded the UCA campus and killed the Jesuit leaders. Cathy is sure that they will assassinate Pope John Paul on Monday when he speaks at the University and blame it on the FLMN." He paused. "The speech is scheduled for noon tomorrow."

"In the turmoil after the assassination," General McComber interrupted, "their mercenaries will come in from Honduras and Guatemala and take over the country, just like she said."

"They can do that in one day?" Admiral Cabe asked.

"You can drive from one end of El Salvador to the other in half a day," Rucker answered. "If they enter where we projected, they won't have a problem. Remember those people have been at war for the past twelve years, what's one more? Also, we are sure that the Miami people have the San Salvador police Colonel, Rafael Gomez, in their pocket. The Army is open to the highest bidder, so there won't be much to stop them."

"I know the Marines could stop them," Admiral Cabe said.

"My God," Hightower exclaimed, "the Pope." He shook his head in frustration. "I just don't know how many of my people I can get down there by tomorrow."

"I would say none," Rucker answered.

"I don't think we can leave something as important as this to amateurs," Hightower said.

"I might remind you that those amateurs found your missing agent and rescued her," the President added.

"I agree," General McComber said. "You can't run a successful operation with two chains of command. I know something of Captain Nordone, and if his friends are half as competent as he is, they will do whatever is possible. Besides, there isn't time to mount any kind of operation from here."

"Jack did ask that we update the Pope's security and do what we can to prevent the mercenaries from coming in."

"Where are we on that?" the President asked.

"The Pope won't budge," the Secretary of State said. "He is a tough old bird and has complete confidence in his security team. He won't break his promise."

That may be," Rucker said, "but I'm sure the Pope doesn't know that El Salvador security is part of the problem."

"I'm sorry," the Secretary of State said. "Without proof positive, we can't accuse any foreign officers. We can only warn his security."

"As to stopping the mercenaries, the Navy is already on station and will stop any movement by sea," Admiral Cabe said.

"Our people and the Hondurans will reach their objectives today. They will cover the few places the mercenaries will have to use to bring in their soldiers and equipment."

"The Guatemalans have been on the fence, but when they hear what we suspect about Pope John Paul, I know we will get their full cooperation."

We all have much to do," the President said as he stood, "so let's get moving and do them. Aaron you keep in touch with Jack, tell him what we are doing about the mercenaries, and see if there is anything else we can do to help."

Chapter 30

San Salvador, Sunday, March 6

When Belden walked out of the hotel it was already hot and humid. He was glad that Gomez was waiting. It was a long, black, reasonably new Mercedes, and Belden wondered if Gomez wasn't getting ahead of himself. He wasn't the Chief of Staff yet. One officer hurriedly got out and opened the door in back. Belden joined Gomez in the spacious interior.

"Buenos Dias," Gomez said.

"Nice wheels," Belden answered, "and thank you for inviting me on your trip."

They drove south down Paseo Escalon to the Plaza Las Americas and the monument of El Salvador del Mundo and took the traffic circle to Boulevard Constitucion.

"Very scenic," Belden commented on the monument surrounded by well-manicured lush green grass, bushes, and trees.

"In El Salvador we love our heroes, and who knows, one day I will be remembered here," he laughed.

They turned south on Boulevard Venezvea to Boulevard del Ejercito National and the traffic thinned.

"We are going to a house on Lago Ilopango," Gomez explained. "It is one of my country's largest and most popular lakes. Blue water is surrounded by volcanoes and mountains. The house is owned by Martinez and the El Sal Corporation and is in a very rich neighborhood. We are holding your CIA agent there. It won't take long now that we are through the city traffic."

Belden was surprised; he thought they would have gotten rid of Cathy by now.

Gomez saw the look and smiled. "I saw her picture and one of my men gave me a vivid description so I thought she deserved a very personal interrogation. I want to know what she knows about our plans for tomorrow and if she told anyone. I will take care of that today." He smirked. "Maybe you would like to interrogate her after I'm through?"

Belden shook his head, feeling angry that he was even tempted. He knew what Gomez was going to do to her and shuddered. He didn't like this scumbag killing an American agent, but there was nothing he could do about it. He had to remember the greater good.

"I'm a little concerned," Gomez said, interrupting his thoughts. "I tried to call the house several times and couldn't get through. I was told that some lines were down, which happens frequently around here, so I wasn't worried. Then about two hours ago I received information that gunshots were reported in the area early this morning. Still, not unusual for a weekend at the lake. I had to come here for the, ah, interrogation so I decided to come out early and see for myself."

They turned onto the paved driveway and were immediately stopped by two officers. The officers talked to the driver, saluted and waved them on. As they approached the house, they saw three parked police cars and noticed men searching the woods. They parked behind one of the cars, got out, and Gomez went into the house followed by Belden.

As soon as they opened the door, they saw five bodies on the floor and Gomez felt his unease grow. "Who is in charge here?" he demanded of one of the officers.

"Captain Romero," a nervous officer answered, and pointed to a man coming down the stairs.

Gomez shook hands with Romero and asked him what had happened.

Romero shrugged, "We received a call early this morning reporting gun shots in the area, but you know how the lake is on the weekend. The sergeant on duty thought it was just another drunk on the lake, made a note, and put it with the other messages. There was a shift change and the next officer got another call, thought the same thing, and filed the report with the rest. After a third call, he decided that he had better tell the duty officer. After the duty officer's investigation, he called me and I called your office."

"Your efficiency is outstanding," Gomez said sarcastically.

Romero flushed, ignoring the comment. "I did send a car to check things out. When they told me what they found, and about the bodies, I came out myself, bringing more officers. We think two of these men were killed on or near the pier and then dragged in here. Two of them were killed upstairs and it looks like the other one was killed coming up the stairs. The door to the balcony in the back bedroom was blasted open. We searched the rest of the house and the grounds and found two more bodies in the garage. My people are still searching the woods."

"Was one of those bodies a female?" Gomez asked.

Romero shook his head. "No woman was found, but after our search, I'm sure there were two women here last night. One was in the front master bedroom and one in the back where the door was broken open."

Gomez scowled at Romero and led Belden outside where they walked down to the lake.

"I just don't believe this," Gomez complained. "No one knew about this place and even if they did, who could do this? These guards were some of my best men."

Belden walked out on the dock and noticed some blood and some scuffmarks. He looked at the lake, the woods, and turned to Gomez. "I know who could do something like this."

"You must be thinking of Joe Ellison and his friend Jack Nordone."

Belden nodded. "I don't know much about Ellison, but from what I've observed, this could have Jack Nordone written all over it."

"One man couldn't do all this," and Gomez told Belden that he had killed Ellison and how close he had come to arresting Jack.

"He is one lucky gringo. We knew that he and some friends were in their room, but when we broke in, no one was there. I don't know how or why they got out. I'm sure they knew nothing of this house."

"I'm sure you pay taxes, have power and water like we do back in the States and if so, there are records. If this house is owned by Martinez or his company, there will be a paper trail and I'll bet his friend found it. This friend and another one flew to San Salvador on Friday to join Jack."

"Jesus, what a mess, and I still don't understand how the three of them could do this. They must have had help. What in hell am I going to tell Martinez?"

Belden shook his head. "I don't think you should tell him anything."

Gomez looked doubtful.

"Worst case scenario. Jack and his friends have Stanfil. She suspects they will assassinate the Pope but doesn't know for sure. Who will listen to her? The Pope always stands by his word, and I know he will give his speech tomorrow regardless. It is also a very long parade route with the caravan and they have no idea where or when it will happen. They can't possibly cover the whole area."

"I just don't know," Gomez agonized," if anything goes wrong, Martinez will have my ass."

"Well, actually, you don't have much choice because it's already too late. The people in Honduras are on the move and probably the people in Guatemala. There is no way of recalling them. You have a job to do tomorrow, have a good plan, and I don't see any reason why you can't complete it."

Gomez mulled it over and smiled for the first time and nodded, "I can do this."

"And we do have one more card to play," Belden said.

Gomez frowned.

"I served with Jack in Vietnam and we became friends. When I heard about his family, I flew to Atlanta to attend a memorial service for them. I was staying at his home and I promised to help Jack find who was responsible for the death of his family and I became a member of his advisory group. They trust me and Jack tells me every move they make. I will call this friend of Jack's telling him I came to San Salvador to help. I'm sure I can find out where they are staying and I know they will be all together."

"You can do this?" Gomez asked and almost hugged Belden in his relief.

Chapter 31

San Salvador, Sunday, March 6

It was late Sunday afternoon. Jack, Walt, TC, Cathy, Victor, and his top two compatriots were gathered in the living room of the house on Delgado.

They were all tired, picking at the food on the dining room table: *pupusas*, tortillas filled with a soft white cheese, beans, tacos, fried plantains, and *plato tipico*, a cup of refried beans with a spoonful of crème.

Edgardo told everyone about the incident in La Liberstad and Ralph had become the best fed dog in El Salvador, if not the world. Every one contributed, and Ralph munched happily.

Jack and Walt talked about the call they had made to Senator Rucker. He had assured them that they would stop the mercenaries from invading El Salvador. They did alert Pope John Paul's security, regarding the possible assassination attempt, but the Pope issued a press release and said he would fulfill his obligations. He was satisfied with his security.

"I have this terrible feeling," Cathy said in dismay, "that they are going to kill that beautiful man. I feel so helpless."

"You're just exhausted," Jack said, "and remember, we wouldn't even be this close if it wasn't for you."

"Something else," Walt interjected, "I checked our Atlanta number and we had a call from Colonel Belden and wonder of wonders, he is here in San Salvador. He said he wants to help and left the telephone number of his hotel." He handed Jack a piece of paper.

"This is a surprise," Jack said as he reached for the telephone, "maybe it is the break we need. He knows a lot of people here that could help."

TC stood up, took the telephone from Jack and replaced it in the cradle. "Let's talk," he said.

Jack looked up and frowned.

"I know you won't like this but I, well we," and he nodded toward Cathy and Walt, "don't trust Belden. We suspect he might be working for the other side."

"I don't follow you," Jack said.

"Think about it," TC answered. "He was at your house when Sister Linda brought you that statue. He disappears and your house burns down. You meet Father Esteban and think he will give you some information about the statue if Cordero isn't around. You tell this to Belden and Esteban is murdered. You're sure that Cordero did it. Joe Ellison, your CIA agent, saw Cordero with Gomez and we know which side Gomez is on. Also, it looks like Cordero might be involved in the theft of Cathy's fax. We don't like Belden's friends."

Jack shook his head, "I just can't believe that Gene would kill Sister Linda."

"Don't forget," TC said, "when he left us in the church parking lot he thought that Sister Linda would be going to the Holiday Inn with us. He didn't know she was in the house."

Jack looked at Walt and Cathy. "Do you both agree with this?"

They both nodded.

"There is more," Cathy continued. "Twice, before I left Langley, Colonel Belden was huddled with Art Clausen. He didn't even ask to see me," she paused. "And I know it had to be Clausen who set me up. When I got back to Washington I went straight to the CIA and told Art Clausen about Pope John Paul. He ordered me not to tell anyone else and to go home and get some sleep. The next thing I know, he is knocking on my door at three in the morning and telling me that Joe needs me in San Salvador. He drives me to the airport and stays with me until I'm on the plane."

"That no good son of a bitch," Walt said.

"Joe was probably dead by then and he had Gomez's officers waiting for me when I got here. I'm sure he didn't tell anyone about the Pope John Paul and Clausen has gone missing."

"I think that ties it," TC said, "but let's think about this for a minute. We are still short of information, and knowing what we do, maybe we can use him to get the information we need."

"Do you want me to call him and arrange a meeting?" Jack asked.

TC shrugged.

"Look, I'm not defending him, but all this is circumstantial. He could be on the level."

"I believe I know a way we can find out which side he is on," Victor said. "If your friends are right, he suspects that you will all be together and if he is working with Gomez they would want you in the worst way. I suggest we give him a false address and watch what happens."

Jack thought about it, "OK," he agreed. "What address should I give him?"

It was quiet while Victor was thinking, then Hector laughed and Victor scowled at him.

"Carraras," Hector grinned.

Victor's scowl changed to a smile and then he too laughed. "Jose Carraras is one of our worst drug dealers, the scum of the earth," Victor explained. "He always has seven or eight armed men around him. If your Colonel is with Gomez, I don't think that they will knock on any doors because they want bodies, not prisoners. They will come in with guns blazing and it will make a great show. We could get two for one."

"And if we are wrong about Gene? What will happen to him in that drug house?"

"Not to worry," Victor said. "I will get him out. Carraras knows me and while not afraid, he doesn't want to mess with me. It would be bad for business and he would just make a lot more enemies. I think he already has enough of them."

"Are you sure the police don't know about this place?" Jack asked.

"I don't think so," Victor answered. "The police stay clear of that bunch and it's their new location. It's perfect for what we want and I will see that we have great seats. The only reason I know about the house is…"

Jack held up a hand. "I know, because you have a cousin."

Victor laughed.

Jack agreed to make the call after they discussed questions that Jack could ask to obtain the information they needed. Jack went to another room and when he came back he said that he didn't learn much. He said Gene didn't believe that there would be an attempt on the Pope and down played the idea. "He did ask if we were all together when I gave him the address."

"Well," TC said, we will soon find out whose side he's on."

"I think I already know," Jack said. "He made a mistake. I know he is aware that Cathy is missing and he didn't even ask about her."

"Because he already knows she was rescued," Walt added.

"I told Belden to be there by seven because we were going to move to a new location."

They all piled into a dark green SUV and drove to a small park on a hill overlooking a few large, well-protected houses.

"The houses are bigger," TC remarked, "and the walls longer."

"Unfortunately they are needed," Victor answered, "there is much crime here."

"Well," TC said, "that mason could make a lot of money in Chicago if he could change the building code."

Victor parked in an empty spot. As they climbed out of the vehicle, a man came out of the shadows and talked with Victor.

"This is Tomas," Victor said, "he has been watching for the last hour or so. He said that nothing unusual has happened except for one car that drove around the house down there a few times." Victor pointed to a large, rambling, two-story brown house on the left.

Jack glanced at his watch. "We have about ten minutes."

It was twelve minutes later when four black Cherokees slowly approached the house. Two stopped at the front while the other two drove around to the back. Four men got out, all carrying automatic weapons. They each took a position at the four corners of the property. After the men were in place, the four black Cherokees crashed through the wrought iron gates.

It looked like about eleven or twelve men rushed out of the vehicles and immediately attacked the house, forcing the front door open. They were met by a barrage of fire from the house and the battle was on.

Victor squeezed Jack's arm. "I guess that answers your question; your very good friend wants to kill you." He nodded to the others. "Let's get out of here. When they figure out what happened, they might come looking for us, assuming we would be watching."

As they climbed back into the SUV, Cathy's exhaustion showed. "I'm beginning to lose hope; there just isn't enough time left." She looked at Victor, "Could you just have one of your men shoot Pope John Paul in the foot at the start of the parade?"

Victor grimaced and then smiled. Actually, it could be a solution, but even then too many things could go wrong.

"We have many people out looking over the parade route. Maybe someone has come up with something and we can find a better solution, and save his Holiness his foot."

Chapter 32

San Salvador, Sunday, March 6

THE LAST OCCUPANT OF THE drug house was on his knees begging for mercy when Gomez shot him. Filled with rage, he destroyed the man's face with three well-placed shots. One of his men came down the ornate winding staircase herding a beautiful dark-haired woman in a long black dress in front of him. She held a hand to her mouth and was crying. Gomez met them at the bottom of the stairs and pressed his gun to her head.

"How many other people have been in this house today?" he demanded.

"No one, no one else," she sobbed.

"What are you trying to prove?" Belden asked in disgust. "You know we were set up. They were never here."

Gomez turned to look at him. "We were set up?" he questioned, and emphasized the word we. "Apparently those dumb Georgia people are not as dumb as you think they are."

"Apparently not," Belden answered ruefully, "but that isn't going to help." He motioned towards the woman.

Gomez hesitated, and then lowered his weapon and told the woman to go.

"Look at the bright side: from what I surmise, you just busted a big time drug dealer. You will be a hero."

"Not to a certain police chief, a few judges and some politicians I won't."

Belden nodded in understanding.

"And I have two dead officers, three wounded. What a mess. When Martinez hears about this he won't be happy."

Gomez was further angered when he returned to his office and found that Maria had been freed. He slammed the officer that told him up against the wall, demanding an explanation.

The man, sweating profusely, told Gomez that Francisco Marroquin, the radio station owner, a judge and two local policemen came to the office with a writ or something. Captain Navero told him to let her go. Navero said it was all legal and he didn't think it was a good time to get into a fight with the locals, especially this close to the election.

"Damn!" Gomez exclaimed after the officer left.

"Why is she so important?" Belden asked.

Gomez told him that Maria had a connection to Jack and Victor.

"She has been our guest for a few days. Unfortunately, some of my men have big mouths. I'm afraid of what she might have heard. I have to find her before she finds your friend, Jack, and the others. I will send two officers to her hotel and I will check the radio station."

Belden frowned and held up a hand, "Hold on a minute, I have an idea. I know Maria is a friend of Jack's and spent some time with him. I think that I should go to that radio station."

Gomez frowned, "Why would you go?"

"I'm thinking that if she spent all that time with Jack, there is a good possibility that Jack mentioned me. She might trust me. She can't know about anything that just happened because she was in jail."

Gomez still looked skeptical, "Why would you go to see Marroquin?"

"I will tell him Joe Ellison told me to see him if I had any problems in San Salvador. That he was a very influential person and would help. There is no way he can check that out. It's a win-win situation for you. If she is there and takes me to Jack, you follow and we get them all. If she won't take me to Jack or doesn't know where he is, you can arrest her."

Gomez smiled. "I like it, and I hope this plan will work better than your last one." He gave Belden a small hand-held radio. "Just click the button twice when you want us. I think it is time we end this."

***

Francisco Marroquin thanked the judge and police officers for helping him on a Sunday and drove Maria straight to his office. She had wanted to go to her hotel to get some things, but Francisco knew that Gomez would come looking for her. The hotel would be the first place he would look and, probably, his office would be next, so they had to work fast.

Maria told Francisco some of the things that she had overheard at the jail. That she now believed that her husband and the other leaders of the FMLN might still be alive. She thought they were being held somewhere in San Salvador and heard that something important was going to happen on Monday. She was afraid that it meant that Roberto and the other FMLN leaders would be killed.

When Francisco arrived at his office he drove around to the back and parked behind a dumpster, partially hiding the vehicle, before letting Maria out. There was a skeleton crew manning the station and he didn't want anyone to see her. Once inside they used a back hallway to his office, avoiding the employees. He directed her to the empty office next to his.

"I don't think that our friend, Rafael, will let it end like this. I'm sure that he will come looking for you and when he finds out that I helped you, he will look here. We must find Victor, or Senor Nordone, as soon as possible."

"How about the American, Joe Ellison?" Maria asked. "I'm sure he would help me and would know where Jack is."

Francisco shook his head and told her about Joe.

Maria put a hand to her mouth. "Oh, so many, I am so sorry."

"Use the telephone on the desk," Marroquin directed. "Start calling your friends and relatives. One of them is sure to know where Victor is. I will call some of my contacts. We must hurry."

Maria connected on the fourth call and ran into the editor's office. "I've got it," she said, "I know where Victor and his friends are."

Marroquin breathed a sigh of relief, still expecting Gomez and his goons to appear any second. He again urged Maria to hurry as they started toward the back door, but he stopped when he heard a knock on his door and motioned Maria back to the other office before opening the door. An older, heavy-set woman looked up at him in surprise.

"I didn't know you were here," and she gestured towards the front. "There is a man there, in uniform, American I think, and he is demanding to talk to you. I told him you weren't in, but he insisted that I look for you and refused to leave."

"Did he say what he wanted?"

The woman shook her head and told Marroquin that he was still waiting in the vestibule.

"I had a little paper work to clean up so I came in the back way. You can tell the man I will see him." As soon as she left, Maria re-entered the room.

"You heard?"

Maria nodded.

"Do you know anything about this?"

"No, except that Jack has some friend helping him and one of them is a Colonel Belden. Why he would turn up here, I have no idea."

Marroquin gave Maria the keys to his car. "It's your call. You can leave now, or you can talk to him."

"You talk to him first and if his name is Belden, I will see him." And she stepped into the next room and partially closed the door.

Marroquin admitted Belden and asked his name and what he wanted.

"My name is Belden, Colonel Gene Belden, and I am looking for some friends of mine."

Once she heard the name, Maria walked into Marroquin's office and when Belden saw her he held out his hand. "You must be Maria. Jack told me a lot about you and even his glowing description does not do you justice."

Maria blushed and took the hand, hoping Jack didn't tell him everything. "You must be Colonel Belden."

Belden nodded. "I'm really surprised to find you here. Actually, I didn't think I would find anyone, but I was getting desperate. Jack or his friends weren't at his hotel. I also couldn't find Joe Ellison at our embassy. He was the one that gave me your name and told me to go to your radio station if I had any problems in San Salvador and that you would help. You are Mr. Marroquin?"

Marroquin acknowledged that he was, wondering why Joe Ellison would tell the man to see him. It seemed coincidental, his arriving at a time like this. His job and twelve years of war taught him not to trust coincidences.

He did remember something and asked. "Weren't you stationed here some years ago as a military advisor?"

"I was," Belden admitted, "and was happy when my tour was over. Nothing against your country, it's very nice, but the people in control weren't."

Marroquin was still skeptical but worried about Gomez so he turned to Maria. "It's your choice, what do you want to do?"

Maria smiled, knowing that Marroquin still had doubts.

"Jack spoke of the Colonel many times and I know they are good friends." She made her decision and turned to Belden. "I know where Jack and his friends are and I will take you there."

Chapter 33

San Salvador., Sunday, March 6

THE DINING ROOM TABLE WAS cleared of food and dishes when Victor placed a map of San Salvador on it. The Pope's parade route was marked in red. They all gathered around the table looking at it, feeling tired and discouraged.

Jack stood alone, thinking. After several conversations with Cathy and adding what he knew, he was positive that Nelson Martinez and his friends were responsible for the deaths of Nancy and Tim. He was also sure that Gomez was involved and shocked that Belden was a part of it.

Cathy thought that Belden and Clausen had been working with the Miami group from the beginning, either for money or misguided patriotism, maybe both of the above. It explained why she was sent to Rome and then set up to be kidnapped in San Salvador.

Jack guessed that Clausen didn't know about the assassination of Pope John Paul, or he wouldn't have sent her to Rome, and when he found out about it from her, he knew she had to disappear. It was all starting to come together, but it had to be put on the back burner. It was much more important to help save Pope John Paul. After that he would concentrate on his problem. He would take care of Gomez, return to the States and do the same to Martinez and his crew. He wasn't sure what he could do about Belden and Clausen.

Victor, standing at the head of the table, dropped his marker and slowly shook his head in dismay. "There are just too many places. It could happen anywhere."

"Well," TC said as he looked at his watch, "we have some tough decisions to make and better make them soon."

"As you know, I sent many people out to check the parade route, looking for possible assassination sites. Everyone is back except Hector." Victor shrugged. "So far we have nothing.

With all the repainting and building repairs, it could happen in any one of them."

There was a babble of voices, offering different opinions, when the front door opened and Hector hurried into the room with a roll of papers under his arm.

"Where have you been?" Victor snapped, showing his frustration.

"Doing what I was told to do, getting information," Hector retorted and then smiled. "And, I'm not sure, but I think I found something."

All conversation ceased and they looked at him expectantly.

"I work at the University," he explained to the Americans, "in the maintenance department and know a lot of people there. I saw that the parade ends at the Science building and thought it would be a good place for me to start. Being Sunday, there weren't many people around and I was about ready to give up when I ran into a friend of mine, who is also in engineering and he told me a weird story. For some reason, all the maintenance and engineering workers in the science building were replaced with security people. My friend said most of them don't even know how to turn on the water. He was curious and tried to get to the basement but was turned away by two armed guards who told him not to come back until Tuesday, unless it was an emergency."

"Why would they need armed guards in the science building," Cathy wondered aloud.

"That's what I asked myself," Hector continued, "so I went to all the shops and restaurants nearby asking questions. I found a restaurant that has been selling take-out to the security people for the past five or six days. The owner guessed the food would feed three or four people."

"That's it," Cathy almost shouted, "now I know why they will assassinate Pope John Paul."

They all looked at her.

"Victor, didn't you tell us that the three leaders of the FMLN have been missing for the past ten days?"

Victor nodded.

"Don't you see," Cathy continued. "I'm sure my scenario is right, but it puzzled me why Martinez would take the risk of assassinating Pope John Paul in this predominantly Catholic country. If anyone ever found out, he would be toast, so why take the chance?"

Cathy paused and rubbed her chin.

"So you think the three leaders of the FMLN are being held in the basement," Jack said. "The Pope's caravan will park here," and he pointed to the right of the science building. "They will have to cross in front of the building on their way to the park where the Pope will give his speech. This is where they will kill him."

"Then Gomez will kill the FMLN leaders and blame the assassination on them," Victor finished.

"I will bet Gomez already has those FMLN guys' fingerprints all over the murder weapons by now," TC added.

"The assassination of Pope John Paul will cause chaos in my country," Victor said, "and will be the perfect excuse for Martinez to move his people in without opposition. They will take over the country. Then after they prove that the FMLN was responsible, they will be welcomed with open arms." Victor shook his head. "We will be right back to where we were twelve years ago. We must find a way to get into that basement."

***

Maria drove down F.D. Roosevelt Avenida, past the General Cemetery, and turned right on Avenida Cuscatian. She questioned Belden about his relationship with Jack. He told her that they met in Vietnam. She felt better when he told her about Jack's wife and son and that he had been there for the memorial service.

Maria made one more turn, drove half a block and then turned into a driveway, stopping at a locked gate. She got out of the car, searched under some bricks, came up with a key and opened the gate. She drove through and parked in a small courtyard. The house was a walled, two-storied stucco, and it was completely dark.

When Maria got out this time, she relocked the gate and walked to the front door, followed by Belden.

"It doesn't look like anyone is home," he said.

Maria opened the door and turned on the light. The house had three fair-sized rooms downstairs, a kitchen, dining area, and living room. While not opulent, it was nicely furnished, clean and neat.

"No one is home," Maria answered. "Don't worry though, Jack and his friends will pick us up in about thirty minutes. This belongs to a relative of mine who is out of town. It will give me time to take a shower. I have been in that filthy jail for a lifetime and don't know if I can ever get clean."

Belden didn't like it but couldn't object so he checked for another staircase. He didn't find one and when he heard the water run, he picked up her keys and went out to unlock the gate. He returned to the house and sat down in a brown leather chair that gave him the best view of the stairs. He hoped Gomez and his men would be patient.

There were times when he wished he had never gotten involved with Martinez; he was one mean son of a bitch.

Reagan was right though. We had to stop those Commie bastards somewhere. Nicaragua was already gone and El Salvador was next. We couldn't have Russian missiles in Mexico, so it was all for the greater good.

Chapter 34

San Salvador, Sunday, March 6

THE NOISE AND SMOKE THAT filled the room were getting to Cathy. It reminded her of the old movies where everyone had a cigarette. She knew Ralph must feel the same way because his tongue was hanging out and he was drooling rivers. She decided to take him out for some fresh air. Besides, they were going nowhere; everyone had his or her idea and this was leading to more arguments than solutions. She was beginning to feel helpless again; there was no way they could help that holy man.

TC also had enough and put an end to it with his best top sergeant voice. Even those that didn't understand the language understood TC. All conversation ceased.

"Unfortunately," TC said, "we don't have time to come up with the perfect plan. I suggest we work with the information we have and come up with something."

Victor agreed, translating for his friends, and Jack added that their first priority would be getting into the basement and freeing the prisoners.

"We know they will be well-guarded, so we have to find a way to get us and our weapons on campus and into the science building without attracting attention. If we are successful and free the prisoners, we will also be in position to help Pope John Paul." Jack shook his head. "It's a big campus and we must find a way."

"I have been trying to tell you something," Hector interrupted as he unrolled the papers he had been carrying and placed them on the table. He told them he had gotten them from his engineering friend and explained they were the blueprints of the underground area around the science building and all adjacent buildings.

Hector pointed to one of the maps. "This is the lecture hall, directly behind the science building. It has a little-used passageway in the basement connecting the two buildings. My friend said it leads from the lecture hall to a small storage area in the science building. He gave me the keys to the doors but said they were seldom locked. The storage room is just around the corner from the engineering section where they must be keeping the prisoners."

Victor looked at the plans and smiled for the first time. "You did good," and Hector beamed.

"That should solve our biggest problem," Jack said, "so now we just have to find a way to get us and our weapons to the lecture hall. I'm sure it won't be as well-guarded as the science building, if at all."

"I can help you with that, too," Hector said proudly.

Hector told them about a vending company that had its offices and distribution center near the University because they serviced all the vending machines there and the University is their biggest customer. They usually service their machines early Monday mornings so as not to disturb the students. But when they learned about Pope John Paul and the parade, they decided to do it Tuesday, instead of Monday, because of all the traffic and security caused by his speech. "My friend's wife's sister works at the vending company."

"That would be perfect," Jack and TC said in unison.

"Do you know where this sister lives?" Victor asked.

"About two or three miles away," Hector answered.

"Do you think she would help us steal a truck and some uniforms?"

Hector hesitated and then nodded. "I'm sure she would, especially when she finds out why we need them, and my friend said that security was pretty lax there."

"Wow," Jack exclaimed. "That would give us a legitimate reason to be on campus, and we could hide our weapons in the confection bags."

"I think we have a solution," Victor beamed, "and if you weren't so ugly I would hug you."

"Well I don't think he's so ugly." Cathy, who had returned from her respite, said, and she gave a reddened Hector a big hug, applauded by the others.

"Hey, I fed Hector when he came in," Walt offered. "What do I get?"

Cathy smiled.

"O.K.," Jack said. "We have a plan and it may not be perfect, but it's probably as close as we can get. How will we split up?" Jack deferred to Victor.

"We will take four in the vending truck: you, TC, Hector, and me. And just in case we are wrong about the Science building, I think another hot spot would be crossing the street to the park. We will send Walt and Cathy there along with three of my people."

"Do you think the police will be blocking off all the entrances to the University and that they might know that the vendors are not working Monday?" TC asked.

"I don't think so," Victor answered. "If we are stopped we will tell them we didn't get the word. It happens all the time in San Salvador. We will try and talk our way in and if that doesn't work, we will go to plan B."

"Which is," TC asked?

"We will sleep on it. I am sure that one of us will come up with plan B," Victor answered.

"Need any help with the trucks and uniforms tonight?" Jack asked.

Victor smiled, "No, my cousins will take care of that. We should try and get some sleep."

***

Belden looked at his watch again. The shower was still running and she had been in there almost twenty minutes. He knew women needed more showering time, but this was ridiculous. Belden was also getting impatient. Jack and his friends would be here in a few minutes and would she still be in the shower?

His impatience turned to suspicion and he walked up the stairs to the bathroom, listened at the door and knocked. There was no answer and he knocked louder. Still no answer, so he tried the handle. It was unlocked and the bathroom was empty. There was a message written in lipstick on the mirror, telling Belden to wait. They would pick him up in a few minutes.

"Shit!" Belden exclaimed as he pushed the red button on the radio while he checked the two bedrooms and returned downstairs.

When the officers broke through both the front and back doors with drawn guns, they found Belden sitting in a chair with raised hands.

"Where is she?" Gomez demanded.

Belden told him what happened. "I don't think she will be coming back for me."

Gomez's eyes blazed and he cursed, kicking over a table.

Belden rolled his eyes. "Get control," he ordered. "It really doesn't make any difference. There is no way for us to stop what will happen and there is no way for them to stop it. They just don't have enough time."

"So you think they will try?" Gomez asked.

"I'm sure they will if they believe Cathy about the assassination attempt. I don't think they will be able to get much help and our biggest asset is the length of the parade. They have no idea where it will happen and can't possibly cover the whole area."

"You still don't think we should tell Martinez?"

"No, like I said, everything has gone too far to stop. I would tighten your security, but you have a good plan. I don't think anyone will be able to stop it now. Stick to the plan and it will all work out."

Gomez nodded in satisfaction. "And my reward will be getting my hands on Jack Nordone. I just hope he is still alive when this is over."

Chapter 35

San Salvador, Monday, March 7

Jack awoke with the first light and stretched, feeling a lot better. Victor was right, sleep-deprived people make mistakes. He had learned that in Nam and it had been a rough week. Cathy and Maria's return probably had something to do with his good night's sleep. He felt much better with the two ladies back.

Last night, just before they were ready to hit the sack, there was a knock on the door. Everyone grabbed a weapon but when Victor opened the door, he found Maria.

Victor was speechless for a moment and then embraced her in a long hug. "We have been so worried about you," he said. "How in the world did you get out?"

TC checked the outside and admonished Ralph for not giving them any warning, but Walt intervened. "Look at that face," Walt said, following TC. "I think he's smart enough to tell the good people from the bad, even if you aren't."

TC gave Walt a long look that broke into a grin, locked the door and returned to the living room where the greetings were winding down. One man went to the kitchen to get Maria something to eat while she told her story.

She explained how Marroquin and the judge were able to get her released and her going back with Marroquin to the radio station. How Belden showed up unexpectantly, telling her that Jack asked for his help. Belden said that Joe Ellison had told him about Mr. Marroquin and where to find him. Maria laughed as she told them about leaving Belden at her aunt's house. How she slid down the roof and then slid down the pillar. She and her cousin had done it many times when they were kids.

Jack was curious to know why Maria didn't trust Belden because he remembered telling her about him. She admitted that she really did believe him, but reminded Jack what she told him in Ocotal, to 'never trust anyone'. She said she was just being cautious. If everything was all right, they would have gone back to get him.

"I faked the first shower, and now I need a real one and some sleep."

After breakfast, Hector gave them their uniforms. "I went back to see my friend and his wife, and his wife's sister was there. She gave me a key to the office and the security code. We didn't have a problem getting the uniforms or the truck. My friend also assured me that the passageway from the lecture hall to the science building was open and no one would be in there. Once we open the door to the science building, though, we are on our own.

Six of Victor's men had already left for the Metro Center, where the caravan would start. Six additional men were assigned to watch from available rooftops along the route. They all carried weapons and hand-held radios. Victor decided to take Maria with them in the truck and the others agreed. Now they had to decide what would be the best time for them to leave.

"I don't think they will bring the FMLN people up from the basement until the last minute," TC said. "I know that they have the building under tight security but, as we all know, shit happens. I know I wouldn't want them hanging around up there in plain view. It could cause trouble."

"I think you're right," Victor said, "and with Gomez in charge of the caravan, he will see to it that the Pope passes in front of the building at the scheduled time."

"Looking at the map and time schedule, I think that would be about eleven-thirty," Maria said. "That would give them enough time to get to the park."

"If you're right, it means they will bring the prisoners up a little after eleven," Jack added.

"Then we will leave at nine," Victor decided. "I'm sure that the south entrance will be covered, so we will use the north entrance. Hector said he didn't see any police activity up that way."

"That could change," Jack interjected. "I think we would be better off hanging out on campus, or in the lecture hall, than take a chance on getting there too late. It will also give us more time if we have to come up with plan B."

Victor nodded, "good point. Let's get into our uniforms and head for the University. Put your weapons in the bags with the vending food and attach your repressors, I'm sure we will need them."

Police HQ

The meeting had broken up with the officers scurrying out to take care of their assignments. Only Gomez and Belden were left.

"What do you think?" Gomez asked.

"I believe it went well," Belden said as he looked at the maps of San Salvador and the UCA campus. "I think you covered all the bases and it will go off as planned. However, I do think you should put some men at the north entrance to the campus."

"The University is giving the students a holiday and many students will be going in and out. It will be a mess." Gomez answered.

"I know," Belden agreed. "I would still like to know what is happening up there."

"I'll take care of it," Gomez said, reaching for the telephone.

UCA Campus

The traffic was already building and Hector drove along the Autopista Sur and turned left on Albert Einstein Avenue. He saw a questioning look from Victor and explained that he was taking a short cut, which would avoid the crowded streets and get them there quicker.

They were all tense as they turned the corner and approached the North Entrance. The place was swarming with police officers, and Hector drove on by, turning left at the next street and pulling to the curb.

"Now what?" he asked.

There has got to be another way in," Victor said.

"We can look," Hector shrugged and drove back onto the road. They made a half circle of the campus finding every entrance blocked and again parked the truck.

"We better come up with plan B pretty damn quick," TC commented.

"I still think we can talk our way in," Victor said.

"But if that doesn't work, we're dead in the water, and so is Pope John Paul." Jack said.

"Maybe I can give us an edge," Hector mused as he pulled away from the curb. "I'm going back to my friend's house and borrow his car."

"I don't understand," Victor questioned.

"I will drive to the entrance and join the line of cars going on campus. As soon as I have an opening, I will accelerate on through. They will certainly give chase and in the turmoil, you might get through. Let Maria drive; I know I wouldn't stop her."

"No," Victor exploded, shaking his head, "it's too dangerous."

"I know the University as I do my own home," Hector said. "With the head start I will have, I know exactly where to go and leave the car. I will make a sharp turn on one of the side streets, jump from the car and they will never find me."

Victor hesitated.

"I think that's our best chance," Jack said, "but I'm going with him."

"Hell, no," TC protested. "I'll go with Hector."

"We don't have time to argue so I'm pulling rank. You stick with Victor and Maria. They will need your help saving Pope John Paul if this doesn't work. That is the most important thing."

Hector was back in fifteen minutes with the car and told Victor that if everything went well, he and Jack would meet them at the administration building. "If we don't show, you know where the lecture hall is," Hector added.

They all shook hands and Jack and Hector got into the borrowed car.

Maria parked the truck a short distance from the entrance where they had a good view and watched nervously as Hector turned slowly into the entrance. When it was his turn to be checked, he accelerated through the crowd. Everyone screamed and scattered to avoid being hit. To add to the confusion, Jack shot the tires out on the nearest Jeep as they passed it.

Maria waited a few minutes, took a deep breath, loosened the top two buttons of her blouse and turned into the north entrance.

Chapter 36

Honduras, Monday, March 7

THE LAST JOLT SHOOK HIM to his teeth and almost knocked him out of his seat. He let out a string of profanities.

"This must be the road from hell," Brad Loring shouted and wondered how his men were doing. Their trucks had wooden seats that would make this trip brutal. The seats of the jeep were a little more comfortable, providing a dirty cushion, a very thin one, but better than nothing.

Carlos Camejo laughed, "I watched them build this road. They dumped many loads of rocks, some dirt and then drove over the mess with their trucks."

"A bulldozer or grader would have helped," Loring answered. "I have ridden over more rocks today than I have in a lifetime."

"That kind of equipment is unknown here. Remember our country is the poorest of the poor."

"How big is that town down the road from your place?" Loring asked.

"I'm really not sure. I don't get down there too often. There is not much there. I would guess that it is around fifteen thousand people."

"I'm assuming they have a police department," Loring continued.

Camejo nodded.

"Don't they give you any trouble? I mean with the type of business you run, I noticed that everything was pretty much out in the open."

Camejo shook his head. "We have very good relations with our local police. We take care of the chief, and a few of his officers, even help the town. We give them a hospital or library and we provide many jobs. It is a win-win situation. We are very secluded here with the mountains and forests and are pretty much left alone."

"It sounds like a sweet deal," Loring said as he looked at his watch. "Maybe we should have left a little earlier with a road like this."

"Not to worry," Camejo answered. "The road does get better as we get closer to the border. We only have a little more of this. Keep in mind that they don't want us to come into El Salvador until after the assassination."

"I know that will fool everyone. Like we just happened to be in the neighborhood, and when we heard what happened in San Salvador, we offered to help." Loring couldn't keep the sarcasm from his voice.

He spent the rest of the trip trying to enjoy the scenery. It was breathtaking, the lush forest and the nearness of the mountains. He kept looking for a White-Faced Monkey but with all the noise the convoy was making, there probably wasn't a monkey within miles. Loring knew his men were getting anxious after all the training and were looking forward to a little action.

They soon pulled off the road and the troopers jumped out of their trucks, in obvious relief. They started to unload their equipment when Loring sent Sergeant Kowolski with three men as scouts to see what they would be getting into. They had about an hour to kill and the men were getting a little restless by the time Kowolski and his men returned.

The sergeant pulled Loring aside.

"It looks like we have some big problems," he said. "Someone let the cat out of the bag. There are a lot of soldiers up there dug in on both sides of the road that leads to the border. They have some pretty heavy equipment. It looks to me like they are just waiting for us."

"I thought we might walk through," Loring answered, "but hell, sergeant, this is what we trained these guys for, this is what we are being paid for. You've seen Camejo's people and I'm sure the people on that road are the same ilk. I don't think we will have a problem. It will be a turkey shoot."

"Yeah," Kowolski answered, "but it gets worse. We could be the turkeys."

"Explain," Loring demanded.

"About half those soldiers are Americans. I'm sure they are Rangers."

Loring stopped in his tracks. "What in the world would American Rangers be doing down here?"

Kowolski shrugged.

Loring knew he didn't have to ask him if he was certain so he went to the side of the road and sat down. The sergeant squatted next to him.

Loring had been in this business for some time and had done some questionable things. Some he wasn't so proud of, but he did what he was paid to do. He drew the line at this, though; he would not fire on American troops.

The sergeant read him, smiled for the first time and stood up. Loring did, too, but lowered his voice. "Don't tell our guys about the American soldiers yet. Just tell them to have their weapons ready and stand by. Our host might not be too happy with what I'm going to tell him."

Loring saw Camejo talking to one of his lieutenants and broke into their conversation. "I have some news," he told them. "I sent some scouts ahead to check things out at the border crossing. They just reported back. They found American and Honduran troops dug in on both sides of the road."

"How could they know?" Camejo wondered aloud. "But I'm sure that together we can handle them."

"I wouldn't bet on it," Kowolski interrupted, "it's a Ranger unit."

Camejo looked unconvinced.

"It really doesn't matter," Loring said. "No one told me that there would be Americans here. I will not fire on American troops."

"You will do what you are paid to do," Camejo demanded.

Loring shrugged. "As I see it you have three choices," he said quietly. "One, you could try and force us to go with you. I don't think you could do that, and even if you did, there wouldn't be enough of you left to take on the people at the border. Second, you could try and break through with your own men. Having served with the Rangers and observing your people, I would rate your chances as zero. Or three, you already have a good thing going here and I wouldn't mess with it. I suggest we all go back to camp and you throw a big party and afterwards we will fly home. You charge this off as a good deal gone bad."

Camejo hadn't survived in his business by being stupid. After gaining control of his temper, he slapped Loring on the back. "I love fiestas."

Guatemala

The Guatemalans didn't want to get involved. They also didn't like someone training soldiers in their territory so they moved an army unit close to the training camp. When they heard about the possible assassination of Pope John Paul, they reacted immediately, surrounded the camp, and disarmed the participants. Two boatloads of mercenaries tried to get away by sea but were discouraged by the U. S. Navy and returned to their base, which ended the Guatemala threat.

Chapter 37

San Salvador, Monday, March 7

MARIA WATCHED AS SEVERAL POLICEMEN piled in to two black Cherokees and a Jeep and took off in chase of Jack and Hector. She said a short prayer for her two friends, and then looked at her two companions. Victor and TC nodded their confirmation, so taking another deep breath to calm the butterflies in her stomach, she started the truck, driving to the north entrance. The scene was still chaotic with people running in all directions. Maria thought they might have a chance to slip through without being stopped until she saw an officer running toward her, motioning her to stop.

Maria considered pretending she didn't see him, but, the thought of being chased by those black Cherokees changed her mind. She rolled to a stop. Victor and TC hid their weapons as Maria rolled down the window.

"Where do you think you're going?" the officer demanded.

"I'm following my Monday morning schedule, officer," Maria said smiling, "going on campus to fill the vending machines. The students empty them every weekend." Maria slid a little lower in her seat and leaned out the window. It gave the policeman a much better view of her cleavage, and he took advantage of it.

He scratched behind his ear. "I don't know, we have some big problems here," he said in a softer tone.

Maria tried to put the panic she was beginning to feel in her voice. "Please, officer," she begged. "This is my first week on the job, I desperately need it. My new boss has a thing against women employees, and if we don't fill those machines he will find a reason to fire me."

The policeman was about to respond when another officer ran up to him.

"Quick," the officer shouted! "We have to alert someone. That runaway car turned left, toward the park where the Pope will give his speech."

Victor gave Maria a large bag of candy, which she handed to the policeman.

He took it, frowned in indecision, and then waved them through.

"Nice job," TC said. "For a minute there I didn't think we were going to make it. Now I know you just need a bag of candy and a pretty woman to get what you want in San Salvador."

"Let's drive to the administration building," Victor said, "but go the long way around and keep to the back streets. We can't afford to get involved in that chase. When we get there, Maria, you stay with the truck. TC and I will go in to make a pretense of filling some machines. We will wait for Jack and Hector as long as we can. Unfortunately, that won't be long."

TC and Victor entered the administration building. The few people working paid no attention to the two men in uniform. TC saw three vending machines in a corner. They walked to the machines and dropped their bags. They moved the machines around, tried to look busy, and finally Victor stood up and shrugged. "It's time, we have to go."

TC wanted to object, ask for another five or ten minutes, but knew he couldn't. Too much was riding on the next phase, and now they were shorthanded. He made the sign of the cross even though he wasn't a religious man. He hoped Jack and Hector were all right.

They looked through the windows, checking the street and sidewalks. Seeing nothing that threatened them, they joined Maria in the truck. TC felt a wave of relief wash over him when he opened the truck door and saw the smiling faces of Jack and Hector.

"What happened to you and why didn't you let us know you were here?" TC grumbled.

"They got here soon after you left," Maria said defensively. "They were just going in to tell you when Hector spotted a police cruiser turn the corner. They hid in the back. The police stopped and checked my identification and asked if I had seen anything suspicious. I told them I saw some people go into the cafeteria that didn't look like students. Anyway they went to check it out. They just left a couple of minutes ago."

"Good thinking," Victor said to Maria, "and, I'm glad you're back," to Jack and Hector. "Now we just have to get into the lecture hall."

"We have been watching it," Jack said, "and there is good news and bad news. The bad news is that the lecture hall is under surveillance. The good news is the officers are very consistent. They should be coming around any minute now. After they turn that far corner, we will have ten to twelve minutes to get in."

"There they are now," Maria said.

"I think that as long as the police already checked the truck, we will leave it here. If we move it, someone else might get suspicious, and it could give away our location."

When it was clear, they each grabbed a bag with their weapons, locked the truck and hurried into the lecture hall. Hector fished for a key, but the door to the hall was unlocked, as promised, and they entered the building. A quick search showed the building was uninhabited. They went down to the basement and found the door leading to the science building.

They dropped their gear, found some metal folding chairs and sat down, checking their weapons. They were all tired, stressed, and there wasn't much conversation. It wasn't long before Victor's radio crackled. He picked it up, talked for a minute, and then put it back in his pocket.

"I think it's time to go," he said. "The Pope's caravan is about forty-five minutes out. Jack, Maria and I will take the basement and free the prisoners. TC and Hector will clear the first floor, but stay away from the entrance. If there is time, check the top floor and then join us in the basement. Once we take care of the guards, we will wait for them to send someone down to retrieve the prisoners."

Victor opened the door to the passageway as they ruefully made their way through the pipes, dirt, and spiders to the science building. They drew their weapons, waiting with apprehension, as Victor opened the door. They found themselves in a small, almost empty, storage room. They all stared at the next door, it was the big one and they wondered what they would find on the other side. Before opening it, Victor reached into his bag and brought out a bottle of *Aquardiente*, a fiery liquor made from sugar cane. The others looked on in surprise as he opened the bottle and took a large mouthful. He swished it around in his mouth, spit it out and sprinkled some on his uniform.

"A drunk is not half as threating as a sober man," Victor explained. "This could lower their vigilance, giving us a chance to get closer to the guards and adding some needed seconds." He handed the bottle to TC.

Jack and TC shook their heads in admiration. "You don't miss a trick do you?" TC said.

"Also," Victor said to Maria, "You will be our other distraction. Take off your cap and let your hair fall, and could you unbutton your blouse?"

Maria looked surprised and then smiled. "Anything for the cause," she said.

"Don't worry about the noise. We must act like we belong here and that we are very drunk."

Victor put out his hand, palm up. It was covered by the others. "Good luck and may God be with us."

With that, Jack opened the door.

Chapter 38

San Salvador, Monday, March 7

Gomez and Belden rode in the lead car, just in front of the Pope's limo and behind the motorcycle escort. He could control things better there. Gomez was not a happy man. The last two days were near disaster, and he still worried about not telling Martinez. He grimaced as he answered another call on his radio, knowing that it was trouble. He listened, gritted his teeth, and when he hung up he told the driver to slow it down a little.

"More problems?" Belden asked.

"You were right," Gomez admitted. That was one of my officers from the north entrance. He said a car with two men ran their blockade and turned left toward the park where the Pope will give his speech."

Belden frowned, "Are you sure there were just two men in the car?"

"He said he had a good look. There were only two men."

"If that was Jack, where the hell are the rest of them? We know he has help."

"Maybe it was just some wise-assed students, showing off." Gomez said.

Belden shook his head. "I wouldn't count on it. It would be too coincidental. I think we have at least two of the enemy on campus and should keep a sharp eye out for them."

"I don't like it," Gomez said. "They found the wrecked car but not the two men. They are still searching for them."

"O.K., let's think about this. We know we have two of the enemy loose on campus who might try to stop the assassination. If this is true, there is a good chance that there are three or four others. They will probably concentrate on the park. Even that is a lot of area to cover. No, there is no way they can stop this unless they get into the science building. I don't think they have even given that a thought. To be on the safe side, you might alert the guards."

Gomez breathed a sigh of relief. "That makes sense. No matter what, it will all be over within a short time. We will be turning off the expressway very soon now and drive past the students' park to our parking area. There will be a large crowd there so watch carefully."

Once they exited the expressway, they found both sides of the street lined with people waving flags and religious articles and shouting.

The car was moving very slowly now and Belden noticed a blind man with his dog standing in the front row. The man was wearing dark glasses, and something about him clicked, but Belden pushed the thought away. What could a blind man do? Then he saw the man's companion. He frantically punched Gomez and pointed. "See that blind man with the dog, standing in the front row?"

Gomez nodded.

"The lady with him is Cathy Stanfil, your missing CIA agent."

Gomez leaned across Belden, pushing him back onto his seat. He studied the two, noting their dress. As soon as the caravan entered the parking lot, Gomez jumped out of the car and cornered two police officers. There was a brief discussion and the officers checked their weapons and hurried toward the street.

"What are you going to do?" Belden asked.

"Those are two of my best men. I gave them the description of the blind man and his friend. They should be easy to find. I told them to kill them both."

"In front of all these people?" Belden questioned.

Gomez smiled. "In a few minutes all these people will be mine. You will be surprised at how many of them won't hear or see a thing."

Belden shrugged. "Since, I won't be of any use to you down here, why don't you get me a rifle. I will go to the roof of the building and look for any others."

Gomez reached into one of the Cherokees and took a rifle and a clip of ammunition and gave it to Belden, along with a pass that would get him into the building. He watched Belden leave and started to arrange the entourage for the short walk to the park. He stalled until he heard three gunshots, then smiled and moved towards the science building, assuring the Pope's security that everything was under control.

***

"What the heck are we doing here anyway?" Walt Kutch asked, "Or rather, what am I doing here?"

Cathy smiled. She understood he was out of his element and was glad to be with him. It gave her a chance to help him for a change. She knew she really owed him when she found out about all the things he had done for her. She smiled again; she didn't know anyone she would rather be in debt to.

"Right now, we are here to observe," Cathy pointed out. "Victor thinks something will happen here if it doesn't happen at the science building, and he could be right. Look for anyone acting aggressively, pushing to get closer to the front, especially if they are wearing a coat or long jacket in this weather. Also, look for someone carrying a package or bag, one big enough to carry a weapon."

"These dark glasses of mine cut some vision but I better not take them off."

"Victor was right about the people here," Cathy told Walt. "They really do respect their handicapped. The people just parted and made a path for us to get up front. I hope the people Victor sent across the street are doing as well."

"Remember they don't have a blind man and his dog to help them. And thank goodness we didn't see a rabbit," Walt added.

Cathy laughed, again remembering Jack saying that Ralph would make a great service dog, as long as a rabbit didn't run by.

"Oh, Oh," Walt said softly.

"What?" Cathy asked, alarmed.

"I was watching two police officers push their way through the crowd. They appeared to be looking for someone and when one of them looked in our direction he poked his partner. They are heading straight towards us."

"I'll bet they are Gomez's people and somehow spotted us. Heck, they had me for two days; my description must be plastered all over the city. Get behind me," Cathy ordered as she reached into her purse for her gun.

Either Walt didn't hear her or he ignored her because instead of getting behind her, he pulled Ralph with him and stepped in between Cathy and the advancing officer, who was also reaching for his gun.

The officer shoved a woman out of his way as he cleared his weapon from his holster and moved toward Walt, looking for a closer shot. He was just starting to raise his weapon when Ralph broke free and leaped at the officer, his jaws clamping down on the man's wrist. The officer screamed in pain as his gun slid from his hand. The other officer knocked a boy down, shot Ralph, and was trying for a shot at Walt, when Cathy shot him in the head. A chaotic scene followed with the people screaming and running in all directions. The first officer bent over, reaching for his fallen gun, but Walt got to it first, picked it up and clubbed him over the head with it.

Some of the PNC officers around the science building heard the commotion and rushed to the area. Cathy tried to pull Walt away but he wouldn't leave without trying to pick Ralph up. Luckily, two of Victor's friends observed the confrontation and came to help. One stayed behind to give the police misinformation while the other helped pick Ralph up, leading Walt and Cathy to a sports field. He made a call on his radio and then helped Walt carry Ralph as they ran.

The police had trouble pushing through the crowd and sorting things out. Victor's friend pointed in one direction while the crowd pointed to the sports field. The police finally saw the three people running and took off in pursuit. The police were gaining on them when a panel truck raced through the field. It stopped briefly to pick up the runners and Ralph, and then took off in a cloud of dust. The police had to hold their fire because of the crowd.

The truck jumped a curb to get back on the road and Walt shouted at the driver to get them to the nearest vet as quickly as they could.

Chapter 39

San Salvador, Monday, March 7

THEY WERE APPREHENSIVE AS MARIA opened the door to the science building. The door emitted a small squeak and Maria held her breath as they examined both corridors. They were empty. TC and Hector took the staircase to the right, with TC giving Jack a quick salute. Victor, Jack, and Maria turned the other way and started down the corridor that led to the boiler room.

Before they turned the corner, Jack moved his Berretta to the top of his bag, while Victor reached into his bag and took out a wicked-looking knife, which he stuck in his belt, covering it with his shirt. They both put their arms around Maria and started forward, talking loudly. They rounded the corner and saw two men, each armed with an AK-47, who berated them in rapid Spanish, and then questioned them. Victor explained that they were from the vending company, refilling the machines.

"There are no machines down here," the older man said suspiciously and demanded to know how they were able to get into the basement.

"Maybe no machines," Victor replied, "but they do have a bed in that storage room back there," and he leered at Maria. "We came through the passageway from the lecture hall."

Maria smiling at Jack, reached up, and gave him a long kiss. Both of the guards became aware of Maria as she moved closer, especially aware of her exposed breasts. The heavy-set guard, smiling, moved toward her.

"Maybe you would like to have her for a while?" Victor offered.

The fat guard, excited, licked his lips, moved closer to Maria and took a whiff of Victor. He grimaced in distaste. "This one is very drunk, I think."

The older guard relaxed, lowered his AK-47, and ordered his companion to back off. He told Jack, Victor, and Maria that they couldn't go out that way and would have to go back the way they came.

"I'm not backing off until I get a little feel of those tits," the fat guard protested, reaching down into Maria's blouse. Victor pretended to stumble into him, pulled his knife and shoved it into the man's heart. Victor grabbed him before he could fall. The older guard started to raise his weapon, but he was too late. Jack lined up a headshot, changed his mind at the last second and shot the man in the right shoulder. The bullet drove the man against the wall as his AK-47 slipped from his fingers. Jack quickly kicked the gun aside and gagged him. Victor gave him a puzzled look.

"I just thought that we might, ah, convince him to tell us what to expect upstairs."

Victor smiled, "I knew we would make a good team."

They searched the guards, found a set of keys and opened the door to the boiler room. When they entered, they dragged the body of the dead guard into the room and pushed the wounded guard in front of them. The room had an acrid smell, an odor of unwashed bodies. They saw the three prisoners across the room, chained to an iron pipe. One of the prisoners glanced up with disinterest as Jack, Maria, and Victor walked across the room with the wounded guard. Then his eyes widened, his mouth popped open and he nudged the other two. The man chained on his right, with long dark, unkempt hair and a shaggy beard, looked up in disbelief and muttered hoarsely, "Victor?" When he said that, Maria ran to him, knelt down and took him in her arms.

"My God," the man exclaimed as tears ran down his face and mingled with hers, "Maria, my love, I, I, don't understand, what are you doing here? How did you get in here?"

Victor and Jack unchained the prisoners, secured the guard, and quickly outlined the plan the Miami ex-patriots hatched to kill Pope John Paul.

"That explains it," Roberto said. "We just couldn't understand why they were keeping us alive."

"They were keeping you alive for today," Maria said, "so they could blame you for this horrible crime."

Victor took out his knife and knelt by the wounded guard. "I am sorry amigo, but we are in a hurry, so I will make this quick. If you tell me exactly what is going to happen up there, I will come back when this is over and take you to a doctor. If you lie to me, I will come back and kill you. You have twenty seconds to decide."

"If I tell you, how do I know you won't kill me anyway?" the guard asked.

"You don't," Victor retorted, "Now you have fifteen seconds."

The guard looked like a trapped rabbit. His eyes found Maria's. She smiled encouragement and nodded.

"Five, four," Victor flatly intoned and when the guard nodded his head vigorously, Victor took the knife away. The guard gasped for breath, quickly telling them everything he knew.

"Very soon they will send two police officers down here to collect the prisoners. They will take them to the first level and make them lie down behind a large desk near the elevator. We are supposed to clean up down here." He paused, and Victor motioned with his knife.

"In the lobby," the guard continued quickly, "there will be the three assassins on the right side, near the entrance, and two backups on the left. The shooters will have a good view as the

Pope walks by and they will kill him. As soon as he is shot, the killers will come back through the lobby, kill the prisoners and put the murder weapons in their hands. Then they will go out the back entrance. The shooters are wearing gloves because the prisoner's fingerprints are already on the three rifles. Gomez and some appointed officers will shoot towards the building and will claim to have killed the assassins. The crowd will be enraged, and the police will see to that. The people will rush in, drag the bodies to the park, and burn them."

TC and Hector joined them in time to hear what the guard said. TC added, "That fire will burn up a lot of evidence."

"There was only one man on the first floor," Hector said, "and we took care of him. We didn't go near the lobby."

Jack undressed the dead and wounded guards and gave one uniform to Victor and put on the other.

"So," Jack began, "when we get to the lobby we will have three shooters on our right, two backups on the left, and possibly one or two behind the desk. Hector and TC can take care of the two on the left and Victor and I those on our right. If we're quick and quiet it will work out. Everyone's attention will be focused on Pope John Paul."

They tensed when they heard a pounding on the boiler room door. Victor directed TC and Hector to stand against the wall and cover both sides of the opening. Victor and Jack, dressed in their guard uniforms, opened it, keeping their heads down. The two officers entered, asking where the outside guards were. Jack hit one of the men with his Beretta and Victor took care of the other with a piece of pipe. It was over in seconds with a minimum of noise. The men were semi-conscious, as Victor and Jack stood them up, stripping them of their uniforms and chaining them to the far wall. He gave the uniforms to TC and Hector.

"O.K.," Victor cautioned. "You all know what you have to do, so let's do it. If there is someone at the desk, I will take care of him." Victor looked at them. "We cannot screw this up. Jack and I will lead; Hector and TC will follow with our rescued prisoners. Maria will stay here and watch our new prisoners."

"Our advantage is surprise," Jack said. "I'm sure they will not be looking for trouble behind them, and with these uniforms, we should be able to get close enough to take them down. It will be a walk in the park."

"A pretty damn dangerous park," Hector muttered.

They were halfway up the stairs when the noise increased and they raced to the top. They hurried down a short hallway and entered the lobby from the left. There was an attendant at the desk, surrounded by a table and some cabinets. Victor motioned for the others to hold up while he approached the desk and talked to the man. Victor said something to him and the attendant started to answer when Victor hit him behind the ear with his revolver. The man collapsed on the floor. No one appeared to notice because the noise and outside activity commanded their complete attention. The former captives, now armed with the guard's AK-47s, knelt behind the desk. TC and Hector moved toward the two men on the left, and Jack and Victor went after the three men with the rifles on the right.

The noise of the crowd grew louder so they knew the Pope had arrived. The three shooters were starting to raise their rifles when one happened to glance back and saw Jack and Victor coming down the steps with their weapons. Jack shot him as he turned to warn the others, killing him instantly. Victor killed the other two before they could react. The sound was lost on the crowd outside. One of the officers on the other side of the entrance rushed over when he saw the bodies fall. Hector and TC intercepted him and his companion before they had a chance to figure out what happened, disarmed them, and took them behind the desk.

Jack and Victor hid their weapons inside their uniforms and went down the steps to check the bodies and watch the Pope pass. Pope John Paul was just approaching when Victor's radio crackled. He answered it and his face drained of color.

"The lookout on the auditorium roof told me there is a man on the roof of our building. He is wearing a black hood and carrying a rifle! He is not one of ours!"

"Oh, God, no," Jack cried in anguish as he turned to rush up the stairs, closely followed by Victor.

Jack's heart was hammering and he wondered where the stairs were that led to the roof. After all their planning, he couldn't believe this was happening. He knew Victor had sent a man to the roof but he was probably dead. When they reached the top floor, Jack took one passageway and Victor another. After one dead-end, Jack found a way to the roof and saw a closed door. He prayed it was open. If not, he would blast it open. That would at least distract the hooded man. The door wasn't locked and Jack opened it cautiously. He was at the back of the building and his view to the front was blocked by a plaster board structure. Jack edged his way around the corner and saw the hooded figure leaning over the edge of the roof with a rifle in his hand.

Jack drew his Beretta and shouted for the man to stop, but his words were drowned out by the sound of a rifle shot. Jack was stunned, all that work for nothing. He watched as the man turned toward him. He wasn't sure if the man was raising his hands or his rifle. Taking no chances, Jack shot him twice. The man dropped his rifle and fell. Jack knelt down and hung his head as Victor came up, out of breath. Jack pointed at the fallen man, telling Victor that they had failed to save the Pope. Victor crawled to the fallen body and pulled off the hood. Jack looked in total surprise at Colonel Gene Belden.

Chapter 40

San Salvador, Wednesday, March 9

ELECTION DAY AND THE DAY after exceeded everyone's expectation. It was incident free and the favored ARENA party swept into power while the FMLN showed some support in the outlying areas.

Victor felt safe moving back to his home after a five-year absence. Many of the friends who had helped him and Jack were invited to celebrate. The party gave them the opportunity to congratulate each other and to re-hash their stories. Walt and Cathy were there, and when they saw Jack and TC walk in, Walt rushed across the room and asked about Ralph. Jack assured him that Ralph was healing and would be ready to travel in a few days. The vet said the bullet went through his leg but didn't break any bones or hit any arteries.

Walt smiled in relief and shook his head. "If it hadn't been for him, Atlanta would be short one banker. That SOB was so close he couldn't miss."

"Walt's right," Cathy confirmed. "I was trying to get my gun out and told him to stand behind me. Of course, he didn't listen," she admonished, and then couldn't stop the smile that broke through. "I know I would have been too late to stop him, but I wasn't too late to get the other one though, the one that shot Ralph."

"I wish I was the one that shot him," Jack said.

"We had no idea what was happening at the science building," Cathy said, "but hoped that all the commotion we caused, along with the gunfire, would deter Pope John Paul's procession from crossing the street. We didn't know if there were any assassins in the crowd, and the one thing I was sure of was that we had to get out of there in a hurry. I knew the place would soon be swarming with Gomez's people."

She described how she grabbed Walt and tried to drag him away, but he wouldn't leave without Ralph.

Jack looked at Walt with a wry smile and moist eyes.

"Luckily," Cathy continued, "two of Victor's men saw our predicament and came over to help. One aided Walt with Ralph while the other called a friend. We started across a soccer field feeling sure the pursuing officers would catch us when a panel truck bounced across the field and picked us up. We escaped in all the confusion and took Ralph to the vet."

"You were lucky," Victor said. "I'm sure the officers were afraid to shoot because of the crowd." He then told them about the trouble they had getting on campus and what had happened at the science building.

We had no idea that Belden killed Gomez, we were sure he killed Pope John Paul. Victor told Jack that he was just about to go over to police headquarters and go through the records that Gomez kept in his office, before the other people tore the place apart.

"Why would they let you go through all the stuff in his office," Jack asked.

"They have already appointed a new Colonel, and he is a cousin of mine," Victor said with a smile. They all laughed, Jack the hardest of all. Jack never found out if he was Victor's cousin, but they were greeted warmly, with respect, and directed to the office Gomez had occupied.

After an hour of searching, they were amazed at the documents they found, proving that Nelson Martinez and the other Miami people were behind the whole thing. They also found that Martinez got help from two Americans, Colonel Belden and Art Clauson.

"I just can't believe that he would leave all these papers lying in the open," Jack said.

"Don't forget," Victor answered, "he thought he would be in charge of everything by now and that he didn't need to hide anything."

After a few minutes, Jack figured they had found all they needed. Victor nodded his agreement, handing Jack a calendar. "Look at this," he said, and pointed. Jack saw that a message was written on the calendar the day before Joe Ellison was killed. It told of the meeting Gomez had scheduled with Bill Thomas.

Jack grimaced and clenched his teeth. "If that bastard had anything to do with Joe's murder, I'll kill him myself."

When they returned to Victor's house, they told everyone what they found. When Victor mentioned Clauson, Cathy blurted out, "That lousy traitor, he knew he set me up."

"He is probably on the run right now," Walt said, "but eventually they will find him and take care of him."

"And I would like to take care of Bill Thomas right now," Jack added.

"Well, you will get your chance tonight," Cathy interrupted. "Our embassy is holding a reception celebrating their candidate's victory. If you go, I want to go, too."

"Don't forget the Velados," Victor reminded them. The Velados had reclaimed their home with the help of their new radio friend. "The party is special, a party for their American friends and, of course, Ralph," he added.

"We wouldn't miss it," Jack answered, "this won't take long."

Victor stared knowingly into Jack's eyes. "But it's still not over for you, is it?"

Jack returned the look. "It's never over until it's over."

Chapter 41

San Salvador, Wednesday, March 9

Jack met Cathy in the lobby and commented that she looked lovely.

"Thank you, I'm just glad I remembered to get my bag after my rescue. Walt wanted to come, but Victor and I talked him out of it. Where is TC?"

Jack shook his head, "I don't have the foggiest. I called his room a couple of times and even left a message. I thought he would be fighting to go with me."

They took a taxi to the embassy. After showing their credentials, they were admitted.

"So what now?" Cathy asked.

Jack shrugged, "I really don't know. I can't prove that Thomas had any involvement in Joe's death, but I hate coincidence.

"Walt had a long talk with Senator Rucker this afternoon and I think that Mr. Thomas will soon be looking for a new job," Cathy said.

"It couldn't happen to a nicer guy," Jack said.

They were directed to the parlor where the reception was being held. Jack saw Thomas in the far corner talking to a small group of people. Jack steered Cathy to a table laden with food and drink.

"I'm not sure how this is going to go down, so you stay here. Remember, you still work for these people. I'll call you if I need you." Cathy didn't like it, but she nodded.

Jack picked up a large glass of red punch on his way over to see Thomas. He pushed himself into the middle of the group. Bill Thomas looked at him with surprise and annoyance.

"What in the hell are you doing here?"

"I just came by to offer you condolences on the death of your friend."

"What friend?"

"Your good friend, Rafael Gomez."

"Do you mean that police officer that was killed saving the Pope?"

"That's the one, only your facts are a little distorted. He was trying to kill the Pope, not save him."

Thomas shook his head. "I don't have the faintest idea what you're talking about, and besides, he is not a friend of mine."

"This calendar tells a different story," and Jack waved a page of the calendar under his nose. "It shows you set up a meeting with Gomez the day before Joe Ellison was killed."

"Gomez is not a friend of mine," Thomas repeated. "It was just embassy business and not your concern. Also, this reception is by invitation only and we do not want people like you here." He called for the two Marine guards and told them to escort Jack out. The two Marines, a sergeant and a corporal, were about to grab Jack when stopped by a loud commanding voice.

"As you were, Marines!"

"The corporal didn't move but the sergeant moved over to TC. He knew a Top's voice when he heard one. TC told him that Jack is a decorated Marine officer, a veteran who always took care of his men, and stood out front. He also told him that Thomas might be involved in the murder of the CIA agent. The sergeant gave a barely perceptible nod, leaned toward TC, and told him that Thomas was a pompous ass. He suddenly bent over and groaned in pain, telling the corporal to help him to the bathroom.

Thomas looked at them in frustration. "You will pay for this," he yelled at their retreating backs.

After that, Jack threw the full glass of red punch in Thomas's face. It ran down, covering his tux. In a rage, Thomas struck out at Jack, knocking him into a table. Jack put his glass down, ducked the next punch, and hit Thomas in the gut. Once Jack had regained his feet, it was a short fight with Thomas ending up on the floor.

"I was going to call you a piece of dog shit," Jack said, "but actually any piece of dog shit is better than your are." Jack turned and walked out of the parlor, followed by Cathy and TC.

***

The celebration was going strong when Jack and TC arrived at the Velados' house. They all gathered around the two of them, asking questions.

Jack shook his head. "No, I didn't kill the bastard, or even hurt him, except for his pride. I went for humiliation instead of mayhem," and he told everyone what happened.

"He won't get off so easy," Jack said. "I'll have a little chat with Senator Rucker. With Victor's information, I'm sure that Mr. Thomas's career in the State Department is over."

Jack had thought it would be awkward, seeing Maria with Roberto, but he was wrong. She gave him a warm hug and told him she cherished their time together. She introduced him to her husband, explaining that Jack was instrumental in his freedom. Roberto thanked him and as they talked, Jack formed a respect and admiration for the man.

Victor came over, gave Jack a Pilsner, and they wandered into an empty room to reminisce about the past few days.

Jack took a long swallow of his beer, looked at Victor, and shook his head. "I had no idea what we were doing to you people down here. No wonder you hate Americans."

Victor sighed. "I certainly didn't have any love or respect for them." He put his beer down. "Then you came along and I realized that it wasn't the American people that hurt us, it was your government's fear. After Nicaragua fell to the Communists they thought we would all fold and Communism would spread to Mexico. Actually, their policies forced us to the left. No one should back a regime whose only power relies on killing and torturing its dissidents and the poor."

"I read a lot of papers and still had no idea. They never did get me a true picture of what was happening here."

"You may have a free press, but it appears the papers have their own agenda."

Jack nodded. "The old newspaper days are gone. We are learning not to believe what we read in them."

"Enough of this kind of talk," Victor said and raised his bottle. "We are here to celebrate."

Jack also raised his bottle. "I'll drink to that and to the friends I made down here, to all your cousins, and to one man in particular whom I have grown to like, admire, and who has my complete trust."

"And here is to the man who taught me that hating is not good," Victor answered. "He also taught me I am not too old to learn. I never thought I would ever trust or respect a gringo. I was wrong."

Their bottles clinked and they drank.

Victor drained his bottle. "I also hope you understand that I am going back to America with you," he said.

Jack looked up in surprise.

"I know exactly what you will do when you get back and I want to be there with you."

Victor waved off Jack's protest. "It's not just our friendship. If those people are capable of doing what they tried to do, my country will never be safe as long as they live. Like you said, it's not over until it's over."

Jack was surprised but not shocked, and he nodded, "As I said before, I couldn't think of a better person to back me."

TC, Cathy, and Walt, with his arm around Cathy, came into the room.

"We think you boys have had enough time together," Cathy said, and filled them in about her conversation with the CIA Director. "Art Clausen has gone missing and they are sure he is out of the country by now. They have proof that he and Belden were working with the Miami people."

"Also," Cathy continued, "None of the mercenaries were able to enter El Salvador. In Honduras, Captain Loring, the head honcho of the invaders, refused to fight the American soldiers that were with the Hondurans, and they went home. Guatemala finally acted, surrounded the mercenary's camp, and the mercenaries quit without a fight."

"That's settles that," Jack said, "and I still can't believe I was so gullible about Belden."

"Look at it this way," Cathy said. "In the end he solved one of our problems."

Jack shook his head. "I think my heart almost stopped when he got off that shot. I had no idea Belden killed Gomez, not Pope John Paul. It makes sense though. I think Belden knew it was all over and Gomez knew too much. He still had his hood on when he turned, his rifle was pointing right at me and I didn't recognize him. I just acted instinctively. I had no idea I killed the Colonel. At least I let him die a hero. Gene would have liked that."

"Well," TC said, "we did manage to save Pope John Paul and he was part of it. Maybe he did die a hero."

Jack stood up. "I have no problem with that. Now it's time to go home and take care of the people responsible for all this, bringing it to an end, one way or another."

Chapter 42

Atlanta, Georgia, Two Weeks Later

Jack sat on the balcony of his condo sipping a cup of hot coffee. Walt had done a good job. The condo was close to his work and had a great view of downtown Atlanta. More importantly, they accepted dogs. Walt had returned to Atlanta a couple of days earlier than Jack, found the condo and rented it for him. He was a great friend and Jack wondered if Walt was still ticked off at him. They had not spoken since Walt found out he wasn't invited to their Miami party. Now, looking back, that seemed a lifetime ago but it was only what, nine days ago?

Ralph rolled over on Jack's foot. Jack reached down and scratched him behind his ear. He was rewarded with a soft groan when Jack bent down and gave him a hug and thought what a dumb thing it was, taking him to Central America. He gave him another hug, but he and Walt might not be here if he hadn't. Jack contemplated the unopened letter from Cathy Stanfil that sat on his table. He just wasn't sure he wanted to go back there. It was finally over, and then with a sigh, he opened it.

There was a short note and a news article cut from the Miami Herald. In the note she told him that everything was cool at work and that she was being transferred to the Atlanta office, per her request. There was no sign of Art Clausen yet, but they were still looking. She thanked Jack for not taking Walt on the Miami trip and was aware that Walt wasn't too happy about it. She felt he was beginning to like the spy business but knew he would get over it. She also asked about TC, who was wounded in the Miami gun battle. She knew that it wasn't serious and that he was recuperating.

Jack stared at the newspaper article a long time before finally picking it up.

The Miami Herald:

Five men were shot to death last night in the home of Nelson Martinez. Four of the men were businessmen from El Salvador who fled their country in the early 1980's to avoid their civil war. The other man was a security guard reported to be employed by Mr. Martinez. There was one survivor, an elderly businessman. He told police that he was in the upstairs bathroom when the gunfire broke out and stayed there until it was over. He didn't see anything nor did he have any idea why it happened. Names are being withheld upon notification of relatives. The police suspect a drug deal gone bad.

Jack let the article slide through his fingers and it fell to the deck. His mind drifted back to that night. He, TC, and Victor had approached the house from the sea in a rubber boat with an electric motor. It all went as planned, short and sweet. After the battle, he had checked the second floor while TC and Victor checked the lower level. Jack didn't find anyone in the three bedrooms and was about to check the bathroom when the door opened and an old man walked out. Jack raised his weapon for a quick shot, but the man just stood there looking at Jack, unarmed and unafraid. When Jack hesitated, the man said quietly, "Go ahead and shoot. I deserve it; all those people died because of us. I should have done more to stop Martinez."

Jack stared at the old man and then lowered his gun. He turned, walked down the stairs, and told TC and Victor it was all clear. It was strange, after all the bloodshed, that one act set him free. Maybe now he could go back to work and join the living. He knew his life would never be the same, but he knew that Nancy and Tim were together, in a far better place.

He reached across the cluttered table for his checkbook and wrote a check for $100,000 to Tim's school in Ocotal. He sent it to Bob Wood and told him to buy the kids some erasers.

About the Author

PETE MOELLER'S WRITING TALENTS WERE recognized early, while attending the University of Wisconsin—Milwaukee, where his creative writing professor invited him to join the Allied authors group. Upon graduation, he served aboard an aircraft carrier during the Korean War.

After retiring from a successful insurance career in Atlanta, Pete wrote his first novel. Wanting a professional critique, he entered this book in a writer's contest at the Southeast Writers Conference in St. Simon's Island—earning second place, before making any improvements to the first draft.

Pete is a member of the Atlanta Writers Club and the Southeastern Writers Association. A widower, Pete enjoys spending time with his four sons and eight grandchildren. He is currently working on his next book project.